He blinked and bli

Two tall nutcrackers stood on each side of the front door, and more lights danced around the porch. Animatronic Santa Claus waved merrily, plus two aliens wearing reindeer ears? He parked in front of the inn and saw guests strolling along the decorated paths between the trees. Jonas felt a sense of wonder he thought he'd lost as a child.

He spotted Micki among her family and she bounced down the steps to greet him. She was a bundle of energy, the good kind that radiated off her in happy waves. It seemed to make her glow, but that could be the lights, although no one could think the warmth in her wide brown eyes was anything but real.

"Hey, teach," Micki said to him with a warm smile.

"Teach?" The one word was a question from his lips.

Micki's smile widened. "As in *teacher*. Never mind. What do you think of the decor?"

"Was it all here this morning?" Jonas asked, half-confused. "I think I would've remembered an alien wearing reindeer antlers."

"This stuff wasn't lit up, so it was easy to miss. Gideon brought Santa out today—we're a little ahead of schedule," Micki explained. "Margo had the aliens up for Halloween and insisted they stay for Christmas. Omar came up with the antlers."

"Ah," Jonas replied, not knowing what else to say, still looking around and taking it all in. Especially the beautiful woman beside him.

Dear Reader,

You would love London, and those of you who have visited know why. It's my second home, the place I feel happiest. With my extended family there, it is always a good time. Family, fun and food—yes, food, is our love language, and we embrace it all while we are there.

Jonas and his family came about thanks to a family barbecue in Aldershot. My cousin's in-laws are fantastic, and we couldn't help but love them immensely. My husband never felt more comfortable in his life. There is a picture of him somewhere, barefoot in the yard with the guys around a grill. Being a diverse, blended family, we are rich in culture that both sides share. It's very important to our lives, our children and the love that binds us.

Similarly, my character Jonas was meant to be with his Micki at Ballad Inn, and their lives had to happen the way they did for their happy-ever-after. I hope you enjoy the third book, where winter has now come to the inn, and the honeysuckle hides until the sun returns.

Kellie A. King

A HOME FOR THANKSGIVING

KELLIE A. KING

Harlequin

HEARTWARMING

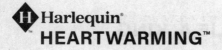
Harlequin®
HEARTWARMING™

Recycling programs for this product may not exist in your area.

ISBN-13: 978-1-335-05128-8

A Home for Thanksgiving

Harlequin Enterprises ULC
22 Adelaide St. West, 41st Floor
Toronto, Ontario M5H 4E3, Canada
www.Harlequin.com

Printed in Lithuania

MIX
Paper | Supporting responsible forestry
FSC® C021394

Kellie A. King is the *USA TODAY* bestselling author with a hint of Caribbean spice. Born and raised in Barbados, she now lives in Charlotte, North Carolina, with her large family. Kellie is married to her longtime love—her "Sarge" is always with her for every adventure. As an author of color, Kellie features strong heroines with a proud cultural heritage. Writing is her passion, and she hopes to inspire your imagination within the pages of her books.

Books by Kellie A. King

Harlequin Heartwarming

A Home for the Doctor
A Home for the Marine

Visit the Author Profile page at Harlequin.com.

To my favorite glam-fam,
Ashley, and her wonderful husband, Jack.

Thank you for inspiring me. My love to all.

CHAPTER ONE

"THE BEST YEARS of my life are yet to come," Micki sang along with the car radio and hummed the parts of the tune she didn't know. It was her nightly pastime while she drove home to her Sardis Woods, North Carolina, neighborhood from a class she had on a nearby campus.

Fall had come in a hurry that year, bringing with it the reds, yellows and oranges. The changing leaves dropped idly to the pretty streets, blown along by the cool breeze. It had been a warm enough Halloween that kids could trick or treat in costumes only, but right after that, the chill had descended over Charlotte, making everyone pull out thicker coats for going outside.

It was the time of the year when her family kept a stack of firewood close to the back door. Fireplaces were lit in the inn after dinner, and you could just feel the holidays approaching. It was her favorite moment at the B and B, with pumpkins and bales of hay in the front yard and beyond. Gideon, her brother-in-law, had begun to decorate the large Victorian house in earnest. Her sister Margo always insisted the Christmas decorations be up one week before Thanksgiving. And then on Thanksgiving after dinner, they light everything up. Hunter, the inn's regular landscaper, had already hung the white lights and the icicles that would look like snow. It was the only simulation they could muster, since Charlotte had a tendency for snowstorms that consisted of five and a half snowflakes. Yet the entire area would shut down for the day while people bought all the meat, milk and bread they could find.

"Time for those meat and bread sandwiches," she murmured as she approached Ballad Inn.

The bed-and-breakfast slash family home was always a comforting oasis, especially around holidays. Micki stopped her jeep in its usual spot before grabbing her backpack and purse from the passenger seat. Outside the vehicle, she paused and looked at the property that had changed so much in almost three years. There was another path that led to the new houses on the property, where her sisters Mia and Margo lived with their own families. She was the only one in the main house now, apart from their beloved housekeeper and cook, Enid, whose two-bedroom cottage would be ready by spring.

Then it really would be just herself and the staff that came in daily or nightly to see to the guests.

Enid and Margo still ran the kitchen and evening meals were always special shared with their guests and/or their family that had grown exponentially. Besides her adopted son, Omar, Mia and Ryan had little Georgina Grace, who was just born on August 5. Micki had immediately nicknamed her Gigi. A month and two weeks later on September 20, Margo and Gideon gave his Claire a baby brother, Andrew, who weighed in at a whopping ten pounds, three ounces. Gigi, Andy and their respective siblings had brought so much joy to the Ballad family that the walls of the inn were bursting with love.

In the midst of all the brand-new additions, Micki wondered where her place was. She didn't want to push herself on her sisters and their families. Even at dinnertime, she often felt like an eighth wheel, as if she were intruding It made her wonder if it was time to take off, see the world like her parents had been doing for decades. But she still had school—her bachelor's in criminal justice was almost done, and she was planning on starting law school hopefully next September.

Her dream was to work for a nonprofit that helped people in Charlotte, but did she have to do it from Ballad Inn? More and more she thought she should just get an apartment closer to the university and come by as the cool aunt a few times a week. With a sigh for her muddled thinking, Micki opened the door to the inn and stepped inside. At the reception desk was a new guest, signing the register. Mia was talking to him in her professional but friendly voice. This new guest would make it an even six they would be having for Thanksgiving— a full house, and a flourishing business. Micki tried to sneak past, but Mia saw her and waved her over enthusiastically.

"And here is my other sister, the third owner of our happy bed-and-breakfast," Mia said warmly.

Micki tried to shake her head at her sister, to let her go in peace. But it was too late. The man had turned to face her and suddenly it felt like time had slowed down. Tall at around six feet, blond hair cut neat with a shock of curls that fell over his forehead. Hazel green eyes stared at her, his glasses slightly askew, and his angular jaw line was clean-shaven. He wore a dark peacoat over a similarly black turtleneck and casual trousers. He looked studious and interesting, and Micki moved forward to stand closer to the desk.

"Sis, this is Jonas Brand, our newest guest and a full-time transplant to Charlotte," Mia said brightly. "Jonas, this is Michelle."

"Micki," she corrected her sister. "No one calls me Michelle ever, but my sisters do it to antagonize me because that's their job, or so they tell me."

"Michelle or Micki, both are lovely." His voice was a soft baritone with a pleasing English accent. He held out his hand. "Nice to meet you, Micki."

"Same here." She shook his hand. "Well, see you lat—"

"You and Micki have lots in common," Mia cut her off and Micki glared at her sister. "Micki is in the process of getting her undergrad degree in criminal justice studies at the university, and you're going to be the new dean of the law school there. What a coincidence."

"Ah, how much longer do you have left?" Jonas asked.

"Not long. This is my final year," Micki replied. "Don't worry, my grades are immaculate, so I won't bring the whole establishment down around your head."

"Good to know. I'm always up for a spirited debate, if there's ever a need." A soft chuckle escaped him. "I suppose I should head on upstairs. Shall I pick a meal now to be brought up?"

"Brought up to your room?" Micki asked.

He nodded. "Yes, isn't that standing procedure here?"

"Not usually, we have a family-style dinner each evening with our guests, unless the group is smaller," Mia explained. "It's the friendly, get-to-know-each-other type of setting our guests love."

"I often eat alone," Jonas said slowly. "I'm not much of a talker, very introverted, eat with a good book and all that."

Micki tapped the front desk with her fingertips. "But you don't mind a spirited debate?"

He smiled. "That's more one-on-one, which I find myself to be good at."

"Ah. Well, here's to learning, then." Micki smiled and fixed her backpack over her shoulder. "Gotta go. I have some work to do. Nice to meet you, Jonas Brand."

"Nice to meet you," he replied.

"I know you had a long flight, and the jet lag must be kicking in, so tonight we'll fix you a tray for dinner," Mia offered. "But starting tomorrow, meals are downstairs in the dining room."

"Got it and thank you for the warm welcome." Jonas took his key and went up the wide staircase.

Micki waited until he was gone before she turned to Mia. "You know the code for *I don't want to be introduced, let me go upstairs* is still the same. Circular finger motion, a cut-it sign or my glare."

"He's nice and someone you can talk to about all this legal stuff you try to drag us in on," Mia pointed out.

"Wow. Sorry if my interests bother you guys," Micki said sourly. "Do you and Margo and the rest of the family discuss how much I talk about law at the table?"

"Micki, it's not like that," Mia soothed. "You're so passionate about the topic, and sometimes we honestly don't have a clue, especially when you bring up different cases and rulings. We only have a vague idea of what you're talking about and you're so darn smart about all of it. Your mind soaks up knowledge like a sponge."

"Don't try to butter me up," Micki grumbled. "I've got to study for an exam."

"Will you be down for dinner later?" Mia asked. "Claire has a cold, so they're going to stay at theirs tonight, so it will be just us, Enid, and the guests. Mom and Dad are off playing cards with the neighbors."

"Is Claire Bear okay?" Micki asked. "Does Auntie need to come deliver a dose of sunshine and laughter to the sweet patient?"

"I'm sure they'd love an extra hand after dinner—you're the best," Mia answered.

"Just playing my role as support staff," Micki quipped.

Mia gave her a look. "You're much more than

that Micki, I hope you know that. You mean the world to us."

"Sometimes I feel like I'm on the outside looking in," she admitted. "Everyone's lives are so full and I'm still trailing along like the tail end of a kite that hasn't caught the wind. Maybe everyone was right, I should've finished college the first time and then I wouldn't be treading water now."

"Oh no, you don't." Mia came around the reception desk and put her hands on Micki's shoulders. "Sis, your path was not meant to be one straight linear path. You are a comet, a shooting star in the sky that can change course on a whim. All you've ever done is live life to the fullest. More people should be like you, daring to dream and to experience everything. You're amazing, Micks, and don't ever forget that."

Micki pulled her sister into a hug. "You always know the right thing to say."

"That's because I'm your big sister and I love you more than words can say," Mia whispered. "You make our families whole. You are never an extra anything but love."

"Okay." Micki kissed her sister's cheek. "I'm going up, see you in a bit."

"Maybe you'll convince our Mr. Jonas Brand to join us for dessert at least?" Mia teased.

"No matchmaking from you," Micki warned. "You won't put that hex of falling in love on me!"

"It happens when you least expect it. You can't dodge it forever," Mia called after her.

"If I can dodge zombies in our annual charity run, I can escape that," Micki replied loudly. "I've got enough on my plate."

MICKI STUDIED UNTIL DINNERTIME, and then ate with everyone around a table filled with laughter and great conversation. The nightly chill had settled in and now they lit the outside heaters on the porch. Standing with one of her favorite throws wrapped around her shoulders, Micki noticed the couples enjoying the starry sky and their crème brûlée dessert. She didn't expect to see their new guest standing next to one of the heaters looking out into the darkness.

What is it about this darn porch? Micki wondered to herself. There was Mia's first conversation with Ryan and then Margo sat out here with little Claire at night. She almost went back inside to escape the inn's porch juju, but Jonas looked lonely, so she gravitated toward him.

"I thought you were jet-lagged?" she commented lightly, coming up behind him.

Jonas looked back at her with the hint of a small smile on his face. "I needed a breath of fresh air. It's so different from London. The air, I mean."

"What do you smell at night when you're in London?" she asked.

"Mostly the food and drink from my local. The pub where I eat in the evenings," Jonas answered.

"Wait. You eat dinner at a pub every night?" Micki asked, amazed.

"I can't cook, unless you're talking about beans on toast or a can of tomato soup," he admitted. "Those you can't mess up too badly."

"Did you enjoy your dinner?" Micki asked.

"I really did. It was marvelous, full of flavor," Jonas said with a smile. "I'm waiting a bit before I have dessert."

"Get it soon because Mia's husband and Margo's have a sweet tooth and tend to come by and raid the kitchen at night." Micki wrapped the Afghan around her tighter. "That also includes Mia's teen son Omar, just in case you head for the kitchen later."

"Is that allowed?" Jonas asked. "Do all the guests raid the fridge?"

"Not really." Micki nudged him with her shoulder. "But I'll make an exception for you. Now, if it's dark when you get there, you turn on the light and they'll freeze like criminals caught in the act. But don't meet their gazes, just grab your dessert and join them."

Jonas chuckled softly. "It all sounds like fun."

"Only child?" she asked.

"No, I have a sister. She's a midwife," he replied. "Her and my parents are back in London."

"Any reason you chose to be a dean at a college in the States?" Micki hoped her tone was more conversational than curious.

His face became a sudden mask of seriousness, but it lasted for only a moment before he spoke again. "The offer was too good to pass up. I guess I'll be seeing you on campus."

"Hey, don't go being all chummy with me when I'm with my friends," Micki said in fake outrage.

Jonas looked alarmed. "I'm so sorry if I offended you—"

"No, you didn't. It was a joke," Micki replied. "You'll have to get accustomed to my type of humor."

"I guess so." His shoulders relaxed.

"Anyway, have a good night, Professor." Micki turned but then hesitated. "I know being dean is going to be a really tough job but be sure to stop and enjoy Charlotte sometimes."

"I'll try to do that, thanks, Michelle," he said, grinning.

Usually. she would have gritted her teeth at

the full use of her name, but from his lips it sounded nice. Micki quickly put that out of her mind. There was no way she was falling into the Ballad Inn trap where love seemed to come calling. She wanted to focus on being the best lawyer she could be, to help people and to live a great life. Yet she wondered if love would maybe enhance her goals instead of hampering them.

In her bedroom, Micki changed and slipped under the covers, feeling left out again—had she ever truly been in love even once in her life?

JONAS WASN'T ONE to lounge around. The Monday after his arrival into Charlotte, he was on the university campus, making his way to the Edgar Richards School of Law building. Looking up at the stately, redbrick building, with Lady Justice blindfolded and her scales etched into the stone, Jonas felt a sense of pride. He had gotten this job on his own, no pull from his family or using his name as leverage to get in the door. This was all him, from the application to credentials, interviews and vetting. Jonas entered and walked across the white marble floor. There were students studying in the large common area, sitting at tables and in various comfortable chairs, with laptops and what he guessed was coffee. He shook his head at how familiar the scene was while he went up to the front desk.

"How can I help you?" The receptionist didn't even look up as she spoke.

"The dean's office, please," Jonas asked politely.

Her shoulders lifted with a huge, frustrated sigh. "The new dean isn't here yet and I doubt he's going to want to deal with grade petitions on his first day."

"I might, since I'm the new dean," he replied casually.

Her head lifted quickly, and she stared at him with wide eyes. "Oh goodness, I'm so sorry, Mr. Brand. I didn't expect…"

"It's absolutely fine. I understand Mondays can be a bit frustrating." Jonas's smile was friendly. "If you can direct me to my office, I'll get settled in and begin learning about those grade petitions."

"I can show him, Debbie, no need to get up." A man walked up to him with his hand outstretched. "Professor Aaron Willoughby. Nice to meet you."

"Dr. Jonas Brand, new dean," Jonas shook the cold, clammy hand.

"Professor Linton asked me to show the new dean to his office and help him out until she returns," the receptionist, who Jonas now knew as Debbie, said with a frown. It was quite clear she didn't like Professor Willoughby. "You're supposed to be teaching your civil law class. It started ten minutes ago."

Professor Willoughby tutted. "Trust me. Those students can wait a few minutes, it isn't like they can understand the complexities of the syllabus without me."

"Debbie can take me," Jonas replied mildly. "The students in your class shouldn't be kept waiting. I look forward to reviewing your class curriculum myself."

"Linton never felt the need to review my work," Professor Willoughby said, lifting his chin.

"As the new dean, I'd like to say that I work a different way." Jonas tried to keep his tone neutral.

From this short interaction between himself, Debbie and Professor Willoughby, he could see the professor was not going to be an easily likable colleague. It didn't matter to Jonas one way or the other—he was accustomed to dealing with difficult people.

"Debbie, if you would kindly lead the way, so the professor can get to his class," Jonas said politely.

"Certainly, Dean Brand." Debbie got up and cast a wry look at the professor before she led

Jonas down the long hallway. "This will be your office, sir."

Jonas grimaced. "No *sir* needed, I'm not my father." He paused. "So, Professor Willoughby?"

Debbie nodded, then frowned. "Watch out for that man, he has been the bane of this college for over ten years. He has been passed over for tenure a few times and has interviewed for your position in the past, too. The students do not like him in the least. He's not fair, and is pompous, as you can see. Professor Linton has had to correct grades for students after the man's class finals. He has one foot out the door, but the board hasn't seen fit to get rid of him yet. Must have friends in high places."

"Not high enough to get him the dean's chair," Jonas quipped, looking around the spacious, neat room.

Debbie laughed. "Good one. But he also likes to throw around his clout, so watch out for him."

"Thank you, Debbie?" Jonas let his words trail away into a question.

"Deborah Sidwell," she answered. "Everyone calls me Debbie."

Jonas smiled and put his satchel on the desk.

"Professor Linton will be in by one. She had to take her thirteen-year-old son to the dentist to get his wisdom teeth removed."

"And she's still coming in?" Jonas asked. "Shouldn't she take the day off?"

"She's got Cain at home to help," Debbie explained. "I'll leave you to get settled. Make yourself at home. Our instructors will pop in through the day to meet you."

"Thank you again, Debbie," he said with another smile that she returned. "I look forward to meeting them all."

After she closed the door, Jonas sat down with a sigh. *Home.* Debbie was right. This would be his new home away from home for a while, which reminded him that he still needed to find other accommodation. Jonas didn't want to drive a rental for too long, nor take up space at the inn long-term. He was hoping to find a house close to campus where he could take the light rail or maybe even walk. He'd researched the area thoroughly before he'd accepted the position. After the Christmas holiday, he'd make it a priority to get a new place to live. Right now, it was more important that he find his feet at the college and truly get to know his new city and country. He was excited to see what spring and summer looked like. He'd read it would be warming up from March on, unlike in England where you had to wait well into May and June to feel the sun.

His personal things would take a few weeks

to get to Charlotte. Meanwhile, what he wanted for his office he'd shipped ahead and the stuff was sitting in the corner, he noticed. He would unpack later, choosing to open his laptop and review the bios on the school's website to get to know the professors in the law school. He'd already met the board via a video call when he interviewed for the position. Engrossed in the files, he startled when there was a knock on the open door. A woman with friendly eyes and a warm smile stepped inside.

"Hi, there, I'm Professor Jennifer Linton, Dean of Students." She balanced two coffee cups so she could shake his hand exuberantly. "Welcome to the law school."

"It's very nice to meet you," Jonas said, instantly liking the woman. "Please, sit down."

"Here. I got you an Americano front the campus coffee shop." Jennifer handed him a cup. "Grade Point Perks has the best coffee this side of Boardwalk Willy's."

His brow furrowed. "And that is?"

"Just the best BBQ close to campus. The place has a little bookshop and there's a coffee spot right next door, owned by the same people," Jennifer explained. "Willy and his wife, June, have been a staple in the community for twenty-plus years."

"I found that the communities in the area that

I researched are very close-knit," Jonas replied after a sip. Jennifer was right—the dark brew was fantastic. "I'm staying in Sardis Woods until I can find a permanent place."

"That's a great little community," Jennifer enthused. "It's only a quick hop on the interstate to get here."

"I'll try to find something closer to the college, when I really get to searching," He enjoyed another sip of his coffee. "This is really good."

Jennifer grinned. "Told you. I see you've been checking out the staff profiles. Just to let you know, the gang's planning a little get-together in the common area on Friday to welcome you officially. There will be cake."

"That's not necessary," Jonas answered. "Really."

"Oh, so you're the quiet, reserved type! Still, it won't save you." She laughed. "You're in the South now—the friendlies will be a little disconcerting, until you get accustomed."

"How long have you been at the college?" Jonas asked, knowing instinctively she was a transplant like him.

"Fifteen years. Came here from the cloudy, rainy state of Oregon," she replied. "Nice catch, you picking up on how I'm no local. So, is there anything you want to know before I leave you to unpack?"

"Nothing the profiles don't cover, but why didn't you apply for this position?" Jonas asked, curious. "You have the credentials for it. I've already read your profile."

"I'm okay with being Dean of Students. Less politics, more interaction with the kids," Jennifer answered easily. "I'll leave someone else to deal with the various personalities and egos in this law school. All the profs are very nice, I swear, but some have a few quirks."

"Like Professor Willoughby," Jonas confirmed. "I met him as I came in. He's quite— interesting."

"That's one way to put it," Jennifer said slowly. "Just know he wanted your job like a breath of air to the lungs, but despite his connections with those at the top, they chose to hire outside the faculty. He will not make your time here pleasant."

"From what Deborah tells me, he makes no one happy, so I will be in good company." Jonas took a seat at his desk. "If he has so many complaints from students and staff, why hasn't he been terminated?"

"Like I said, friends in high places." She walked toward the open door. "But one day, he will go too far and even they won't be able to look away."

"I'm sure he and I will get along famously." Jonas stood to walk her out.

Jennifer burst out with a short laugh, then gave him a sidelong glance. "You're a believer in miracles. I like that."

Jonas grinned. "My door is always open to staff and students. My job is to ensure not only professors have my ear, but students as well."

"I think we're going to like having you here, Jonas. Welcome once again." Jennifer offered a small wave as she walked down the hall.

"Thank you," he called to her and stepped back into his office.

Silence reigned around him, and he looked at the boxes with a sigh. "Better get to it, old boy."

It was his intent to make this office his space, just like he would eventually make his new home comfortable and inviting.

A fresh start meant more to him than he could say, and as he worked on his office, his mind wandered. Would he see Michelle Ballad today?

CHAPTER TWO

JONAS FELT A sense of satisfaction at seeing his things placed exactly where he wanted them and hung neatly on the wall. Professor Willoughby came to his office that afternoon and in his way tried to toot his own horn and assert his authority in the law school. Jonas took it in stride, but also made it clear he would not tread lightly around the pompous professor. The board thought Jonas was the best person for the job and that was how it would be. The professor left with a nod and a thin smile and Jonas knew it would be a battle of wills with this one.

There was another visitor just as he was leaving for the night. Jonas pulled his coat from the back of his chair and looked up. He recognized the face as one of the instructors in the law school but couldn't place the name.

"Dean Brand, I'm Micah West, I teach intro to civil law, and the senior seminar on landmark constitutional cases," he said and held out his hand.

Jonas chuckled, loving the light Caribbean accent he'd come to recognize from his life in the UK. "I've met and shaken so many hands today I think I've built up some muscle mass in my right arm. Now, let me see, Trinidad by birth?"

"Good guess. I'll walk with you since you're leaving. My last class just finished." Micah grinned. "I think we took the same path to North Carolina, except mine went from Trinidad to university in London and *then* to here."

"Ah, a fellow traveler. I feel less alone," Jonas teased.

Micah's dark eyes danced with humor and stood out against his light brown skin. He was the same height as Jonas but built stockier around the shoulders and chest. Jonas felt an instant kinship to him.

"Do you like teaching here?" Jonas asked conversationally as they walked.

Micah nodded. "It's great. I started out in Arizona, but that dry heat is not for me. I love the seasons here in Charlotte and the extracurricular activities in the area."

"What do you recommend?" Jonas pushed on the main glass door as they exited.

"There's the Whitewater Rafting Center," Micah suggested.

Jonas shook his head. "That will be a *no* from me. I have no desire to be careened over rough water in some sort of canoe."

Micah laughed. "I have a cricket group. We meet up every two weeks for a game in the park. You should come out. We'll be having our last game of the season, since the cold is setting in fast. But come spring, you can join up if you like our groove."

"Groove? Are you one of those players that celebrates with a little dance when you hit a good four runs or knock off a wicket?" Jonas asked.

"Why, yes, I am, and I'm not ashamed to say it." Micah laughed. "Should I tell the lads that you'll be coming round?"

"Please do. I would love to join up." Jonas pulled out his cell phone. "Take my number and text me when and where. I'll dig through the boxes in the office, try to find my shin guards."

"Will do," Micah said, before reading off the numbers for his cell. "Where are you staying?"

"Ballad Inn Bed-and-Breakfast in Sardis Woods." Jonas called the number and watched the cell light up in Micah's hand.

"That's a lively area. And with it being so close to the holiday, it's going to be decked out soon with lights and decorations," Micah told him. "You may need sunglasses at night over there! They are serious about mistletoe and garland."

"I'll let you know if I make it to my room safe and sound," Jonas promised with a laugh. "Great to meet you and I'll see you tomorrow."

"Don't make any lunch plans. I'll take you to the best on-campus diner," Micah promised as he strolled away.

"That's a plan I can get behind," Jonas called after him.

His spirits were lifted thanks to his conversations with one of his colleagues and now a new friend. *It's not going too badly for a first day*, he thought, satisfied.

Using the car's navigation system, he was able to find his way back to the Sardis Woods neighborhood, and immediately saw exactly what Micah meant. Not one house was dark; even the trees had been bedecked in colorful twinkling lights and there were inflatable decorations—like Santa and his reindeer—on every lawn. Other neighbors had projectors that created dancing snowmen and similar characters on their houses.

"It's festive. I'll say that for it," he murmured to himself as he drove slowly, merging with the traffic into a single lane of cars.

Jonas assumed that people driving through

the neighborhood to see the display was a usual thing. Back in England, none of this would've gone up before December 1 and not to this level of festiveness, at least not where he'd lived. Still, he stared in wonder as the procession moved gradually forward until he signaled to make the turn into Ballad Inn… *Wow.* He gaped at the scene in front of him. Lights ran up massive tree trunks that blinked merrily. Icicles hung from branches as well as snowflakes and stars. The haystack with the huge pumpkins still sat front and center, but around it was everything from an inflatable Grinch to a small train with a red bow on front moving merrily between the displays.

Two very tall nutcrackers stood sentry on either side of the front door and more lights danced around the entire wraparound porch and every balcony. Animatronic Santa Claus waved cheerily while two aliens were smiling and wearing reindeer ears. Okay, that one was weird, but somehow fit in.

He parked the car, and spotted guests strolling through the decorated paths between the trees. Jonas felt a sense of wonder he thought he'd lost as a child. Micki was standing with her family and when she saw him, she bounced down the steps to meet him as he got out the car. She was a bundle of energy, the good kind that radiated off her in happy waves.

Micki seemed to glow, but that could be all the bright lights, although no one could think the warmth in her wide brown eyes was anything but real. She wore her hair free today, thick tight curls that bounced when she moved. Her skin was a beautiful golden brown that had captivated him from the first moment he saw her. Though a large group had gathered, Jonas's focus was on her. As she came up to him, he noticed her sweater dress that had I Love the 90s in neon pink and green splashed across the front, and ended at her upper calf, which revealed black leggings and boots.

"Hey, Teach," Micki said, greeting him with a warm smile.

"Teach?" The one word was a question from his lips.

Micki's smile widened. "As in *teacher*, never mind. What do you think of the decor?"

"Was it all here this morning?" Jonas asked, nodding toward the busy porch. "I think I would've remembered aliens wearing reindeer antlers."

"The lights weren't on, so it was easy to miss. Gideon brought Santa out today," Micki replied. "Margo had the aliens set up for Halloween and insisted they stay for Christmas. Omar came up with the antlers thing."

"Ah," Jonas said, unsure who everyone was.

"Come meet the family." Micki took his hand and encouraged him to pick up the pace. "Before Enid rings the dinner bell and we all rush for the table. That even includes guests. It's a feeding frenzy."

A little bemused and a lot shy, Jonas allowed her to tug him forward, his senses aware of how right her hand felt in his. They got to the top of the steps, where all her family were smiling and eyeing him from head to toe.

"There's a lot of us," Micki whispered into his ear. "Let's start at the top, shall we?"

"Let's!" Jonas felt a smile pull at his lips. Whatever Micki was, she was magic, because the tiredness of the day seemed to wear off him in seconds.

"This is Mom and Dad, Brian and Rosie Ballad," Micki introduced them. "They live in the cottage between my sisters' houses so they can easily maneuver between the grandchildren."

"Wonderful to meet you," Jonas said and reached out to shake their hands.

"Oh, sugar, we don't do handshakes around here much." Rosie pulled him into an embrace. "Welcome to Charlotte and Ballad Inn."

"Don't mind my wife. It's the Southern living. We haven't met a person yet who isn't a friend," Brian Ballad said, while shaking his hand firmly. "Love the UK, by the way."

"You've been?" Jonas asked.

"They've been everywhere," Micki informed him. "Don't get them started or you'll never meet the rest of the gang. Next up is my oldest sister. You have met her, but not my little smoochie, Georgina Grace aka Gigi. Oh, that's Mia's husband, Ryan Cassidy, pediatric doctor, yada yada…"

Micki proceeded to press kisses on the tiny little hand of her young niece.

"Gee, thanks for the warm introduction," Ryan said dryly. "Nice to meet you, Jonas—I have to ask, are you a footy fan?"

"Chelsea all the way," Jonas answered immediately.

"Good man, you can stay here after all," Ryan grinned. "I've got someone to watch matches with."

Gideon shook his head. "What about rugby? Now, that's a classy sport."

"Guys smashing into each other is not a finesse game," Ryan retorted.

"Finesse?" Gideon said the one word.

"Stop it, you two," Margo said in exasperation. "I'm Margo and the other guy arguing with

Ryan is my husband, Gideon. These are our kids, Claire and Andy."

"I was doing the introductions," Micki pointed out. "Andy is my little sweetums."

Margo smiled. "You still have Enid."

"And this is Enid, our favorite lady in the whole world." Micki kissed her cheek with a smacking sound while Enid rolled her eyes.

"Nice to meet you, Jonas," Enid said drolly. "As you can see, our Micki has a lot of favorites in this family."

Micki puffed up her chest. "My superpower is love. I can put a lot of people in my heart. I have one three sizes too big."

"That's called a health risk," Ryan teased her, and Micki punched his arm.

"What about you, Jonas," Rosie asked. "Any family you left back in—?"

"I'm from London, and I have a sister and parents there." Jonas's heart lurched at the question.

He'd come to Charlotte to escape the dark clouds that hung over his family because of him. In an instant, the problems he'd left behind were right back in the center of his mind. *Would his deep sense of guilt ever fade away?* Jonas's long silence seemed to cause the family to glance at each other before Margo handed baby Gigi to Micki.

"Well, let's get everyone inside for dinner," Margo said brightly. "Jonas, Mia told me you often eat alone, and I think we can make an exception if you prefer the solitude of your room again. We pride ourselves on the family setting here at the inn, but we also want to make our guests comfortable."

Jonas hesitated for a minute, contemplating his original request. "I think I'll eat with everyone else tonight. Sometimes stepping outside of your norm is a good thing, or so I was told."

"Whoever said that was a genius." Micki hooked her hand through the crook of his arm. "Hey, I think it was me."

"But this is the first time we've spoken since our initial meeting when I got here," Jonas said, amused.

"I used my special psychic abilities." Micki made a signal from her temple to his. "Sink into it, my friend. You're one of us now."

"You get used to her, I promise." Gideon laughed. "In the spring we can introduce you to disc golf."

"Disc golf?" Jonas repeated slowly.

Ryan followed him inside the inn. "Trust me. We felt the same way when we heard of it, but Matt, our friend—you'll meet him—was right. It's a pretty cool sport. We just play for fun."

"I look forward to it." Jonas offered a weak smile. *How bad could it be?*

He stopped by a window facing the side yard. There was a lizard wearing a top hat and an enormous orange cat perched on the back of a sofa, peering out the window. The twosome seemed captivated by all the lights as they sat contentedly until the cat licked the lizard, knocking his hat off. Neither seemed to care.

Micki paused behind him and followed the direction of his gaze. "Oh, that's Monty and his best friend Doodle, the neighbor's cat."

"You do know cats eat lizards?" Jonas asked, slightly worried.

"We've been chasing Doodle from the house for years, then Ryan came up with the idea they might want to be friends," Micki explained. "One day we just said enough, and his owner, Mr. Webber, brought Doodle over, and with a watchful eye from all of us they became steadfast buddies. They went right into hugging or grooming each other. Sometimes you can see Monty riding on his back. Now they have sleepovers here at least twice a week, so the friendship appears to be working."

Jonas glanced at the duo again. "If a predator and prey can get along, why can't we as humans figure it out?"

Micki beamed at him and slapped his shoulder. "Right. You get it."

This was possibly the first family gathering that he'd ever been to where everyone wasn't reserved and steeped in formal conversation. Instead, this was a loud, friendly, laughter-filled evening, where everyone talked at once, and sometimes it didn't feel like he and the other visitors were just that, but rather family. Jonas noted that the Ballad gang made sure the atmosphere was warm and inviting. It was only after dinner that people slipped away to enjoy dessert outside or to retire to their rooms. Soon it was only he and the rest of the family in the dining room.

"This was lovely. I'm glad I chose to eat with everyone." Jonas's words were genuine.

"We're glad too. You can't be alone all the time." Micki took a bite of her dessert, a lovely warm bread pudding with fresh ice cream. "Besides, you are a fun conversationalist."

"I appreciate the compliment, Michelle," Jonas replied.

"You're welcome." She smiled at him but quickly inclined her head.

Jonas noted the room was silent and that the others looked shocked. He felt awkward immediately. "Is something wrong?"

"You called her by her real name and she didn't hiss at you not to," Gideon said.

Margo nodded. "Nor did she threaten you with some kind of bodily harm?"

"What kind of sorcery is this?" Mia asked.

"Can I not have a moment of enlightenment and growth?" Micki demanded. "And, it sounds nice when he says it. You people just tease me with it. For years, mind you."

"It's very nice to hear the full name we gave you." Brian moved around the table to give Micki's shoulder a squeeze.

Jonas watched the dynamics with interest. He had a wonderful family—a kind, loving sister who was a midwife, parents who were well liked and known in the community. He'd even loved growing up in the countryside, before the move to the capital. Life was simpler then. His parents and sibling, and all their friends used to sit about and laugh and talk a lot. Now it was quite the opposite, and whether it was his fault or not, it was still the case. His thoughts drove him to want to step away from the warmth Jonas felt, the guilt resurfacing already that he was enjoying himself. Shouldn't he still be paying penance for almost destroying his family and their good name?

"Thanks for tonight," he said. "I—I have to

get some work done for the college. Thanks for dinner. It was delicious."

Micki looked a bit stunned at the change in his demeanor. "Oh, well, okay, but don't forget your dessert."

He picked up the bowl and gave a quick smile. "Right. Thanks. Good night, everyone."

"Good night."

They all said the words in different tones and speeds, but he could feel every one of them staring at him curiously as he turned toward the stairs. It was too early to get invested in the people at Ballad Inn. Only his second day and here he was acting like the past was behind him. *You're here to work, nothing more.* Being too trusting had gotten him into a load of trouble the last time and at the moment he needed to focus on carving out a new place in this world—away from all he knew.

MICKI HAD NO classes on Thursday. In fact, she hadn't had one all week. The entire campus was closed. The faculty called it SSB or student's self-care break and it happened once every semester before the halfway mark in the syllabus when all classes amped up. Then it was a race to papers that had to be turned in and exams to be taken. She was twenty-eight among a sea of eighteen- to twenty-two-year-old kids.

It felt strange. In her heart she still felt like her usual super-young, energetic self, but she could also feel the corners of her personality being smoothed out and refined as she evolved.

She was lucky she could fit in with both groups— kids who still dreamed and older students who tended to have a goal in mind and a path to get there. In one of her classes there was a forty-five-year-old woman finally living her dream to be a college student. Micki was acing her classes, and it was entertaining to butt heads with the pompous Professor Willoughby. Willoughby was a guest lecturer in a couple of undergrad courses related to legal studies, while primarily teaching at the law school. Micki quickly pushed the thought of the man that every student dreaded, out of her mind.

She rolled over and stretched, loving the fact that she could sleep in for the next few days and regain some of the rest she'd lost studying and helping out around the inn. Everyone in the family wanted her to focus on her classes, but she hoped when she went downstairs that she'd avoid Gideon and actually get a few minor house improvements in. She missed the feeling of swinging her hammer.

Another ten minutes went by and finally she tossed the blankets aside and gave a little shiver as she left the warmth of her quilt and a comforter. Mia and Margo thought she was silly for using both and not sweating to death, but she slept with her window slightly open in the colder months and then tucked in. It was much easier to get warm than to get cool in the house where the heat could keep the upper floors a balmy seventy or more.

Her phone dinged and she looked at the message with a smile. Forget a little DIY work, she now had more exciting things to do that afternoon. After her shower, she dressed in a long-sleeved, burnt orange polo, jeans and her comfy boots with the sherpa lining, and bounded downstairs.

Breakfast had come and gone, so the only other option was to forage in the kitchen. When she went through the swinging door, there was Jonas, sitting on a stool pulled up to the kitchen island where Enid worked dough with her hands. Micki had to admit, her heart skipped a beat in a sweet way seeing him sitting there. He drank a cup of coffee, and there was an empty bowl in front of him. Jonas wore a long-sleeved hoodie with the emblem of his favorite soccer—football—team and faded jeans. Even with his dressed-down look he was cute and studious with his glasses on and that shock of hair that would not stay in place.

"Good afternoon. I see you're finally up." Enid smiled at her.

"I needed the extra time to catch up on my sleep." Micki gave Enid a quick hug from behind. "I usually don't get to bed till after midnight given my night classes and then homework."

"I was teasing, little girl," Enid said.

"I'm twenty-eight," Micki answered.

"Still my little girl." Enid winked at her and Micki grimaced, feeling her face warm, knowing Jonas was sitting listening to the interaction.

"Any breakfast left?" Micki asked and reached around the housekeeper to grab a slice of peach from the bowl.

Enid slapped her hand. "Those are for the cobblers. It's the last of the summer peaches we jarred. And you can either make some eggs or have a bowl of oatmeal with fruit like Jonas."

"You won't miss one slice of peach. Eggs it is." Micki kissed the older woman's weathered cheek. "Hey, Jonas, learning to make pies?"

"It's fascinating watching Enid prepare the dough. The butter ratio to what she's doing is so precise, and she folds it in cold so it will create air in the mixture as it's all happening."

"Yes. That's how pie dough is made," Micki said dryly, while she pulled eggs, green peppers and chopping onions from the fridge. "Do you want some eggs?"

"That would be lovely. Thank you," Jonas answered politely.

"What are your plans today?" Enid asked Jonas.

He shrugged. "Stay around here. Check out more of the property. Maybe read in my room."

"And you, Micki?" Enid had finished with the dough and was checking that the oven was on.

"Mrs. Grainger called. She and Mr. Grainger are pressing a new batch of cinnamon apple cider, so she asked if I wanted to come by and help," Micki replied as she cracked eggs into a bowl. "Sally is on bed rest and Bill is frantic with the kids and she knows I like doing it."

"Plus, you'll come home with at least two big bottles of the stuff." Enid's voice held nothing but amusement. "It will go well with dessert tonight, some hot apple cider with a cinnamon stick in it."

"Who says I'm sharing?" Micki demanded to know.

"I do." Enid laughed. "Why don't you take Jonas with you? He might like to see how we make cider here in the South."

"Enid—" Micki's voice held a warning.

"What?" She looked at Micki innocently. "Jonas, have you ever seen how cider is made?"

"No, I can honestly say I have not," Jonas answered. "But Michelle shouldn't be roped into playing tour guide for me."

"It's called Southern hospitality," Enid said firmly.

"It's okay, Jonas, you may like it. Plus, you'll get to meet the neighbors too," Micki replied. "In case you decide to get a place in this area."

"I was thinking nearer the university, actually. Those lovely condos are very appealing near the North Davidson District."

"The less formal name is NoDa," Micki explained. "I've seen those condos. I think they're amazing. Very roomy. And modern."

"When did you see them?" Enid asked, clearly curious.

"I went with a friend to see them a few months ago," Micki said quickly and didn't meet Enid's gaze.

She didn't want any of her family to know that she was thinking about maybe moving away from Ballad Inn. At least, for a few years. Yes, her house was in the process of being built and she would furnish it using part of her savings but she was thinking more and more about having some freedom away from the inn and her family. Sure, she'd be close enough to visit and even stay over, if need be, but she longed to have her own space away from their childhood home.

"We can head out after we eat," Micki's voice was bright. "Just beware, don't eat too much of Mrs. Grainger's apple taffy. That stuff can be addictive and also give tummy aches."

"That only happened to you, Micki." Enid chuckled. "You could never understand the concept of too much candy."

"They shouldn't make it so delicious, then." Micki refilled Jonas's mug before making herself a cup and then bringing them both a plate of fluffy eggs.

"The notion of candy being delicious, then for children to show restraint in eating it is confusing to say the least," Jonas added.

Micki gave Enid a smug look. "See? He gets it."

"Don't encourage her, Jonas." Enid sighed.

Micki and Jonas looked at each other and smiled before digging into their eggs. They ate silently while watching Enid put together the cobblers that would be served tonight. After she stacked their dishes and cups in the dishwasher and gave Enid a quick hug, she went to grab her coat from the closet downstairs while Jonas jogged up to get his from his room. In a matter of minutes, they were heading outside to her car.

"Enid said we get to bring home the apple cider?" Jonas asked.

Micki made a careful turn at the stop sign. "No. Cider ferments so they won't touch this batch for a few weeks, but she'll send me home with a few gallons from the last one. The Graingers have a thriving apple orchard and their farmers market has been ongoing in this area for as long as I can remember. Their operation grew from being a little stand to a thriving business that hires many people. It's loved in the community."

Jonas propped his arm on the rest. "And you still go to help out?"

"I've been doing it since I was fifteen," Micki replied, then admitted, "I always had way too much energy and not a lot of focus. It's Attention Deficit Hyperactivity Disorder. Holistic ways that channeled my energy always worked best for me."

"And that helped? Cider making, I mean?"

"That and the fact that I can build almost anything, so as I got older I took over the handyman work at the inn, until I broke my arm last year." She sighed. "Then my sisters insisted we hire a full-time professional and Gideon came to take the job. Then he and Margo got married and I went back to school."

"Might I ask, and you don't have to answer if you don't want to, but you started university later than most," Jonas pointed out gently.

Micki nodded. "It's not a problem, really. I started school for architecture when I was younger but left after a year. It didn't feel right, and it took a little while to find the path I wanted to be on."

"And that's the law," he added.

"There is this really great nonprofit here that helps people who don't have the money to pay for legal fees. Their lawyers cover the gauntlet from custody or child separation cases to ones where the defendants might have been wrongly convicted." Micki drove along the leafy street, keeping a careful eye on a couple of kids cycling. She loved biking through her neighborhood when she was younger. "I want to work for them. I've been volunteering for over a year, just compiling research, looking up precedents and small stuff like that, but I love it. And the coordinator said I have an eye for the law. This felt right, so, criminal justice studies it was."

"I get what you mean. The law calls to you, often to help people, and then you can never let the feeling go."

"What about you? What's your law story?" Micki glanced at him quickly before once again focusing on the road.

"My father is—was a lawyer and I grew up with his law books. When I got older, like you I was his researcher," Jonas said with a fond note in his voice. "I passed the bar when I was twenty-two."

"Wow. That's impressive," Micki commented, and then slowed down and stopped. She rolled down the window. "Hey, Julius! Don't forget, Mr. Webber needs that tree trimmed before we get an ice storm."

Jonas waited for her to roll up the window before he spoke again. "It's not that impressive, I wasn't a prodigy. I had been technically clerking for my father since I was fourteen. I knew more law cases and outcomes than simple math equations."

"Shouldn't everyone?" Micki laughed.

"Good point." His laugh was a lovely sound. A little husky but with a hint of base. She liked it.

Jonas continued. "I went on to work for a large law firm in London for several years, made a ton of money, abhorred every minute of working for a high-powered firm that stepped on the little guy. Got out and worked for the Crown—"

"The Crown?" Micki asked, confused.

"What you would call the public defender's office," Jonas explained. "I worked there for two years and then went into teaching for seven before coming here."

"So, by my calculations you're about thirty-four." Micki had tried to do the math while he'd been talking.

"Right on the money," he confirmed.

"Oh, Professor Willoughby must love you." Micki gave a snort. "He's been teaching at the campus for fifteen years and he can't get your job no matter how often he tries."

"I've met him. He's a real character."

"He's something all right," she quipped before deftly changing the subject. "And here we are at Grainger Farmers Market."

Sally and Bill's business was decked out for Thanksgiving. The couple felt that each holiday should be given its due. They refused to decorate for Christmas until after the Thanksgiving holiday was over, so pumpkins and cutout turkeys lined the entrance. There was a small pumpkin patch outside of the main building where other vendors sold a variety of products, from homemade candles and soaps to fresh-baked breads and artisanal cheeses from small dairy farms from around the state. Scarecrows dressed for autumn wore big, painted smiles. Young parents pushed children in strollers and other folks at work stopped in for lunch. It was much busier on the weekends, so Micki understood why Sally had sent her a message about pressing apples today.

"Remind me to grab some blue cheese for the

inn from the Wren Dairy booth on our way out," she told him.

"Blue cheese?" He wrinkled his nose in distaste.

"Oh no! You did not just diss blue cheese." Micki gasped in shock.

"It's terrible," Jonas protested.

"I shall change your mind," she declared.

"But I don't want to change my mind."

"It's already out there in the ether," she said, walking away.

Jonas ran to catch up. "You sound like my sister."

Micki beamed. "Aw. Thank you."

"You both only hear what you want."

"Hey!"

His laughter floated past her as he took the lead and opened the door for her to go inside. Sally was sixty-five, with long dreadlocks that went from black to gray at the roots. Her husband, Bill, was a tall man originally from Norway, who wore his gray hair like the Vikings of old, long and braided. Their story always fascinated Micki because they were homesteaders in Alaska from the seventies and then moved to Charlotte after having their first child.

"Micki, you made it!" Bill strode forward and embraced her in a hug that lifted her off her feet.

"And who have you brought with you? Is this young man courting you?"

"What? No!" Micki sputtered out. "He's a guest at the inn. I'm just showing him around the area."

"Bill, stop teasing her." Sally came out from behind the counter and she too gave Micki a hug. "How are you?"

"Good. I've been busy with classes. I'm sorry I haven't been around much lately."

"Not at all. We're just so happy you're chasing your dream." Sally smiled. "Now introduce us to your friend."

"This is Jonas Brand. He's the new dean of the law school at my university," Micki told them. "Jonas, this is Bill and Sally Grainger."

"Nice to meet you both. Micki tells me you have the best cider in North Carolina."

Bill's laugh boomed out. "She is the best advertising we ever had. Are you two ready to get your hands dirty?"

Micki rubbed hers together. "We are indeed. I need to put my energy into apples."

"Come on." Sally waved them forward. "Jess, you have the front register, Dale is managing outside."

Her cashier smiled and nodded before focusing on a customer who held a large loaf of apple bread. The place changed from a storefront to a processing room that was spotless and well organized.

"Roll your sleeves up past the elbows," Micki told Jonas while handing him a white apron from one of the hooks. "It's about to get messy."

"Oh dear," Jonas murmured.

His words made her grin.

The process of making apple cider had a few steps. First, the grinder turned the apples into pulp. Bill was certain that the old ways were best, so the grinder was hand-cranked. He claimed it made the cider taste better because it had a personal touch and hard work behind it. And then that pulp was strained via cheesecloth over a large metal tray. The cheesecloth was laid on top in a certain way so the essence of the fruit could be squeezed out. The heavy presses were also hand-cranked and when it became too much for her and Jonas, Bill took over with arms that had done this job for over thirty years.

Both she and Jonas watched the juice run in rivulets into the containers before helping Sally with the pulp that was leftover. That would be included in breads, cookies, crisps and even ground finer when it was dried to make apple sugar and added to apple butter. Nothing was wasted and that was what she loved about the process and Sally and Bill's technique. What couldn't be used was composted and fed back into the orchard in a sort of circle of life. She hopped up and down and did a spiral, she was that content.

"Michelle, um," Jonas said her name hesitantly as he took his turn cranking the large handle.

She glanced curiously at him. *"Oui, monsieur?"*

He grinned. "You have a very unique personality."

"Thanks."

The happiness in his eyes was evident when it seemed like he was actually relaxing and having fun. Now was a good example of that. Otherwise, Jonas tended to pull back and come across as serious, if not brooding. She wondered what made him tick. Why would being at ease with people bother him so much? As she'd heard many times before in her family, it was his story to tell, when he was ready to tell it, if ever.

"Was that what you wanted to say?" Micki asked when the silence reigned a bit too long.

"Yes. No, not exactly. There's a cricket match one of the professors invited me to. It's their last game—I wanted to know if you would perhaps join me on Sunday?"

"I can honestly say I didn't know they played cricket in Charlotte, and I'm pretty much aware about most events in our area," Micki mused.

"That's how I got my family into the zombie run."

Jonas's brow furrowed. "Zombie run?"

"It's a thing my family does. Don't worry, I'll invite you next year," she promised.

"So do you want to go to the match, or will it be too boring for you?" he probed gently.

"No, I think I'd like to come," she said. "I know of the game, saw it on TV a few times with friends at the Big Ben Pub. Tell me what time and I'll be ready."

"I'll let you know when I know," he said. "Then maybe you can take me to this pub that boasts the name of our iconic clock tower."

"Deal," Micki said automatically. "You're going to love it."

"Okay, kiddos, we've finished for the day." Sally joined them, smiling. "Come on in for something to eat and rest those feet."

"We've been here for hours," Jonas said, sounding amazed, looking at the time on the clock.

"Time flies when you're having fun." Micki took off her apron and waited for him to do the same before she put them in the hamper.

They had chicken salad and apple sweet tea for a quick lunch before Bill resumed his tasks and went back to the orchards. On their way out, Micki and Jonas were graced with three gallons of the fermented cider, plus bread and cookies from Sally.

"It was nice meeting you, Jonas," Sally said and handed him a Dutch apple pie. "This is for you."

"Marvelous." Jonas inhaled the scent. "This is going to be a treat. Thank you, Sally."

"Hey, how come he got a pie?" Micki demanded to know.

"Because you've had more than a few dozen since we've known you." Sally kissed her on the forehead. "Come see us again soon. Bring Jonas with you. Bill and I like him."

"I will," Micki promised.

"Bye." Jonas waved with his free hand as they walked to the car. "They're lovely people. Thanks for letting me tag along."

"It was fun." Micki unlocked the car so they could slip inside. "You're going to share that, right?" She pointed to the pie.

"Sally did say it was mine," Jonas hinted. "But you can have all that blue cheese you bought."

Micki laughed. "Touche," she said sweetly.

As they drove home, they talked nonstop, shifting easily from one subject to the next, which showed Micki how much they had in common. By the time they arrived back at the inn, they were both laughing at something he'd said. Some might consider his joke stuffy, but she found his dry wit amusing. A smile crossed her lips when she opened the front door and found most of the family was already there at the main house, helping set up for dinner, talking about how the week had passed and generally lounging around.

"Hey, guys, we're home!" Micki called. "There's cider, cookies and bread. But Jonas got the big-ticket item. One of Sally's famous Dutch apple pies, in the sixteen-inch pan, mind you."

Ryan, Gideon and Omar moved in for a closer look.

"The one with the sticky top because she does that glaze thing?" Ryan asked, staring at the pie long enough that Jonas stepped back.

"The very same." She threw Jonas a devilish look. "And he doesn't want to share."

"Gasp!" Omar held his stomach. "I feel faint."

"Bro, you're going to change your mind about that, right?" Gideon came closer. "We made you part of the family."

"When did this happen?" Jonas asked, a smile playing on his lips.

"When you came inside with a pie the size of the moon," Ryan answered.

"Don't mind them, Jonas, go store your pie in the fridge. These dessert fiends already have cobblers." Margo pulled Gideon away with some difficulty.

Ryan looked back at the pie longingly but took Gigi from Mia, who shook her head and laughed.

"You set me up," Jonas accused Micki as he walked to the kitchen.

Micki sighed. "Large families, dude. The needs of the many outweigh the one."

"Smart," Jonas replied. "Harsh…but smart."

LATER THAT NIGHT when the house was dark and the guests were in their rooms, Micki timed her entrance into the kitchen perfectly. When she turned on the light, three men and one teen boy were sitting around the island, eating. Their heads whipped around at once to see who had caught them.

"Ha. It's like catching a bunch of owls with a bright light," she said.

"Owls with pie." Omar stuck his fork into his thick slice with a happy sigh.

"I see they let you into the brotherhood," Micki said to Jonas dryly.

"Well, Michelle, after I paid my dues with this glorious pie." Jonas took a bite and closed his eyes. "My word, this is heavenly."

"You're all weird and I'm telling your wives

and mother," Micki replied. "Do they know you guys left the house?"

"How about a slice?" Jonas suggested.

Micki narrowed her eyes. "I know a bribe when I see one."

"So?" Gideon handed her a plate and fork.

"Gimme the pie," she said, smiling smugly. "I told you I'd get my share."

Jonas laughed. "This was your devious plan after all. Well played."

"Thank you," she replied.

"Turn the light out," Gideon told her. "We eat by the clock light on the range."

Micki shuffled over and clicked off the light. "We need to have a family discussion about y'all's eating habits."

The back door opened, and her father came in bundled up in his coat. "Am I too late?"

"Dad?" Micki said in shock. "They pulled you into this, too?"

He waved his hands in front of his face as if performing some kind of trick. "You didn't see a thing. I'm not even here."

"Right," Micki said slowly and made her way back to her bedroom before anyone else discovered the brotherhood's kitchen hangout.

She had no doubt the women in the family knew about these dessert jaunts to the main house. *These guys are so cute... Let them think*

no one knows, Micki thought. It warmed her to
see Jonas included. She liked him already and
that might be a problem, since she'd decided
that she wanted no part of that love vibe thing
her family had going on.

CHAPTER THREE

HITTING THE GROUND running was an understatement when it came to his new job. Accepting the post, he knew the board wanted change within the law program, specifically to bring it more up-to-date with how other universities organized their academic offerings and operations. One of his first tasks was to restructure, then tackle the budget so that the law school could update common spaces for the students and technology for the professors and administrators.

That meant a dinner would need to be planned to introduce himself and possibly get donors interested, especially alumni. He had a meeting lined up with all the law school's administrators and directors to do that, but first he wanted to speak with all the teaching instructors and professors, as well as the support staff that kept the law school running smoothly. He'd been glad to find out he was inheriting one in good stead. He'd offered Debbie the position of his personal assistant, which she'd been happy to accept, and filled her old job with another qualified front desk coordinator. The auditorium was filled with murmurs when he stepped in, but everyone quieted quickly as he reached the podium. Debbie claimed a seat in the front row.

"Good morning, all. I've tried to meet each of you, but for those I've not had the pleasure of talking to as yet, I'm Dr. Jonas Brand, the new dean of the law school." Jonas used a brisk but polite voice. "I passed the bar at twenty-two, did all my graduate and post-graduate work in the UK—well, you all saw my credentials when you were notified I was chosen for the job—no need to go through all of that, yes?"

There was general agreement and a dash of laughter before he continued.

"First, I want you to know my door is always open," Jonas said and made sure he met their gazes. "Now, after this semester I'll be incorporating changes into our academic structure. We'll be adding more classes on women in law and their contribution to the rule of law from the suffrage era to the present. And with that we'll be hiring at least five new female law professors, since there are only ten with us now and I'm not comfortable with that ratio at all."

"Yeah!" one instructor whooped and more laughter followed.

Professor Willoughby spoke up. "More women's roles in the shaping of law? I'd say the topic is sufficiently covered as we have it now. They weren't given the right to vote until 1920."

"But were allowed to practice law from 1879," Jennifer countered. "If you think that women didn't have a hand in shaping the law in this country, then you are sadly mistaken. We may have been overlooked but we were there, bringing cases forward, setting precedents in more ways than one."

Jonas held up his hand for quiet. "This isn't the time or place for a debate, which is exactly why we need these classes. A broad view of the law and how it was shaped needs to be beyond just a cursory gloss-over of a chapter in a textbook or a single lecture. Studies that focus on women in the law need to be expanded so that students may know the full scope. I put this to the board after I created the restructured academic program and they've agreed, so it's not up for discussion. It will be happening."

Jonas looked about the room and saw nods of approval while other people were diligently taking notes. He took a breath, giving the space a chance to settle before speaking again.

"The board is offering additional tenure to those professors who qualify. I have a short list of seven that will be interviewed by myself and a panel of department heads in closed-door sessions." He paused, waiting for questions. When none came, he went on. "With the committee's recommendations, the board of trustees will then make the final decision."

One professor he hadn't yet had a chance to meet asked, "Do you have a list of names?"

"I haven't given formal notification to any of the candidates as yet…" Jonas said hesitantly. "But if you are all in agreement, I can announce the candidates now."

Everyone agreed and sat forward expectantly to hear the names, and as he stated them, there were handshakes and small rounds of applause.

Again, Professor Willoughby interjected. "How is Micah West on the list? He is only on year three of his contract here."

"Thanks for keeping track for me," Micah said casually. "Come on, Aaron. It's just a list of candidates, not a done deal."

"It *is* a big deal," Jennifer said. "Congrats, Micah."

The younger man looked down shyly for a brief moment and then beamed with pride. "Thanks."

"To answer Professor Willoughby, I'm sure you're aware that the standard can be changed to include exemplary teaching services by any instructor and be nominated to receive a permanent post." Jonas chose to list Micah's accomplishments in case any other faculty thought the same. "Professor West's name was put forward because of glowing reviews by students, and in the short time he's been here he's published multiple articles in law review journals, which have highlighted the school in a positive manner. He was given a research grant for his team of students that won them the Ferguson Award, and the Patterson Foundation donated a substantial sum to this school because of his work on The Innocence Project. He has done more than enough to deserve tenure."

"Agreed." That was the consensus of more than a few instructors who'd chosen to speak up.

"I have to say if anyone is disappointed not to be nominated for tenure, then they must search within and ask why and make positive changes to be eligible for this prestigious accomplishment," Jennifer said. "Professors can't rely on individual laurels, rather on the evolution of their work and efforts to enhance this school and its students."

Well said, Jonas thought, but didn't voice it. Part of his job was to remain neutral and to have a sense of detachment while being fair. Speaking of fair, he'd reviewed Willoughby's record and even if he did have friends on the board, they couldn't deny the fact that the professor was well below percentage in many areas where others were excelling. His syllabus hadn't changed in years to evolve and meet the new criteria and advancements in his particular field.

"If that's settled, we can now move on to other business I want to get tabled before we adjourn."

Jonas gave a wide smile using the term they'd all be familiar with to lighten the mood. Professor Willoughby shot dark looks in his direction, but Jonas wasn't fazed in the least. By three o'clock, when they were finally finished, Jonas had a low-grade headache building in the back of his brain. On the way to his office, he decided to stop first and pick up a late lunch from the student union dining room. After paying and taking his box, he was heading out the door to take the short route back to his building, when he spotted Micki bounding up the steps with a pink backpack on her shoulder. They both stopped, each on an opposite side of the railing, and smiled. How could just looking at her make him feel lighter—happier?

"Hey, Teach! How's it going?" Micki said.

"It's going okay," he answered. "I just need at least an ounce of your energy to get through the rest of the day."

"That's called being caffeinated." Micki laughed.

"We have to be drinking different types of coffee," Jonas replied. "Heading in for a bite to eat?"

"A quick bite. I have a thirty-minute window before my next class."

"Oh, then I'll let you get to it." Jonas smiled at her again. "See you later?"

"You can't miss me," she teased. "Bye."

He turned to watch her run up the rest of the stairs, a flash of black jeans, green canvas high-tops, a long-sleeved green plaid sweater with a white collar. Seeing her gave him a boost of energy and he walked jauntily on the path back to his office. The leaves were still green in some spots, but also yellow, red and orange in others. They fell softly to the ground whenever the chilly wind blew. It was a marvelous landscape. One that he liked immensely. With every minute passing, Jonas felt less out of place and more like he was where he was meant to be.

Eating at his desk so that he could continue to work was helpful but as dean it still didn't give him the time to teach his own class. From the spring semester on he too would be in the classroom. So while he had to get the law school in shape, he also had to build his curriculum. Intent on his own work, he didn't hear his phone buzz until the second time around, and he looked at the screen. It was his mother's number. While he wanted to talk to her, it brought back everything he was running away from at home.

Jonas pressed the connect button and soon his mother's face popped up with a wide smile and kind blue eyes that assessed him in her usual fashion. Her blond, short cut was parted in the center, rather than to one side. Everyone always said he was the spitting image of his mum. Maybe that was why they were so close. He instantly felt the ache of missing her, of not being close by. Beverly Brand gave off a positive energy even through the screen and despite the huge distance separating mother and son. While she talked, she was standing in the wide stone kitchen of the farmhouse making something.

"You look tired, JonJon," she stated flatly.

"Mum, not the name," he groaned.

"Why not? You're alone. If not you'd say, Mum I'm in a meeting, and I would then say, why hello, Jonas, how are you, in very formal fashion." His mother made a silly face.

He couldn't help but laugh and he could hear the love in his voice when he spoke again. "Hello to you, too. I didn't think I would miss you this much already."

"You're the one that chose to leave and fly

thousands of miles away from me," she replied. "Are you eating?"

"Yes, Mum," he drawled out and rolled his eyes. "The bed-and-breakfast where I'm staying for now has a terrific cook. I can even sneak into the kitchen at night and enjoy an extra dessert."

"JonJon, I taught you better," his mother gasped.

"It's not just me, Mum," Jonas said quickly and went on to tell her about the Ballad family and their unique relationships.

"They sound absolutely lovely." She smiled. "I'm glad you've got kind people there to take care of you, but don't forget your mum and family here."

"I would never," he promised. "How is everyone?"

"Emily is delivering babies left and right, but still won't give *me* any grandchildren," she complained.

"Mum, I've been gone two weeks—did you plan to have her married off and pregnant in that time frame?" Jonas teased.

"A mother can hope," she replied crisply.

"I'm sure there's more to this and Emily will tell me when she can call." He set aside his empty food container and there was a long silence.

"Dad is fine too," his mother said gently. "He'd

love to talk to you, beyond the cursory hello, how are you and goodbye."

"I think that's all we've had since what happened, happened," Jonas admitted. "It's been complicated by—well, you know."

"Not as complicated as you'd like to think," his mother said. "You and your father need to clear the air. He's not upset. He's more unhappy that you were caught up in it by a so-called friend."

"The fact that I put his good name and esteemed career into it doesn't factor in at all, hmm?"

"Your father loves you more than any of that. I wish you'd listen to him and understand that didn't matter to him." His mother spoke gently. "He would've given it all up for you in an instant, but anger—his initial anger from him and then you made the situation worse. I hope this time apart can somehow bring you two back together again. I hate to see the close bond you have ruined because of someone else's actions."

Jonas pinched the bridge of his nose. "Let's just—Mum, can we put this on hold? I'm starting a new life here—"

"And forgetting the old one you had," she finished sadly.

"No. I'm trying to build back from it," he replied, hoping she'd understand. "Listen, Mum, I have to go. It's almost six here, so I know its eleven for you and you shouldn't be in the kitchen making—what are you making?"

"Kimchi. It's supposed to be good for stomach health and your dad needs it," his mother answered.

"Dad won't eat that. You know his view on fermented foods." Jonas grinned.

"He will when I sit and watch him," his mother said firmly. "I love the man. I want him to be around for a long time."

"I love him, too," Jonas admitted. "I've got to go, Mum. My love to everyone."

"We love you, JonJon. Good night," his mother said and disconnected the video call.

Jonas went back to work, directing his attention to the schedules and files in front of him, instead of sinking into his memories. He didn't move until there was no more work for him that evening. With a heavy sigh, Jonas closed down his computer, got his coat and turned out the light, locking his office before he took the elevator down to the main floor. As he trudged to his car, he felt tired of all a sudden, exhausted mentally and emotionally. He couldn't imagine when the events of the last two years would finally be dull enough that he could think about his father without a lump forming in his throat and a fist tightening around his heart. Would he ever stop feeling like a failure to everyone, especially his father?

The thought followed him all the way to the inn. Not even the cheerful lights and decorations could crack his gloomy mood. The house was quiet. He knew dinner would have come and gone, and no one was sitting outside that night. The blustering winds had made sure of that. He used the code that was on his card to open the front door and stepped inside, finding the place dim except for the lights in the dining room. Micki sat at the table alone, surrounded by stacks of books, head bent over a laptop as she typed furiously. He could've snuck upstairs and she wouldn't have noticed but something propelled him forward into the room and Micki looked up.

"Hey," she said in a friendly tone. "You are pretty late tonight. Dinner is in the kitchen, warming, if you're still hungry."

"Not really. I raided the vending machine a few times," Jonas replied.

Micki tsked softly at him. "You better not let Enid hear you. She'll start packing you a lunch."

"That's an option?" he asked teasingly.

"Be careful what you ask for, the rest of the professors might get lunch envy," Micki said playfully.

"What are you working on?" Jonas asked.

"Homework and some research for The Innocence Project." Micki's eyes took on a look of concern. "You're hurting."

Jonas was surprised. Did she mean his emotions or his actual physical pain of a lingering headache? "How did you know?"

"I can recognize the signs of a migraine. I used to be in acupuncture and reflexology school." She stood and pushed him into an empty chair. "This will help."

"You don't have to—" Jonas's words fell away when she pressed an area of his neck and he felt the pressure behind his eye and at the back of his head ease almost immediately. "Oh, bless you."

"Never doubt my powers," Micki teased. "Close your eyes. Let me work my magic. If you're anything like Margo when I do this for her migraines, you'll be half asleep by the time I'm done."

"I don't blame her for nodding off." Jonas slowly relaxed. "It's like your hands are just pulling the headache away."

"Shh," she whispered.

Jonas obeyed and soon felt relief all over. By the time Micki was finished, her words rang true—he did want to go fall across the bed and sleep for ages.

"There you go." Micki kissed the top of his head. "Now you can rest properly tonight."

As she went to step away, Jonas caught her hand and squeezed. He looked up at her and in a low voice that he didn't recognize, he said, "Thank you, Michelle." And meant it.

A spark ignited between them, and the air changed. To Jonas, it was as if the connection that had slowly begun to form between them solidified. Micki leaned in and lowered her head. Her tender lips kissed him softly, with a sweet friction that was his undoing.

"Why did you do that?" Jonas asked when the kiss ended.

A slow smile crossed her lips. "I felt it, too. Good night, Jonas."

"Good night."

He rose and walked out of the room but stopped to look back. Micki was again sitting with her books and laptop. She smiled at him once more and then focused on her work.

Jonas shook his head bemusedly while climbing the main staircase. *She kissed me*, he thought, and he grinned like a loon as his mum would say. He'd honestly forgotten the feeling of excitement that the first hints of something special always brought. But instead of overthinking it, Jonas took a shower and fell into bed, letting the sweetness of the moment lull him to sleep.

THERE WERE ALWAYS adventures at hand in the
Sardis Woods community. Micki loved that
about the historic neighborhood. It didn't matter whether there was a holiday or reason to
celebrate. As it happened, Thanksgiving was
approaching, and the town was ready. All sorts
of events that embraced turkey season—as
the locals liked to call it—had been planned.
Dreamboat of a Steamboat—yes, that was its
name—was a staple and had been existing on
the same spot since Micki's parents were newlyweds. The vessel hosted the yearly Thanksgiving Country Dance—an event that locals and
visitors were sure to enjoy. Mia always put it on
the guests' itineraries, and those who wanted to
attend had free admission. This time, everyone
had signed up, including Jonas.

Micki and a few of the others milled around
the inn's lobby, waiting so that everyone could
walk together to the dance. Many friends and
neighbors would do the same. The warm sense
of togetherness they'd feel would hopefully keep
the conversation flowing and the chilly evening
air at bay.

Her family gathered, including her parents,
while her sisters' kids were being babysat by a
trustworthy friend and her daughter. The chatting in the lobby went down to nothing, making
Micki look up to the top of the stairs, and even

her mouth fell open. Jonas descended, wearing jeans so new they still had the pressed crease, polished brown cowboy boots and a blue-and-white plaid shirt tucked into the jeans. A large silver belt buckle featuring the horns of a steer embossed the front. His brown cowboy hat matched the boots.

"What in the name of cowboys everywhere is happening here?" Margo shook her head.

"Too much?" Jonas asked uncertainly when he joined the group. "Gideon told me to go wild when I went to the shops."

Micki threw her brother-in-law a dark look. "He did, did he?"

Margo wore a smile, but Gideon looked pained. Micki knew that look—her sister had pinched him on the sensitive skin of the inner arm.

"You look great, buddy," Gideon said.

Ryan clapped Jonas on the back. "We should've gone with you to rein you in a little bit. 'Go wild' was too broad."

"Okay. We can solve this." Micki took his hat and started to re-crease it so it didn't look like it still wore the tag—which it did, so she removed that as well. "Ryan, trade belts with Jonas."

"Folks, if you could please wait for us on the patio," Mia said politely.

"But this is so much better," one guest teased.

"I saw the review from the couple who stayed here when one of you was dressed in a dog costume that was possessed. I didn't believe it, but if the aliens outside the house didn't prove it, this does."

"Well, we appreciate the compliment—I think," Mia said brightly and they walked outside.

Micki looked at Ryan. "The belt, please, and Jonas, open a few buttons to expose the T-shirt beneath, then roll the sleeves up to your elbows."

In a few minutes, Jonas looked less stiff and formal. "Perfect." Micki put her hand through the crook of his elbow and noticed the amused gaze that passed between her sisters and parents. "Shut it."

"What?" Mia feigned innocence.

Micki glared at them. "Don't even think it."

"We're just noticing what a beautiful youngest daughter we have," her father said and patted her shoulder as he passed by. Then he took her mother's hand in his.

"Uh-huh," Micki muttered.

"What's that about?" Jonas asked, looking confused.

"Who knows? My family is an oddity," she said loudly so they could all hear. That generated enough laughter to even make her smile.

"Shall we tell him, Micki, how only last month

you dressed for Halloween like a sand crab that couldn't find its way to the beach?" Margo asked sweetly.

"Or that you were in a mosh pit dressed like a toucan for Carolina Rock Fest, the month before that?" Mia added.

"I was a very pretty bird," Micki said primly and made everyone laugh.

"Are there pictures?" Jonas sounded too eager. "I, for one, would love to see the pretty toucan."

"You show me yours and I shall show you mine," she replied.

"I like the implication of such a trade, Michelle." Jonas grinned at her.

His voice was husky and it made butterflies take flight in her stomach. The short kiss they'd shared had kept her up last night, and if she were honest, she hoped it had been the same for him.

The group got underway and soon rounded the final corner, leading into the marina. *Dreamboat of a Steamboat* was jumping with loud music, streamers waving in the breeze, and a mechanical bull set up with crash mats and circled by hay bales. Micki spotted more familiar faces as people seemed to be drinking and eating and generally having a great time. The annual event seemed to get more popular from one year to the next.

KELLIE A. KING   79

Micki noticed the secondary dining room had the double doors propped open. It was now a large dance floor. There was a bar in each area of the steamboat and there was extra seating on the rooftop patio, enclosed with retractable wood-and-glass garage doors that were so trendy now in the neighborhood's breweries and restaurants.

"Could you take a picture of me so I can send it to my sister, Emily?" Jonas asked loudly over the music. "She's not going to believe this place when she sees it and how I'm dressed."

"Sure," Micki said with a chuckle. "Go stand over there and look like a casual type of cowboy in the saloon."

"How does this look?" Micki asked, handing him the phone.

"Fantastic, thank you," he said and put his arm around her shoulder. "Now some selfies with the two of us."

"For your sister?" Micki gulped.

"Of course. She'll want to know who helped me look as fly as this."

Micki laughed out loud. "*Fly?* Oh, Jonas, never use that word again."

"Not cool anymore?"

She shook her head, amused. "Not since the eighties, but for that you get a few selfies."

A few selfies turned into seven or eight, then

her mother accepted the camera eagerly to take a picture of Micki and Jonas.

"Send those to me," Rosie Ballad told Jonas.

"Sure. Take your phone out and I'll message them to you," he offered politely.

"My phone can do that?" her mother asked.

Micki rolled her eyes. "Mom, I tried to teach you that feature at Gigi's birth, then Andy's."

Rosie looked at her innocently. "I was suffering from new baby fever. I heard nothing and was steeped in happy grandmother endorphins."

"Good grief," Micki murmured and watched while Jonas patiently explained to her mother what he was doing.

After all that, Gideon and Ryan pulled him away to try a new IPA that *Dreamboat* had on tap and to play a game of pool, while she went off to dance with her sisters. The night was fun. Mia still kept an eye on the inn's guests until their mother told her to quit fussing over the poor people. Micki was talking with a few friends—Peter Cage, aka Rabbit, and his new wife, Nina—when Margo hurried up to them.

"Oh, you better come, Micki. Gideon, Ryan and Jonas are going to ride the mechanical bull!" she blurted, laughter in her eyes.

"What?" Micki asked, shocked, and turned to her friends. "I—I'll be back."

"No need, we're coming too!" Peter and Nina followed on her heels.

"Who came up with this wild notion?" Micki demanded to know. "Jonas is an esteemed lawyer and dean of a law school. He does not need to be on a mechanical bull."

Peter looked at her curiously. "Why should any of that stop him from riding a mechanical bull?"

"His cowboy hat still had the tag on it. He's an uptight professor dude," Micki replied.

"Oh. Still, why not? Let the man do his thing," Peter said, grinning.

"I don't want to be blamed for breaking the new dean before he's been there for a month," Micki said loudly above the party noise. "Margo, did Gideon have something to do with this?"

"Hey, it wasn't just my husband," Margo declared. "From what Mia said, the guys were playing darts and Jonas was winning. Then Ryan and Gideon were like, oh well, yeah, you're good at darts but what about a mechanical bull? Jonas said that it was all a matter of physics and he'd seen it on the *telly* and then it came down to bets on who could stay on the longest between the four of them."

"Four?" Micki asked.

"Matt's here and he's agreed to use Jonas's method to stay on the thing. Dad is coaching all of them and Mia is insisting they stop the madness," Margo continued. "It escalated quickly into the usual strange chaos that is our life."

"And here I thought moving to Charlotte from California would be boring." Nina laughed. "I was so wrong."

"You're telling me, sister," Micki muttered.

A large group had assembled outside, where the chilly night air was erased by the portable heaters. Micki strode with purpose toward the mechanical bull surrounded by a cheering crowd. She pushed to the center to find her two brothers-in-law, Jonas, Matt—Ryan's friend, and her father.

"Are you trying to break the new dean of the law school?" she demanded to know, her hands on her hips.

"He started it," Ryan said, pointing to Jonas.

"I technically said it's easy to beat the machine with physics. He dared me to prove it," Jonas answered.

"We've got two teams," her father said. "The naturals who will ride the best they can and the brain trust who will use Jonas's method to stay on for eight seconds or more."

"Dad!" Micki sputtered in exasperation. "You're supposed to be the voice of reason."

"He is, sweet girl," her mother piped up. "I completely overruled his decision to be the tie-breaker."

"You gotta be kidding me," Micki muttered and looked at Mia, who was grinning. "What's so funny?"

Mia shoved her hands in the pockets of her coat. "I'm just here to see who bruises their coccyx so I can tease them like I was teased."

One of the inn's guests poked their head into the group. "Just to let you guys know, five-star rating going up because you're all the best. Now, let's joust!"

"Totally different sport, honey," his wife pulled him back gently.

"Okay! We've got a competition going on at the *Dreamboat*!" the emcee announced so loudly inside the venue that everyone could hear. "Let's ride!"

"And here we go!" Margo clapped her hands as Gideon stepped up first. "Go, baby, go! You're a marine! Oorah!"

"Even you?" Micki was shocked again. "How am *I* the voice of reason?"

Margo shrugged. "This is exciting for us. We've been working and taking care of kids day in, day out. We get our kicks anywhere we can."

Micki sighed. "Okay. I'll give you that one."

Gideon signaled that he was ready. Micki knew that he used to live in Texas when he was still enlisted in the military, so she expected him to stay on for the full length of time. Instead,

Gideon was tossed in four seconds and lay flat on his back, looking upward.

Margo rushed over to the edge of the hay bales. "Are you okay, baby?"

He nodded and rolled over with a groan. "I just figured out I'm not young anymore."

"I'm sorry, honey," Margo crooned and helped him over the side.

Gideon looked at Micki. "Don't stay a word."

"Me?" Micki held back her grin. "Never."

Ryan lasted longer. It was a full seven seconds before he slipped off at the last good buck by the mechanical bull.

Jonas slapped Matt on the back. "Remember, flow with the motion."

Matt nodded. "Gotcha."

He climbed on and got settled before giving a determined nod to start the mechanical bull. Matt held on for fifteen seconds and a used a backward flip to get on his feet from where he was thrown.

"Okay, now he's showing off," Ryan grumbled.

It was finally Jonas's turn and Micki stood next to him, worrying. "Are you sure you want to do this?"

Jonas grinned and handed her his glasses. "I'm going for double of Matt's time. A full thirty seconds. A kiss for luck?"

"Is this your way of trying to sneak a kiss?" A smile hinted around her lips.

"Whatever it takes," he replied. "Lay one on me."

"Fine." Micki stood on her tiptoes and pressed a quick kiss on his lips while the crowd whistled. "Go stay on thirty seconds."

She looked back at her family and gave them the don't-you-dare look, only to see innocent smiles pasted on their faces. Even Rabbit and Nina were grinning.

Micki held her breath as the bull began moving slowly and Jonas looked confident as he held on. The pace picked up and he was still calm, following each motion easily and even using the stirrups to stand as the contraption moved forward and back.

"What in the British bronco…" Margo muttered.

"Where do you come up with these sayings?" Gideon asked his wife.

"He's doing it," Micki whispered and then laughed, saying the words louder. "He's doing it. Hold on, Teach, you got this!"

More bucking movements, and Jonas almost tumbled off but managed to hold on and find his balance. Thirty then forty-five seconds passed. The last huge jerk threw him to the soft mat and the crowd roared, cheering for him.

Jonas managed to climbed over the hay bales before Micki rushed into his arms and gave him a hug. Multiple hands reached out to slap him on the back and congratulate him as she laughed in delight.

"How did you do that?" Micki pushed aside the loose lock of hair covering his eyes, before placing his glasses back on his face.

"Simple harmonic motion. When the velocity of the bull changed, I shifted my sitting position to accommodate the change," Jonas explained. "Even though there is a greater range when the spring moved, I found that those times when I stood, I could handle the jostling much better."

Micki stared at him, impressed. "You just blew my mind."

Jonas grinned. "I'm glad I could do that for you."

They joined the rest of her family and the inn's guests. Jonas stood with his cohorts. "I will expect my winnings in various dessert treats as promised. I especially look forward to the pineapple cheesecake milkshake."

"You guys bet desserts?" Margo asked, clearly flustered. "That's it. All the men in this family are going to dessert counseling."

"That's not a thing," Ryan pointed out as they moved to go back inside the steamboat. "And even if it was, I want no part of it."

"Agreed," the other men chorused.

"A dance?" Jonas asked when the music turned to something slow.

Micki smiled. "I'd like that."

Jonas held her lightly in his arms as their feet found the rhythm easily. She looked at him and smiled. "I should've known a man who could ride a mechanical bull like that would be quick on his feet."

"Thank you." Jonas's eyes settled on her. "You are so beautiful."

His words took her breath away. "I—well, you're handsome as heck."

A soft chuckle escaped him. "I appreciate that. I always felt a little nerdy-looking."

"More debonair and scholarly, I'd say." She caught a glimpse of her family at the tables. Her whole clan was watching them with huge smiles on their faces. Micki sighed. "Don't look now, but my entire family is watching us, smiling like cats with a bowlful of cream, and there's most of the neighborhood as well."

Jonas caressed her cheek. "Then let's give them something to talk about."

Before she could say a word, Jonas dipped her and pressed a kiss on her lips. She clung to his shoulder as they came back up and he held them steady. The kiss went on a little longer. The kind that could make the world tip on its axis.

He lifted his head, and a smile crept across his face. "See. Now, that's a kiss to have a gathering for."

"Yeah," Micki said weakly.

They danced the night away. Jonas even managed to pick up the country line dancing surprisingly well. On the walk home everyone seemed pleasantly happy and quiet, only having an occasional conversation now and again. Micki was acutely aware that Jonas held her hand the entire way home and then pressed a kiss on her knuckles when they parted on the stairs. After she showered and got herself ready for bed, her phone dinged its merry little chime, and she looked at the message from her mother. It was a picture she'd taken at the exact moment that Jonas had dipped her at the end of the tune and kissed her.

"Oh, Mom," Micki whispered, but couldn't stop looking at the picture.

The memory gave her a sense of warmth as she snuggled beneath the layers of thick blankets, then she saved the picture to her phone. It was more than obvious the love juju around Ballad Inn and Sardis Woods was trying to catch her—hard.

CHAPTER FOUR

SEVERAL FACTORS COULD potentially be problems for Jonas. Being attracted to Micki, even though she wasn't a law school student, could still raise a few eyebrows. He didn't want any note of impropriety to ever be attached to his credentials, or hers, so that would be one situation where he'd have to tread carefully. The next was that he didn't come to Charlotte intending to look for a relationship. He was a bit cautious about being hurt by anyone he cared for, including friends.

The true measure of a friend or someone close to you was how they reacted when your back was against the wall. Two years ago, he'd been betrayed by a friend, and the others had faded into the shadows, not willing to be caught up in a fracas. That included his girlfriend, a longtime sweetheart he'd had ever since secondary school. They'd even gone to law school together. But to save face and her career, she'd left just like everyone else. And he'd realized, their love wasn't as strong as he'd thought. The last he'd heard, she was married and at a prestigious firm with her husband. Jonas wasn't mad, it just wasn't meant to be. But it made him wary. Would such an energetic whirlwind like Micki be someone who would be there when the chips were down?

Take a step back. You've known her for two weeks. But he was the type that took every relationship seriously. Never a foolhardy type of man, he always thought about the long term. Still, this might be the perfect moment to loosen up and enjoy life, enjoy Michelle's company just like he planned to that afternoon. It was the last cricket match with Micah's friend, and if he liked the group, he would definitely join up in the spring. After one last look at his white sweat suit, he deemed it okay as an alternative to a pristine uniform to play in, until he could get one.

About to walk downstairs, he almost collided with Michelle when she came bounding from the third floor. They met on the landing. She was again eye-catchingly beautiful, dressed in dark blue jeans, white sneakers and a white sweatshirt that featured a big sunflower in the center. The words Keep Enjoying Sunshine reflected her effect on him exactly. Michelle's heartfelt approach and bright smile seemed to erase his dark thoughts. Calling her Michelle made it special: she was his in that way already. His Michelle. *Maybe Emily is right, I'm a sucker for love*, he thought.

"Good morning, Michelle," Jonas said cheerfully.

"And a good morrow to you, Jonas," she replied with a laugh.

He chuckled. "Very old English of you, I appreciate that. Are you ready to go?"

"I am. We're full from Sunday brunch and we are ready to rock and roll." Together they walked down the stars. "Hey, after the match do you want to go to Big Ben Pub? They have a Sunday band, and we could have dinner there if you'll have worked up an appetite."

"One question. Do they have liver and onions?" Jonas asked.

"I've seen it on the menu." Micki grimaced. "You're going to eat that?"

"It's a delicacy," he told her in shock.

"Enid had to win several debates to get liver anywhere near me." Micki rubbed her hand over her stomach and looked ill. "We had a standoff for an entire night. I even ate my vegetables but not the liver. She gave up around eight and I went to bed without dessert."

"I love it." Jonas grinned. "But we can have fish and chips at the pub, I don't mind."

Micki held her hand up as they went out the front door. "I'm okay as long as I don't have to eat it."

Jonas glanced at the blue sky before he opened the car door for Micki. "A good day for a cricket match. At least the weather warmed up nicely."

"Charlotte's weather is all over the place," she said and slipped into the passenger seat. Then he got behind the wheel. "There can be Christmas Days when we wear shorts and use the smoker for a prime rib."

"That's amazing," he said. "Winter in London is…winter in London. It's cold."

"Well, don't get used to anything because by March you'll be in a light jacket and in May we're outside barbecuing." She laughed.

"Whatever house or condo I buy, it needs to have a balcony or patio so I can barbecue," Jonas said. "I have read up on it extensively and I think I can make fall off the bone ribs and chicken. I even created a recipe for a lovely marinade."

Micki was silent for a moment. "Still, I think that maybe you should let Gideon or Ryan help you with the initial setup of your grill and cooking meat with fire. Enid would be good, too."

"Why?" Jonas queried. "Humans have been cooking meat over fire since their times in the caves."

"Ye-s," she drawled. "But you can't burn down a cave. However, you can a lovely, brand-new condo."

"Good point," he admitted with a laugh.

The cricket match was to be at the university's sports field, which Jonas assumed his group used when no games were being played and in the off season. Right now, they were at the height of American football season for college and pro leagues. He was looking forward to going to one of the college's home games. He parked close to the entrance and waited for Micki before taking his duffel from the trunk that held his batting pads, shin guards, gloves and cricket bat.

"I read up on the sport. The parts I forgot at least," Micki told him as they walked to the entrance then past the gates.

"You know the rules of the game," Jonas said, pleased. "How come, may I ask? Most Americans find it dry and boring."

"Have you watched baseball? It's not exactly an on-the-edge-of-your-seat type of sport," Micki pointed out. "But years ago, when Mom and Dad and us three girls were in London, I happened across a game on TV and got curious. I tend to research anything and everything, so I spent the next six weeks learning the game."

"A researcher's mind." Jonas was pleased. "I do the same thing."

"Hey, Jonas." Micah, wearing the traditional uniform, came jogging up. "Glad you could make it."

"Sorry I don't have my uniform. I didn't expect I'd need it in Charlotte." Jonas shook his hand. "This is Michelle. She's one of the owners of the inn where I'm staying. She came out to watch the match."

"Michelle—" Micah looked at her curiously. "Micki Ballad. I remember you came to those talks my colleagues and I gave to new students about careers in the law. You were really bright, asked lots of good questions."

Micki smiled. "Yes, I'm almost done my undergrad now. Those sessions you did were great."

"Glad to hear it," Micah said. "I thought from your questions that you were probably ready to practice even then."

"I work for a legal nonprofit when I have the time, doing their case research, and I fell in love with it," she added. "It's never too old to find your true calling in life."

"I agree." Micah smiled. "Okay, Jonas, you ready to show us up on the field?"

Jonas sat to retie his laces and put on the shin guards. "I'm more than a bit rusty. I haven't played for about a year. I should ask you to not embarrass me on the field."

"We're here for fun." Micah lifted his bat over his shoulder. "Just a few guys from all walks of life who love the game."

"Then let's do it." Jonas stood and looked at Micki. "I hope you're not too bored by this."

"I'm already intrigued to watch you all play." She moved away to sit in the stands.

"So, Micki Ballad, huh?" Micah said casually when she was out of earshot. "How did you hook up with the most well-known adult student at the college?"

"By happenstance. She's one of the owners of the bed-and-breakfast where I'm booked to stay temporarily," Jonas answered, feeling uncomfortable with the question. "We're just friends, no hooking up involved."

"Still, you might want to think about moving out sooner rather than later. Don't give Willoughby any ammunition to cause trouble for you. Especially if you do end up dating after she graduates."

"That won't be the case. And as for what's happening now, I don't teach until the start of the new year, and I will ensure she's not in any of my classes," Jonas said firmly. "Jennifer has taken care of students before and she will continue to do so."

"I didn't mean to offend," Micah said quickly. "I just know that after my tenure announcement and your tense conversation with Willoughby, he'll be gunning for the new guy."

"He'll have to use something other than some sort of twisted impropriety to complain about me," Jonas replied. "And I'm not offended. I'm just very careful about who to trust and what's said in circles about me."

"I get it, I was once the new guy. If I wasn't teaching, I was defending my right to teach at the law school against Willoughby and people like him." Micah's serious tone perked up. "Hey, let's work this off out on the field."

Instead of the normal eleven players per side, there were only fourteen people in total on the field, so that meant each team would be seven players. Jonas was fine with that. As he'd grown up, he and his friends had certainly played with fewer out in the village. Like Micah said, this group was a diverse bunch but all were talking easily about a game they clearly loved. Some of them were teachers from other faculties and departments and as introductions were made, Jonas pinned them all as a nice lot. The group picked teams randomly and set up their wickets. Jonas looked to where Micki sat. She waved exuberantly, and a whistle came from her lips.

"Looks like we have a student groupie," one

of the instructors said, looking amused. "The first one ever."

"She's not here for you," Micah joked. "Our new guy brought her with him."

A couple of professors raised an eyebrow. Micah quickly corrected the wrong impression.

Jonas firmed his lips. The comment and teasing were rubbing him the wrong way more than they should. His armor might have been tarnished by the past, but he was still an honorable man, and just the thought of inappropriate behavior made him uneasy.

The sun hung high in the sky and the last few leaves in the trees fell with just a light breeze. The grassy field was a mix of brown and green thanks to the shifting temperatures. As he took a deep breath and filled his lungs with the cool air, Jonas knew there was no other place he'd rather be. Everyone was ready to start the match.

Micah's team won the toss and chose to bat first. Jonas' pulse raced in excitement. He put his batting pads on, sensing this promised to be a good, exerting match.

Jonas strode confidently to his position and took his defensive stance with the bat. If the bowler, or pitcher, managed to hit the wicket on the first throw, he would be embarrassed. Cameron, the bowler, sprinted in and Jonas held his breath. The ball was delivered with the grace of a professional cricketer, a wide arch wing of the arm that Jonas tracked. He responded with a precise forward shot that bounced and rolled away from a fielder that was about twenty yards from the wicket. It wasn't how hard you could hit the ball, but where you could send it to get the most runs.

He and his base-running partner, Raj, rotated each strike well, pushing for more runs with each swing of the bat. Micki cheered them on. It wasn't hard to hear her: she was the only one watching. The fielders from the other team slid and chased the ball in determination. In the usual fashion, pristine white cricket clothes were soon streaked with dirt and grass marks. At each turn at bat, both teams went into the game with gusto, trying to keep each other in check.

"Go, Jonas! You rock those runs, go for a four!" Micki yelled and clapped.

"She is enthusiastic," Martin, a teammate of Jonas's, said as he got ready to bowl at the cricketer up to bat.

Raj laughed. "We see who she's enthusiastic for."

"Bring your partners next time, Raj and Martin, and maybe they'll cheer for you," Micah chided them.

"Tess will never come out here, she'd die of boredom," Martin replied.

"Then hush up and bowl," Jonas yelled, not caring about the ribbing from the guys. He was having too much fun to care. He sprinted several yards to make a spectacular catch, even though Martin had bowled clever variations to try to outsmart the batsman. Jonas landed on his back with an oof, but as he looked up in the sky, a laugh escaped his lips.

"You're out!" Micah yelled triumphantly. "Great catch, Jonas!"

There were groans from the other team, but the match continued with an air of camaraderie between them all. Jonas felt friendships forming as the hours progressed and was grateful. Both teams gave it their all, and the match eventually reached its thrilling end in a last-minute tie. They shared handshakes and laughter as they walked back to their bags and other gear, teasing each other unmercifully about old bones and sore muscles. Michelle came from the stands to meet him as he said his goodbyes.

"See you later, Micki." Micah waved, and a few others also offered their farewells. "We could use a bigger fan base. If you could bring others in the spring to boost our egos, that would be great."

"I'll see what I can do." Micki grinned as they

walked away. She stopped and looked Jonas up and down. "Do you need to go home and change before we eat?"

He shook his head. "Not in the least. I've got a quick change in the bag. You head on to the car and I'll use the locker room really quickly then catch up with you there."

"Toss me the keys, I'll get the car warmed up." Micki held up her hand and caught them easily.

"Be back shortly," he promised and jogged off.

He was sore, but in a good way, and he felt invigorated as he changed into comfortable jeans and his navy Cambridge sweater. After he tied his sneakers, Jonas took his duffel and went back to the car. He was looking forward to enjoying the dinner Micki promised and her good company. He'd worked up an appetite for a good pint and a hearty meal.

"Ready to go?" Micki asked when he got into the passenger seat. "Do you want to drive?"

"Since you know where we're going, I don't mind being copilot." Jonas turned to smile at her.

"Then fasten your seat belt, we're heading to a little slice of home," she replied and started the engine.

Jonas took her hand and squeezed lightly. "Thank you for coming out with me today, I truly appreciate it."

"I had the best time." Micki smiled. "Even though I sat most of the time and took pictures of you guys playing."

"You've got pictures?" Jonas asked in surprise.

She nodded. "Yep, I'll show you at the pub. I got a lovely one when you caught the ball and fell on your back. A perfect shot."

"From a most lovely woman," Jonas complimented her.

"To the pub!" she said loudly with a laugh.

Jonas echoed her words, feeling her exuberance. "To the pub!"

MICKI STOOD OUTSIDE the Big Ben Pub and Grubbery. Technically, she didn't know why *grubbery* had been added to the name, but hey, she thought, to each their own. She looked at the pleased smile on Jonas's face while he admired the authentic red phone box that stood sentry outside the pub's front door.

"This is an amazing replica," he enthused.

"It's no replica. Larry had the box shipped here to put a real stamp on the place," Micki told him. "You'd be surprised how many transplants we have from across the pond. Let's go inside."

The mahogany tables and the booths were polished while the single tables sat in the main room. Flags from various soccer teams and a Union Jack hung on the walls along with a series of black-and-white photos. The glass cases and shelves held trophies in chronological order by year. Jonas looked around like he'd found his nirvana and she just grinned, pleased with his reaction.

"Oh, this is so great," he said. "I can bring the cricket lads, here—if that's okay?"

"Why wouldn't it be?" Micki questioned. "You need a proper hangout spot, I think this is yours. I can see you and the guys sitting around a few tables pushed together all talking, yelling at a match on the TV and laughing."

Jonas kissed her cheek. "Thank you, love."

Micki felt a warmth spread through her, even though she knew *love* was a pet name many from Europe used. Still, it felt very personal to her. The hostess told them to sit anywhere, and they chose the high-top table close to the window so they could people-watch while eating. After they ordered their drinks—Micki chose a Ben's Peach Sweet Tea and Jonas ordered an extra cold Guinness—they stared out the window in companionable silence. The early evening was pleasant, which meant more folks walked around and some were doing their shopping for the holidays. The area was already decked out for Christmas but Micki frowned.

"What's wrong?" Jonas asked, concern on his face.

"Nothing, really. I just miss the feeling of anticipation that used to come with the holidays. It's like the stores, and people skip over Thanksgiving and jump right into Christmas. It didn't used to be that way. Thanksgiving had its own vibe and traditions when me and my sisters were growing up. Now it's so commercialized that before Halloween is over Christmas items are for sale, and before New Year's, businesses are already stocking for Valentine's. It's instant gratification, I suppose."

"You miss the build-up to each holiday." Jonas assessed her correctly. "You'll be happy to know that in the village where my parents have their home, the timing is slower. While we don't celebrate your Thanksgiving, you do get that something-is-coming feeling, as you did as a child. The shops still wrap gifts in brown paper with red ribbon if chosen and there's even a toymaker who still creates his toys by hand. I got my very first train set from him and now his son works there, too. When you walk through their store it's like going back in time. You expect someone with a top hat to incline his head and say, *Good morrow to you, sir.*"

Micki stared in wide-eyed fascination. "That sounds amazing. I'm adding it to my bucket list of places I want to see."

"Maybe I'll be there with you," Jonas said in a smooth voice and Micki smiled in response.

Their drinks came and as they looked at the menu, Micki peeked around the laminated card in her hand. "Try the liver and onions, I hear it's sublime."

Jonas's laugh rang out and he glanced up at the server. "I think I'll take her advice. Liver and onions it is."

"I'll have the cheeseburger and onion strings." Micki handed back the menu.

"I'll have that right up for such a lovely couple." The waitress turned and took another order before heading for the kitchen.

Micki thought about correcting the server: this wasn't a date. But the goofy smile on Jonas's lips held her back.

Jonas took a sip of his drink then asked, "What did you think of the match today?"

Micki lifted her glass to take a long gulp of her tea. "It's too civilized for me. I like sports I can really get into, like running, white water rafting, and I hike and camp. I even rock climb. It's a good way for me to clear my head."

"You could run circles around me, that's for sure."

Micki flashed him a wicked smile. "I'll invite you next time I think about scaling a large rock."

"Okay. I place myself in your safe hands," he said.

"You may want to rethink that if you haven't seen the rock yet." She laughed.

He gave her a curious look and shrugged. "Oh, I think I'll be fine. A little danger might push me out of my comfort zone."

"Don't stray too far. You're pretty cool where you are," she murmured.

"What?"

"Nothing," she answered, and their food arrived just in time to divert the conversation.

While they ate, Micki and Jonas talked about the law, their likes and dislikes. The fact that he ate his meal with gusto made her grimace while watching. It was more than a texture thing for her: the taste of liver and onions was just odd to her.

"You should try a bite," Jonas encouraged.

Micki held up her hand in refusal. "How about I don't, and we say I did?"

"To each his own," Jonas said. "I hope they have a good dessert."

"Gasp, you're cheating on Enid's desserts? I'm telling," Micki said in a fake outraged voice.

"I'll not have you getting me in trouble," Jonas said, laughing. "I'm going to get dessert at home."

Micki looked around conspiratorially. "I won't

tell if we share a batch of fried doughnuts and their orange marmalade dipping sauce."

"You're making me an accessory," he whispered. "I don't know if I should."

"Well—"

"I'm in," he said quickly.

"That was a turnaround in two point five seconds." She laughed.

Jonas grinned. "I know a good thing when I hear it—and see it."

"Sweet cotton candy, I might start to think you mean me," Micki replied softly.

It wasn't long before the steam rose from the plate of ten mini fried doughnuts and the dipping sauce in front of them. The smell of the fried, sugary dough wafted up and Micki took a deep breath before rubbing her hands eagerly. Both she and Jonas reached for the same treat. He snagged it and dipped it while she gave him a look that said, *Really?* He put it to his mouth but then held it out for her to take a bite instead. Micki did so and his gaze never left hers.

"Yummy. You get one, too," she encouraged. "If you haven't figured it out yet, the Ballads like food. It's our love language."

"I've noticed and I'm quite pleased with the fact," Jonas answered, taking one of the doughnuts from the plate. "Family dinners in my neck of the woods was mostly me and my sister,

Emily, when Dad was in London for work and Mom went with him. Now my mom's often in the kitchen, cooking, and enjoying every minute of it."

"And your dad?" Micki asked after another bite.

"He's slowing down, but still works from home Thursday to Sunday and in London the rest of the week. My mother is on a mission for grandchildren and Em is not moving fast enough for her. And obviously, neither am I."

"She would go wild for the babies at the house?" Micki nodded. "My mother and dad agree. They seemed to have hung up their traveling bags for grandparenthood."

"And what about you?" Jonas asked. "Do you have plans to go to law school right away, after you graduate, or do more hours at the non-profit until your new studies begin?"

Micki chewed thoughtfully for a moment. "I want to travel. I have tons of towns, cities, countries I want to see before I settle down. Can I tell you something honestly, that you'll keep to yourself?"

"It won't go beyond this table," he promised.

"I think I'm going to move out of Ballad Inn, get my own place off the property." Micki realized how good it was to say the words out loud and be able to confide in someone new. "My sisters have families of their own, and my parents are loving being there for the babies and to support all of them, which is great. Meanwhile, the main house is going to change up, become a full-time business, and while I have a home being built there, I'm not ready to fill it. I have a wanderlust that I want to fill first. Eventually, I'll go home when the timing's right but that isn't now."

"It's totally understandable. One of the songbirds needs to leave the nest sometime, yeah?" Jonas said gently. "It sounds like you've made your choice already—when are you going to tell your family?"

"After the holidays, but I've started looking for a place," Micki said, and she felt a pang of sadness in her chest. Her new beginning would be sad, but she wouldn't be too far away. Talking about it to Jonas made the decision more final in her head. She gave a watery laugh as emotion clogged her throat. "You never know, my condo may be next to yours."

"I'll break out my fondue pot," Jonas teased. "Maybe we can look together? Your family will think you're helping me until the time is right to tell them."

"Okay. I'd like that." Micki smiled. "So, do you have a fondue pot, really?"

He nodded. "I do. It was a going away gift

from my sister. Apparently she thinks melted cheese is an American staple."

Micki laughed. "Oh, I've got a great spot for you to have dinner."

Jonas insisted on paying the check and they left, blending into the dinner crowd on their way to the car. The drive home was quiet but comfortable. She enjoyed watching him look out the window at the sights and the scenic skyline.

"Did you know that the team was trying to tease me about you being a student?" Jonas said casually and gave a small laugh.

"Really?" Micki kept her eye on the road to take the ramp that would lead to her neighborhood. "What kind of teasing?"

"That people may think there's something improper about us. We're in separate parts of the university, so I don't see it. I'm not your head of department or your instructor, and you're not a student in the law school—yet—where I'm the dean, but...I suppose I could be accused of bias?" Jonas replied. "There was some inference that Willoughby might take issue since he didn't get my job when he was up for it again."

Micki was not amused. "Professor Willoughby takes offense at anyone breathing who doesn't sing his praises. The man is pompous and a bad teacher who treats students and peers alike with disdain."

"He is not pleasant, to say the least."

"I'm almost done with my degree. I won't be undermined by this kind of accusation, and not one from him." Micki tried to tamp down her annoyance. "You've only been here for a few weeks. We're friends, just getting to know each other." As soon as she'd said the words, the memory of their kiss came to mind.

"Exactly," Jonas agreed. "In any case, I told them that and they know that I wouldn't be dealing with you in any direct manner on campus. But it may be best if we keep our distance when we're there, so no one gossips."

"So you want me to act like I don't know you on campus and then when we're at the inn, it's all good?" Micki asked slowly. "Making something sordid and unpleasant out of something that is just truly innocent? You are allowed to have friendships and relationships on campus. There are more than a few couples that are married and teach at the college."

"I would assume they were married before starting their positions at the campus or they were both instructors when they met."

"Yeah, you're probably right. And, anyway, I'm just a lowly student," Micki muttered.

"I don't mean that at all, but yes, that is a fact. Even indirectly I wouldn't want it to seem like you're getting some sort of favoritism," Jonas explained. "I'm not saying we can't speak to each other, a hello if we see each other is absolutely fine."

Micki frowned.

Jonas felt the battle was lost already. "I'm trying not to make a muck of this, it's important to me to be the best at my position."

"I understand completely." Micki pulled into the driveway of the inn and stopped. "What you should understand is that I'm a grown woman and if I like you, I like you. I don't go around hiding or behaving like going out together is wrong. It makes me uncomfortable—this whole conversation has made it seem like I'm in some secret relationship and I don't like that feeling, either. So it's best, Dean Brand, that we don't associate in private or public to save your reputation."

"Michelle," he began.

"It's Micki." She held out her hand with the keys and dropped them into his palm. "Have a good night, Professor."

Her feelings were hurt, that was all there was to it. And instead of going into the inn, she took the new stone path toward Crawford Field to see her sisters. She needed one of their special sisterly conversations because this was one of those rare times when she had no clue what to do. The first door she got to was Margo's and she rang the bell and waited.

Margo opened the door, and a look of surprise followed. "Micki, I thought you were out with Jonas."

"I need a sister circle," Micki said, stepping past the threshold. "Unless you have a family thing going on and I don't want to interrupt."

"First, you being here is not an interruption. How many times have you been there for us?" Margo closed the door. "Everyone's over at Mom and Dad's. I was taking a breather and wanted to relax, and what better way than to have my baby sis visit. I'll call Mia, you start the tea. There are fresh chocolate croissants in the kitchen—just pop a few in the toaster oven to warm up."

"Thanks, sis." Micki tried to swallow the emotion stuck in her throat. She wanted to cry.

That realization only made her more upset because Micki really hated to cry.

CHAPTER FIVE

THAT WAS ONE thing she loved about growing up with her sisters. If one of them needed the others, any slights would be ignored, and they would come together to find clarity and solve a problem. Mia glanced around, admiring the still relatively new house and how Margo and Gideon had made it a real home. It reminded Micki that she should step away from the inn, travel the path she wanted to before settling back here. But now was not the time to bring it up, even though she knew her sisters would be willing to help with more than one difficult issue.

She didn't want to mar the holidays by having everyone looking at her sadly, knowing she was leaving. The inn had been in the black for several years. Thankfully, Micki had enough in her savings account to do whatever she wanted. When Mia, always overprotective of her sisters, walked over to the house and joined them, she had a serious look on her face. One of Micki's first memories was of having her arms wrapped around Mia's leg while she stood in the playground, ready to knock a bully senseless on Micki's behalf.

"Who did what? No one messes with my baby sister," Mia said. She pushed the sleeves up of the blue jersey that went with her plaid pajama pants. On her feet she wore the dino slippers that Omar had gotten for her for her birthday.

"Stand down, you look like a prize fighter ready for the ring," Margo said, sounding amused. "Help Micki with the mugs."

The threesome trailed upstairs and into Margo's master bedroom decorated in sunshine yellow. An antique armoire with a set of drawers with hand-painted flowers stenciled on the front was set opposite the bed. In the little sitting area in the corner of the room was an elegant dressing table with mirror and matching chair.

Mia sighed, wistfully looking around. "All the little add-ons you've done really make it an inviting space. Like those built-in shelves by the bed for your books."

"You could always do some upgrades on yours," Margo suggested.

Mia shook her head. "Too disruptive, especially with Gigi. She wakes easily. Okay, enough of that! We're here for Micki and I reserve the right to fight someone on her behalf."

"Then you'd be fighting Jonas," Micki said. "The day was going so well then he went and put his British foot in his British mouth."

"O-kay," Margo said, seeming a little worried. "Tell us what's going on."

"We started out at a cricket match he had with some of his colleagues from campus," Micki began.

"Cricket? They play that in Charlotte?" Mia frowned.

"There are other cultures here," Micki said dryly. "Anyway, it was fun and then we went to Big Ben for dinner."

"A good place, great food." Margo nodded approvingly.

"It was on the way home things took a downward turn." Micki then told them the rest of the story.

"Hmm, tough one," Mia said after. "On one hand, I can see where Jonas is coming from…"

"But he's not her teacher. And he's the dean of a whole other institution. They don't even have direct contact," Margo pointed out. "Plus, she's an exceptional student. Our extra smart cookie is blowing through those last undergrad classes in one year and with a seven-class course load, mind you. She'll be accepted into law school in the fall, no problem. Well, if Jonas is still there...."

Mia nodded. "Who is your dean of students?"

"Professor Linton. I've heard she's amazing," Micki replied. "Jonas wants us to keep our distance at school but it's okay to say a casual hello if we happen to see each other. I don't like the feeling of dishonesty that goes with that. It feels wrong, and I'd rather not say anything at all, which stinks because I like him."

"Like him, like him?" Margo teased and nudged Micki with her shoulder, making her tea splash from her mug.

"Hey!" Micki held her napkin to her lips. "Do you want tea all over your bedspread?"

"It's a few drops, calm yourself. But answer the question, li'l sis. Do you like him?"

"And please tell us, because we very rarely have a sister meeting with a Micki boy problem," Mia added. "You always just take life by the horns, and even if something is wrong, you internalize it."

Micki paused and stared at her sisters. "I like him… Okay, he kissed me and I felt something special. Maybe for the first time."

Margo, as if sensing her distress, moved closer and gently asked, "What do you mean?"

"Guys, they like my energy, they like that I know the fun places to hang out and things to do," Micki explained. "But even if I'm dating one of them, it's superficial. No one asks about my dreams or goals, no one tries to comfort me if I'm insecure or just be there for me. I love who I am, but I kinda wish someone would see something more, and Jonas does. We talk about everything when we're together. It's a mix of a good time and intelligent conversation. I felt seen."

"Oh, Micki." Margo kissed the top of Micki's head. "We see you and we love you."

"But you have your lives, your husbands and kids," Micki pointed out. "I love that for you both, but I guess I thought maybe..."

"He might be someone for you," Mia finished for her. "Do you want me to make him find somewhere else to go?"

"No, that's not right. I'll keep my distance on campus." Micki felt an ache in her chest. "I wish we hadn't kissed twice."

"Twice?" Margo gasped. "When was the first?"

"I was studying, and he came home with a headache. I gave him one of my neck massages that help you when you have a migraine." She told her sister. "Then we kissed, or I kissed him. Either way, the connection was instantaneous, and now look at me."

"This will work itself out and I'm betting in

your favor." Mia put her mug on the bedside table and stretched out.

Soon, Micki was between her sisters, with their warmth and support enveloping her.

"And if he doesn't, he'll be poorer for it." Mia reached out and squeezed Micki's hand.

Micki squeezed back and used her other hand to claim one of Margo's. "Thanks. You guys are the best, I love you."

"We love you, too," Margo replied. "Come over tomorrow afternoon and see Andy and Claire. They'd be thrilled to visit with their aunty."

"Great idea! I'll bring Gigi. Omar will be at school, but we can have a nice brunch and hang out," Mia added.

"I like it, but can we make it Wednesday? Tomorrow and Tuesday, I'm on campus till five," Micki replied.

"We can do that. We need you to become a lawyer in case Mr. Webber sues us for custody of Doodle. That cat's always at my house," Margo stated.

"Who knew Ryan and Gideon would be right about our longtime neighbor looking for friendship when he was always hollering at us about his cat loitering around the inn," Mia mused.

"Who knew our lives would be so full like this in such a short time?" Margo smiled.

"I did." Micki smiled, too. "And we've never been happier."

"True," both of her sisters replied.

The trio lay together, talking about old times and dreams for the future until Micki said goodnight and returned to the inn. She went to bed without seeing Jonas and by the time she woke up to drive to school the following morning, he was gone. Micki breathed a sigh of relief, not having to deal with an uncomfortable conversation in the company of the other guests.

This would be the last week of class before the Thanksgiving break and then it would be the big push for finals before the campus closed down for Christmas. As her day progressed, she had Jonas on her mind. He was so close, but because of what he'd said yesterday, so very far away. She caught sight of him once or twice while going from one class to another but made sure to always turn in the opposite direction. But that strategy didn't work out for her later in the afternoon when she was in the lounge having lunch with Professor Linton.

The professor wanted to get as many senior students to meet up as she could so that they'd all support each other and discuss the requirements for the coming final semester. After a particularly brutal class with Professor Willoughby as guest lecturer, Micki and two others were frazzled, sitting at the table. It was easy to talk to Professor Linton. Not only was the dean of students approachable but a good listener.

"Professor Linton, he's not only patronizing but he made a couple of the kids upset," said Kris, who fumbled with his sandwich. "We sat there asking him questions while he just got angrier and more awful. Right, Micki?"

Micki sighed. "I tried to keep my head down but when you have a nineteen-year-old crying next to you and talking about changing majors just to make sure she doesn't have to take his classes in law school, then that's a problem. He's supposed to be grading a few of our papers. We're afraid maybe our grades are going to suffer."

"We didn't learn anything, and it'll probably be the same the next time," Ronnie said. "And we need those grades to graduate from the program."

"And he wonders why no students sign up to TA for him," Kris muttered. "I don't mind a strict and structured instructor—we've all had bad bosses, but this goes beyond."

"With Professor West likely getting tenure, I'm sure that he'll be offered the chance to guest-teach more often if those classes are in the new year," Professor Linton said in a sympathetic tone. "I will address it again with our new dean of the law school to see if we can curtail Professor Willoughby a bit more. Let's eat and come up with a plan, I know all of you to be amazing students and I will advocate for you."

"Thanks, Dr. Linton," Micki said gratefully. "We can't afford to fail."

Jennifer Linton nodded. "I understand completely, I had one terrible professor when I was getting my doctorate in Oregon. It sours your dreams, and I won't have my students at this college rethinking their choices, especially a career in law."

"How did you handle the situation?" Ronnie asked.

"We boycotted his class," Professor Linton responded, a chuckle quickly smothered. "Not that it's what I'm telling you to do."

"We get it." Ronnie smiled.

Their lunch continued on a positive note. Micki had been able to grab a dozen of Enid's chocolate chip cookies before she'd left the inn, which she and her classmates around her devoured with gusto. In the midst of their conversation, Jonas entered the lounge with a mug in hand. Professor Linton looked up and smiled warmly.

"Dean Brand, nice to see you," she said.

"Oh, I'm sorry to interrupt. I was looking for a fresh cup of coffee," Jonas said, returning the smile. His gaze settled on Micki, and she looked down at her notes.

"You're not interrupting," Professor Linton assured him. "These are our senior students intending to pursue a career in law. I wanted to corral them to give them a pep talk so that they'll start the spring semester on the right footing. It won't be long before we get back from the Christmas holiday. Guys, have you met the new dean of our law school yet?"

Many of them chorused no and gave him a greeting while Micki said nothing.

"I know Michelle. Her family owns the bed-and-breakfast where I'm staying until I find a place to live," Jonas said casually.

"He knows me indirectly and it's Micki, Dean Brand," Micki corrected politely. "I'm not nearly around the inn as much with school going on, and I don't deal with the day-to-day business."

Professor Linton looked interested. "Well, Micki, don't hesitate to take advantage. You can ask him questions and fire theories at him. He's a well-renowned legal scholar in Europe."

Micki shook her head. "I wouldn't want to bother Dean Brand. Ballad Inn is a place to rest and find peace. I wouldn't subject him to my questions or take advantage of having special access to him and possibly give the inference of impropriety. Especially when I can pick your brain, Professor."

"Great compliment," Professor Linton laughed. "Would you like to sit for a moment, Jonas?"

"Thanks, Jennifer, but I've got a call coming in soon and then a meeting," Jonas replied.

If anyone could sense the tension between herself and Jonas, no one gave a sign. Micki noted his frown at her words, but he kept silent as he poured and fixed his coffee.

"You all enjoy your lunch. It was nice meeting you. I hope your dean of students told you of my open-door policy."

"I'll remind them," Jennifer said lightly.

He said goodbye and disappeared into the crowd. Micki made sure her voice sounded as friendly as everyone else's when the discussion resumed around the table. Still, Jonas was on her mind. She couldn't shake the image of how sad his eyes looked when she'd greeted him, but she just couldn't be the "fun girl" in someone's life anymore. There had to be more, especially if she liked that someone as much as she liked Jonas.

TWO DAYS LATER, things were still not right between himself and Micki, and Jonas wasn't happy about that. How was it he could feel so alone without her amazing smile and their daily interaction? But he'd gotten what he'd asked for, which was more disappointing than he possibly realized. He didn't want to mess up his new job or new life, but he seemed to have done just that and hurt the most authentic person he'd ever met in his life. Was he selfish for looking out for his own reputation, and hers, after what happened with his family—to his family—because of him trusting the wrong person? Was he jaded by the events he thought he'd overcome in spite of the strained relationship he still had with his father?

He'd come to the United States and opted for this job to have a fresh start, but by fearing his past mistakes he may have inadvertently upset someone really incredible. He didn't think he could stand the cool, polite distance that Micki had put between them. When she gave him a quick nod and the "Dean Brand," it felt like he was coated in ice from the chill in her voice, and not the November weather.

His office was quiet, too quiet. Regardless of the voices he heard beyond his door, he felt a bit like an outsider. If students were in the lounge, and he walked in to find a granola bar or a cup of tea, silence reigned. He felt like the quirky, gangly kid growing up outside London once again. Instead of a hello and staying for a conversation, he smiled and went back to his office, and when Micki was among the students, it felt even worse.

"I'm a buffoon," he murmured to himself. A knock on his office door made him look up.

Jennifer poked her head in as was her usual fashion and smiled. "Debbie is on lunch, so I thought I'd stop by."

"And if Debbie had been at her desk?" Jonas asked and Jennifer stepped inside.

"I'd have probably crawled past the desk and gently opened the door before slipping through the crack." Jennifer sat down. "She is quite protective of your time. Maybe it's because you treat her so well. You do that a lot."

"She's a sweetheart," Jonas replied and shrugged. "How can I help you today?"

"Professor Willoughby." Jennifer sighed. "We've got to talk to the chancellor and the board about him. Every day it's a new complaint and it's about time that his friends in high places know how he's behaving in general, and specifically, treating the students."

"What is the main complaint?" Jonas pulled his laptop over and got ready to type.

"Patronizing the students, low grades for top-notch papers because they question his theory." Jennifer put a file from her satchel on his table. "This is an account from the last six weeks alone—undergraduate as well as graduate classes. Something has to give here before we get hit with a lawsuit and we're the law school."

"I understand." Jonas nodded. "I'll reach out to the board today and see what options we have. His contract isn't up for another year, so I might only be allowed to reprimand him and place that in his file. Also, his effectiveness as a professor can be rightly questioned. I'll need the statistics on his pass/fail ratio with classes."

Jennifer's face was a mask of concern, no doubt for her students and from being irritated about the situation. "I can compile that information from the students' grades. It may take a bit of time, but I can work back from the students in the complaint file."

"Sounds good. We'll find a remedy to this," Jonas promised. "Anything else?"

Jennifer hesitated before speaking. "How are you faring in Charlotte? Are you liking it, not liking it?"

"Why do you ask?" Jonas kept his tone calm. Hopefully his job performance wasn't in question. It had only been a few weeks since he'd stepped into the position.

"Because I'm a friend," she said gently. "And I've been in the lounge when you come in and see instructors or students in a group there. I can see on your face you want to interact, but you walk away instead."

"I still feel like an outsider, I suppose," Jonas admitted. "Your instructor and student dynamic is more casual here, but I don't want to step on toes. It's easy to say might I join you, and as dean, they'll feel the need to say yes. I don't want to put them in a position of being uncomfortable."

"The students are very versatile," she explained. "To have you sit in on a conversation would make their day, especially the ones already in law school, I can assure you, so next time, just pull up a chair and join in."

"I'll remember that," Jonas promised. "Might I ask you a question?"

"Shoot." She gave him a big, wide grin and took a sip from her travel mug.

"Have you heard of any dean of law school jobs coming available next year?" Jonas asked bluntly.

"Jonas, you just got here. Are you planning on leaving us already?" Jennifer asked with concern etched on her face.

"No, it's more like—I don't want to seem untoward if I meet someone I like who is also on campus."

Jennifer choked on her sip of whatever she

was drinking before asking hoarsely, "Oh, do you want to date this someone, is that it?"

"No—yes—well, it's complicated." Jonas made a frustrated sound in the back of his throat. "Michelle Ballad is complicated."

"Micki, yes, I know her. Good student. Very bright. She'll make a great lawyer."

"She's also kind, funny and will likely be a student in the fall at the law school. For the moment, she's only one third of the owners of where I am now staying, Ballad Inn, I may have told you." He shrugged and continued. "We've actually hit it off quite nicely. I went to an event with her, her family and the other guests from the inn for Thanksgiving, a country bar thing."

"Sounds fun," Jennifer commented. "Go on."

"She's intelligent, a breath of fresh air, the most unusual but wonderfully carefree woman I have ever met," he added. "We had an instant connection, but I might have thrown myself down a hole I can't get out of."

"So, you said something dumb," Jennifer surmised.

He took off his glasses and pinched the bridge of his nose. "After a cricket match with Micah West and a few more instructors here at the campus—"

"And you said to her—" She waited for his answer.

Jonas grimaced. "That we should just greet each other like we don't associate."

"Wow, just—wow," she said slowly. "You're not even guest-teaching in any courses in her department yet, right?"

"Right. I will be teaching by then, at the law school, though. Two night classes."

"Then make sure she isn't in your class or becomes your teaching assistant. Micki had enough credits from her previous college history that she came in as a very high junior. She's fast-tracked through her undergrad requirements and could jump ahead in her law school studies, too. You'll need to keep that in mind," Jennifer said. "Meanwhile, you have and will have zero connection to her or her grades, so what's the problem?"

"I guess I didn't want gossip," he told her. "Been there, done that."

"You dated a student before?"

"What?" Jonas met her gaze and then realized how his comment sounded. "Oh no, nothing like that. It was a family issue."

"It's up to you, but there is no professional reason why you can't see her in a personal way," she said. "But will she even talk to you after your bout of foot-in-mouth fever?"

"We'll have to see," Jonas muttered. "I'll have to get her to stop avoiding me long enough to listen."

"I'm sure you're a very inventive man and will figure it out." Jennifer stood. "Okay. Back to the salt mines for me, before Debbie returns to her desk and gives me one of her side-eyed looks."

"Stop hiding from my assistant," Jonas teased. "I find chocolate makes her smile."

"Such a charmer. You should be able to use that to get Micki to talk to you," Jennifer shot back.

"Ha ha, you're a funny lady," Jonas said but then sobered. "Thank you for being a friend."

"And thank you for being who you are. You'll fit in around here just fine. Don't forget to step outside the comfort zone."

"I'll endeavor to do so." Hadn't he given himself that very advice?

"Hey, Debbie!"

Jonas heard Jennifer greet his assistant in the hallway and laughed softly to himself. Talking to her had given him clarity on a few things, but he knew before he went home, his biggest task would be to speak to the chancellor about their problem professor. Dealing with such an issue so early in his new position was not something he'd anticipated, but happy and well-taught students made for a better program review and graduation numbers. He made the call, admitting to himself that speaking to his higher-ups about a sensitive topic might be easier than getting Micki to talk to him again.

CHAPTER SIX

"How do you apologize to a woman like Micki for being a complete goose?" Jonas asked Ryan and Gideon.

They were the first two people he saw when he got to the inn that evening and it seemed only plausible that since they were her brothers-in-law, they would know her best. Quite honestly, he was too afraid to ask her sisters directly.

Luckily, he'd spotted Gideon and Ryan across the street with the older men he now knew as Mr. Marley and Mr. Bolton. When he'd gotten out of his car, they'd waved him over and he'd gladly gone over to sit with them on Mr. Marley's porch, around the portable heater.

"This is rather nice," Jonas said appreciatively as he settled in.

Mr. Marley handed him a cup. "Gideon found the heater on sale at one of the discount warehouse places and got me a good deal. Take a sip. That's a little hot chocolate toddy."

"It means he put bourbon in the cocoa," Mr. Bolton said with a snort of amusement. "Not too much, of course, just enough to warm the belly."

"What's up with you and Micki?" Ryan asked.

Jonas took a sip of his drink. "Mmm. Good chocolate, thank you—can I ask a question of the male hive mind?"

Mr. Bolton puffed up his chest. "I knew our experience would come in handy. Tell us what's going on, son."

Jonas glanced at Gideon and Ryan, who shrugged and waited for him to talk. "Okay. Here's the situation in a nutshell."

He went on to tell them about Micki and his lack of common sense. Each man visibly winced when he explained what he'd said and how she was treating him now. That could not be good.

"Any ideas?" Jonas asked hopefully.

Mr. Marley shook his head. "The Ballad girls' ice-out is not for the faint of heart."

"Especially Micki. When she shuts you out, it's like a Siberian winter," Gideon added. "When she was mad at me, the way she said *Gideon*, made me shiver."

"She's usually not mad at me," Ryan said. "I learned from that one time to avoid it at all costs, and she cried, too. I just bring her cotton candy, chocolate-coated potato chips or candied popcorn in her favorite blueberry flavor."

"Why would someone cover chips in chocolate?" Jonas grimaced.

"You're losing focus, man, step back in," Mr. Marley insisted.

"So, I should bring her an assortment of snacks that will raise her blood sugar?" Jonas questioned. "That can't be healthy."

"The girl moves around like a firefly. She burns that off, always has." Mr. Bolton shook his head. "Remember when she tried to zip-line from tree to tree when she was around eighteen?"

Mr. Marley laughed. "She is by far the most entertaining, except when Mia did that kooky stunt and almost broke her coccyx. Fortunately, she wasn't hurt, apart from her pride. That was when Ryan came to town."

"Ballad girl down!" the quartet said in unison and began to laugh, while Jonas looked at them still clueless.

"Suggestions, anyone?" Jonas asked helplessly.

Eventually, Gideon answered. "Still waters run deep, and Micki thinks everyone expects her to be this carefree person, which she is, but she is also not truly understood. She has more sides to her, just like we all do. What she seems to want is someone who'll see past the image and actually see *her*. The true her. I'd suggest, since you've spent time with her, that you find a special moment you've had and recreate it and use that to help you apologize."

"She likes lot of different things… But origami is one of her favorites," Jonas said. "What can I do with that?"

"What time is it?" Ryan asked, pulling out his phone.

"Around seven," Gideon answered. "Oh, Jonas, Margo said to tell you that your dinner is in the kitchen in the warmer oven with a cover thingy, so it doesn't dry out."

"How did she know I would see you?" he asked.

"She knew that we'd be over here." Gideon gestured to Ryan, who was talking on his cell. "Who are you talking to?"

Ryan disconnected the call. "A friend who's an artist. Luckily for you, Jonas, he wasn't busy. He's on his way, with a load of quick-dry resin and some molds. Who knows how to make origami?"

Mr. Marley raised his hand. "Believe or not, I'm a man of many talents. Actually, I just like watching all those handy videos online. You can learn a lot from them. I can do a crane, a dragon and—"

"Can you make an elephant? She loves those." Jonas recalled when Micki had said she wanted to go to Africa to see one of the majestic creatures.

"If I see a video, I should be able to do it," Mr. Marley answered.

"To the work shed?" Gideon asked, pushing up the sleeves of his sweater.

"To the work shed," the others answered in unison.

"Let's get this heater turned off before I burn down the house and I have to live with you, Bolton." Mr. Marley chuckled.

"I don't think my wife would appreciate that." Mr. Bolton stopped and turned red while everyone looked at him in shock.

"Wife, what wife?" Mr. Marley's face bloomed in realization. "You and Enid got hitched."

"Lower your voice, man!" Mr. Bolton shushed him and looked around. "We aren't telling anyone until Christmastime, and then we're going on a honeymoon to St. Augustine to get out of this cold."

"How do you think we're supposed to keep this from our wives?" Ryan asked, obviously alarmed. "Mia can see right through me."

"I just start blurting things when Margo looks at me funny," Gideon added. "Those sisters have that sixth-sense thing."

"You three better keep those lips zipped, you

hear me?" Mr. Bolton threatened, pinning them each with a stare.

"Why are you looking at me? How am I in this?" Jonas asked.

Mr. Bolton snorted. "With Micki, you'd fold like a cheap suit. Keep it quiet or I'm telling Enid to cut off the dessert train."

"You wouldn't," Gideon gasped.

"I would," Mr. Bolton promised with a dark glare.

"Have I been flung into bizarro world?" Jonas asked. "Are you people always like this?"

"Yes," they all answered.

What could he say, he was part of this now, it seemed. A smile hinted at his lips as they walked casually across the street then hid in the shadows of the trees to hopefully get to the work shed unseen.

"Y'all know we can see you, right?" Margo's voice came from the inn's porch.

"Cheese it, boys! We've been had!" Mr. Marley called out and began to move faster.

"What are they up to now?" Mia asked.

"Who knows? The five of them hiding behind trees like they're super spies…" Margo huffed. "They are getting more unusual by the minute and now they've pulled poor Jonas into it."

He grinned as he heard the voices talking about their band of merry men. This was the most fun he'd had in a very long time and the venture was all to say sorry to a woman he couldn't get out of his head. They made it to the shed and closed the door behind them until there was a loud knock. Ryan's friend was a tall, redheaded man with a braided beard like a Viking's. He was also strong enough to carry all his supplies in one trip.

"This is Orne, guys. He's a nurse at my hospital," Ryan introduced him. "He's also an artist who uses a few mediums, like glass and resin."

"He's a pediatric nurse?" Mr. Bolton asked skeptically. "Shouldn't he be raiding a village somewhere?"

"My forefathers were the warriors, I'm a healer, an artist and a bard," Orne said, stretching to his full height of what Jonas assessed to be around six-five. He wore thick trousers and a leather tunic over a vintage muslin shirt, so Jonas wasn't too sure that Orne wasn't part warrior.

"A bard," Gideon repeated.

Orne grinned. "Yep. When Ryan called, I was just leaving an ax throwing competition."

"Of course, you were," Mr. Bolton muttered.

"I can teach you guys how to do it," Orne offered. "It's pretty easy and the ax is only about ten pounds."

Ryan clapped him on the shoulder. "How about we leave that until the summer, my friend."

"Okay." Orne glanced at the assembled group "So, what are we making?"

"We want to encase three origami paper animals in resin, then quick dry and polish," Ryan said.

"A circle, a square and maybe a pyramid," Jonas clarified. "How long will it take?"

"With this clear mix, about six hours, but it needs a full twenty-four hours to cure," Orne explained. "Although, with more dry heat and this clear resin, we can cut it down to, say, twelve. Who's making the animals?"

Mr. Marley stepped up. "I am. Learned it in my spare time. We're going to make a dragon, elephant and crane."

"I have a special type of paper that won't crumple under the weight of the resin." Orne began to open his tub of supplies. "We can add a few more elements, like a water lily for the crane, and a stark tree from the plains for the elephant, But for the dragon, we can add the—"

"Stars. She loves them, and with the dragon it would be fantastic," Jonas said. "Can we do all that?"

Orne pulled on his red beard. "Let's do it."

"One sec." Gideon pulled his phone from his

pocket and pressed a button before putting it on speaker.

"Gideon, what are y'all doing?" Margo asked in lieu of hello.

"Helping Jonas with something," Gideon replied.

"Well, it better be an I'm sorry, because he hurt her feelings," Margo said bluntly. "And why are our neighbors with you?"

Her words made Jonas feel worse.

"They're helping, too," Gideon replied. "Is Micki at home?"

"No, she went straight to the nonprofit after class," Margo told them. "Later she was meeting Rabbit and Nina for dinner, so she said she would just stay with them for the night and go back to school from there tomorrow."

"We got time, boys," Mr. Marley said. "A reprieve to finish this!"

"Why are they out there? What are you doing?" Margo asked again.

"Hang up," Mr. Bolton said urgently.

"Wait!" Margo said, sounding exasperated. "Gideon Holder, you better not hang—"

"Gotta go, babe, love you," Gideon said just in time.

Jonas watched the scene, amused before focusing on Mr. Marley, who was already sitting at the worktable and folding thick, textured paper. Orne produced other colors and patterns from his tub. Jonas helped Ryan prep the mold, while the artist and Gideon mixed the resin to the exact consistency needed. While they waited, Jonas recalled something on the bulletin board in his building on campus. Using the app on his phone, he found the event he was looking for and, with a grin, looked at the men as new friends.

"Do you think this will be done by eight or nine tomorrow night?" Jonas asked.

"Oh, sure, sure." Orne nodded. "Why?"

"The Leonid meteor shower is happening then. There's a watch party from the roof of the astrology department," Jonas explained. "What better way to apologize than under the stars and give her the gifts we crafted?"

"The boy is getting it," Mr. Marley said in clear approval.

Jonas excused himself and stepped outside. "Let's see if she answers the phone or hangs up on me."

He pressed the key for her number and listened with anticipation for her voice.

"Good evening, Dr. Brand," her tone was cool.

"Michelle—"

"Micki."

"Michelle," he repeated, longing for her to understand. "Can I ask you to meet me on the roof of the astrology department's building to-morrow night?"

"The meteor shower. I was already going with friends."

"Go with me?" he asked gently.

"Aren't you afraid to be seen with me?" Micki reminded him of his words. "In public we're only to be distantly polite with each other."

"I was a buffoon for saying that."

"You're right," she agreed and simply left it at that.

"If you would do me the honor of watching the stars with me, I will apologize properly." Jonas took a quick breath, his nerves starting to get the better of him. "Please say yes."

She hesitated for a moment before answering. "Yes. I guess so. I'll grab a couple of blankets and some other things for us."

"No, love, I invited you—I will take care of everything," Jonas said quickly. "And Michelle, thank you for saying yes."

"We'll see how tomorrow goes as to whether this was a good decision or not," Micki replied. "I'm with friends now. I'll see you tomorrow night at around eight thirty?"

"See you then," Jonas promised and hung up, smiling. Back inside the work shed, he announced, "She said yes, my friends."

"Outstanding and you're just in time to sink

our little projects into the resin." Orne slipped
on a pair of plastic gloves and handed more to
Jonas. "I'll walk you through the steps. We are
going to use these tongs to push them below
the resin slowly and we reposition before doing
anything else."

"How do we add the stars? With the same
process?" Jonas asked as he carefully did as
Orne instructed. Then Orne added more resin
to the mold to take the amount to the very top.

"Yes, these are metal but hollow, so they
won't sink any further than where we place
them," the artist said.

"This is great, guys." Jonas looked at the
men, appreciating their help, their camaraderie. "Thank you, all. There are no better friends
than you lads."

"I think that means he's taking us out for a
tomahawk steak dinner with all the fixings,"
Gideon said.

"You name the time and the place, gents, dinner is on me." Jonas chuckled. "We'll need two
or three of those steaks. I'm sure Orne can eat
one on his own."

"It's like he knows me." Orne grinned.

By ten o'clock that night, they were shaking
hands for a job well done, and parting ways till
the next afternoon when Jonas would meet Orne
at his studio. Then, they would trim and polish

the pieces before placing them in a gift box and put them in his satchel for his meeting under the stars with Michelle. He wouldn't let doubts get in the way of what might be a good thing forming with the beautiful woman that filled his thoughts. Tomorrow couldn't come soon enough in his opinion. The apology would be first and then hopefully they would kiss again, something he would savor like the last time their lips met.

MICKI LOOKED INTO her closet with a frustrated sigh before whipping the sweater over her head. She wanted to look casual, yet sophisticated. If Jonas only knew how his words had played on her insecurities. She was learning alongside students who were sometimes ten years her junior, and like many other adult students, she felt a bit out of place. In any case, that was hers to deal with, and right now, Micki's stomach clenched nervously at seeing Jonas again on a personal level. She'd almost convinced herself it was okay that they just kept their distance. But while she had her doubts and wanted to say no, her heart had said yes. She admitted she wore it on her sleeve and no matter the worst heartbreak, she couldn't be any other way.

"Micki, you in your room?" Mia called.

"Yeah, come on in." Her voice was muffled

as she pulled on a dark yellow off-the-shoulder sweater and added a teal scarf.

"Hey, what are you up to?" Mia asked, stepping inside the bedroom.

"What do you think of this outfit?" Micki demanded to know.

"Cute. I like the boots with the jeans and the sweater looks great with the scarf," her sister replied.

"Cute? Ugh."

"Micki, cute doesn't mean not beautiful," Mia said gently. "I like the mix of casual, with a bit of sass. Where are you going so late anyway?"

"Meeting Jonas at the astronomy building," she answered. "He called and asked to take me to see the meteor shower and apologize the right way."

"Wonder if that had anything to do with what the guys were doing last night," Mia mused.

"What?" Micki glanced at her sister in the mirror while she tried to sort out her hair.

Mia sat on the bed. "It was unusual. The men of this family, minus Dad, but including Jonas, Mr. Bolton and Mr. Marley went sneaking from across the street to the work shed. Margo and I were on the porch near the back, and we saw them immediately and called over to them. Mr. Bolton said 'cheese it and run'—something like that."

"That's hilarious." Micki laughed.

There was a quick knock on the door and Margo walked inside. "I heard y'all talking. I was taking Enid her medication refills I picked up. What's going on?"

"Micki is meeting Jonas to watch the meteor shower and I was telling her that his apology probably had something to do with the men being in the shed last night," Mia explained.

"Oh, the cheese-it gang." Margo laughed. "What does that mean, anyway?"

"It's slang for get going, we don't want to get caught, or along those lines." Micki adjusted her scarf.

"Who are you?" Mia asked while they stared at her in shock.

Micki shrugged. "I like research and I tend to find obscure references interesting."

"It definitely has something to do with last night," Margo said and went back to the initial conversation. "Gideon called to ask where Micki was and then when I asked what was going on, Mr. Bolton said again—'cheese it, she's on to us.' Gideon was tight-lipped when he got home."

"Yeah, they're hiding something," Mia mused. "Ryan looked shifty last night before bed. I tried to pry it out of him, and he chose to go be on diaper duty when Gigi cried."

"Oh, something is truly up if he chose stinky

diapers over talking," Micki said. "I'll let you know what it's about from my end."

She sighed, looking at herself in the mirror again. "Are you sure I look okay?"

"Add the teal beret that goes with that scarf, and you have an outfit, m'lady," Margo answered.

"Don't refer to her as cute—she might change again," Mia teased.

Micki checked the time on her phone. "I have to go, this will have to do."

"And you look gorgeous," her sisters said and moved closer to give her a hug.

"Not the huddle hug." Micki's voice was muffled between them, but the laughter was still in her voice. "Okay, that's enough. It's over ten seconds."

They pulled away, smiling broadly at each other.

"I love you guys," Micki said suddenly. "You're the best sisters a girl could have."

"We love you, too," Margo said. "Now go knock his socks off and tell Jonas he is super lucky to have a person like you next to him."

"Oh, he's gonna know it. I'm Micki Ballad and I'm sunshine in a bottle," she said with pride, belying her inner turmoil.

"That's our Micki." Mia kissed her on the cheek on the way out.

She followed them downstairs and, after a

quick goodbye, got into her small RAV4 and pulled away from the inn. The drive from Sardis Woods to the campus took about twenty minutes on the highway. The night was cool and clear, making Micki smile as she cracked the window to let some of the fresh air in and hummed along to the radio. The campus at night was fairly quiet and was beautiful even after the sun went down. The red cobblestoned paths had the vintage light poles that once featured gas flames. Now they were powered by electricity but still offered the same amber, ethereal glow. People were heading up the steps of the astronomy building and into the wide main foyer where others milled around, chatting softly. They carried thermoses with hot drinks, portable chairs and blankets to keep warm. There would also be four large heaters placed at each corner of the roof.

Jonas stood by the stairs with a pile of supplies at his feet. It was the most casual she'd seen him since the night of the Thanksgiving party at *Dreamboat*. He wore a sweatshirt that was monogrammed with the school logo and sweatpants with sneakers and a baseball cap. He also carried a bag with a long strap over his shoulder and when Micki walked up to him, his wide happy smile made her feel more at ease.

"Hi, have you seen Jonas Brand?" Micki

said, looking around. "I apparently lost him and you're standing in his spot."

"Funny lady," Jonas said with a smile. "You don't like my clothes?"

"I didn't know you owned clothes like that," she replied. "You had pressed jeans for a country bar."

"I'm loosening up," he replied. "Also, my assistant insisted on going to the student union store to grab these for me."

Micki laughed. "I knew it was something. So, what's all this?"

"Hot chocolate, canvas folding chairs, blankets and hand-warming mittens," he answered.

"And in the bag?"

"Something for later," he replied and began to gather their things.

"The same something that had our neighbors and my brothers-in-law involved?" she asked. "Here, let me help. Two sets of hands are better than one."

"Thanks. You heard about that, huh?" Jonas noticed how easily and freely she slipped the straps of the foldable chairs over her shoulder and together they walked to the elevator.

She chuckled. "My sisters saw you all, and then Gideon called to ask where I was, so it wasn't hard to figure out."

"Okay. I can see that," Jonas answered, amused.

"But you'll have to wait for when we're settled on the roof. Does this department have special events often?"

"For solar and moon eclipses and any other wonderous celestial occurrences that pass close enough to earth throughout the year."

The elevators opened, and they stepped off, following others up the short flight of stairs and outside the glass doors to the roof. A crowd was already setting up areas to get comfortable. Jonas waited for Micki to choose a spot for them. As she pulled the chairs from their bags and folded them open, he got some of their supplies out.

"They'll be students with their massive telescopes and professors charting the sky," Micki continued. "I think they're all hoping to discover a planet or something cool in the sky."

"Well, they'll get to name it and it will be documented for life with NASA. Who wouldn't want that?" Jonas asked as they sat down. "Here's a blanket."

"Thank you." Micki accepted the soft fleece. "We should start to see the first bands by ten and then it picks up until almost midnight."

Jonas looked up at the sky, and Micki marveled at how the stars stood out in the inky blackness. "I often wonder about the vastness of space," he said, still fixated on the stars.

"Would you have been one of those intrepid explorers who took the first steps to live among the stars?"

"Maybe." He shrugged. "Who wouldn't want to see what's out there if there are other places like ours? I always thought that some planet would have violet grass and waterfalls that ran into crystal clear pools."

"That's beautiful." Micki spoke softly. "Or, if you're a science-fiction junkie like me, there's aliens and a battle for mankind."

His laugh rang out loud. "Or that—I have something for you." Micki watched as he placed a black bag in her lap. "The culmination of secret activities last night."

Micki unzipped the bag to reveal a box with a smooth, matte finish and she looked at him, curious.

"Open it," he encouraged her.

She lifted the lid and took out each block, marveling at the origami animals inside. The dragon with stars suspended in the sky with swirls of midnight blue made her gasp. Each was intricate and beautiful, a true piece of art.

"Did you make these?" Micki asked in awe.

"I had help from my friends. Mr. Marley made the animals. He learned how to do it by watching several hours' worth of online videos," Jonas explained. "Ryan had the friend who is an artist and brought the supplies. Gideon and Orne, the artist, mixed the resin, and I set the animals and added the color. Mr. Bolton sang old bard-type songs with Orne and made us promise not to reveal his wife— Oh, shoot."

"Wife? What wife!'" Micki almost fell out of her chair, but instead quickly covered her mouth with her hand. "He and Enid got married?"

"Shh, you don't know. You didn't hear a thing!" Jonas pleaded. "They don't want to announce until after Christmas, I think—I am so deep in it now. He threatened to convince Enid to stop making us extra desserts if we disclosed his secret. I can't be the cause of the loss of dessert for the lads."

"When—where?" Micki asked in shock.

Jonas shrugged. "I don't know any of the details. I think he blurted it out himself, probably the result of his hot chocolate toddies. Don't say a word, I beg of you. Just act surprised when they tell everyone."

"This is an interesting, juicy tidbit." A slow smile crossed her face. "What do I get for my silence?"

"My complete fealty."

"I was hoping for a cheesecake milkshake, Cajun chicken combo and seasoned fries from Tabletop," Micki replied. "After this is finished, maybe. The joint is open twenty-four hours a day."

"That sounds really good. Okay, deal."

"I love these animals, by the way. I meant to say that before you dropped the marriage news on me." She leaned over and pressed a fast kiss on his lips. "Thank you. I will treasure these always."

"Does that mean you forgive me?" Jonas took her hand and dropped a kiss in her palm. The action so personal and intimate, it sent a shiver down her spine. "I'd really like to see where this connection between us can lead to."

"Jonas, I throw my heart into everything I do, and if we start this, that will mean you, too," she admitted. "I know I seem like I have this tough exterior, but I just don't bruise, I hurt, so I ask you, please, if you're not serious about this, then let it go and we can just be friends."

"I don't know what the future holds, but I know I feel alive when I'm around you, like I'm meant to be in your presence," he told her honestly. "The last few days have been miserable without you, without seeing you smile at me and knowing it's just for me, no one else.

"Next week is Thanksgiving and on Friday, there is a gala being held by one of our top donors to the law school," Jonas said. "I'd love it if you would go with me."

Micki looked at him in alarm. "Won't all the board be there and the chancellor?"

He nodded, "And most of the faculty who want to attend."

"Are you sure you want me there?" She felt her stomach drop. "I'm just an undergrad and not even in the law school…"

"Absolutely, I want you there," Jonas replied. "Go with me and save me from the pretentious conversations that are sure to come."

"Okay, I'll go. No one can say that I don't try new things." She laughed nervously and rubbed her hands together to ward off the chill. "The temperature is dropping."

"I have just the thing." Jonas pulled out a pair of mittens. "They have an area for these heat packs that when you crush them, they warm up."

Micki gave him a look and answered dryly, "Yep, I know what they are."

She slipped her hands into the warming mittens and Jonas passed her a cup full of hot chocolate. While they sat in companionable silence and watched the sky and sipped their beverages, the world went on around them. The first few meteors streaked across the sky and Micki closed her eyes and told him to make a wish. She kept her own wish to herself. As he watched him open his eyes, the murmurs of excitement from others on the roof began in earnest. The sky show had begun.

"Look," Micki breathed out, her head tilted to the sky. "Beautiful."

"Yes," Jonas said huskily.

Micki turned to look at him and Jonas's eyes were on her. Time seemed to melt away. They inched closer together as if they were being drawn together. When their lips connected, the sweet friction made the roots of her hair tingle, and a warm flush that had nothing to do with the hot chocolate stole across her face. He lifted his head away from hers and as she sank into the rich hazel green of his eyes, a smile lit his face.

Sitting back, they held hands, and the hands tucked beneath the blanket only added to the closeness that she felt with Jonas. The meteor shower finally slowed down around midnight and then he followed her to the diner that was open all night. They ate and laughed and laughed some more.

Later, back at home, it was easy for her to slip into his arms on the porch and kiss once more. *It's the start of something wonderful*, Micki thought as she stepped inside and hoped her instincts weren't wrong, because even though she hadn't been looking, love might have arrived after all.

CHAPTER SEVEN

KENDALLWORTH MALL WAS packed with holiday shoppers. Micki paused in front of the massive snow globe covered in crystal stencils. The structure housed Santa Claus and his elves for the season while parents and couples waited in line to take a picture with jolly old Saint Nick. She and her sisters stared at the lit-up holiday garland hung from the high roof as the sound system played holiday music on repeat. Trying to find a dress in the huge mall that had a go-cart track outside and a place where you could even buy boats and outdoor equipment was probably a mistake.

"Do you think Jonas would like camping?" Micki asked suddenly. "Peter and Nina are going up to Kings Mountain for the weekend after Thanksgiving and invited us." She shrugged. "He lived in the countryside," Micki said, sounding hopeful.

"In a manor house with an amazing stone

kitchen," Margo replied. "He showed me the pictures of his mom and, yeah, that's a manor house."

"He doesn't strike me as the outdoors type," Mia chimed in.

"You should see him play cricket and Ryan invited him to join indoor rugby for some hospital charity thing," she told Mia. "I didn't know your husband could play rugby."

"I didn't either, come to think of it," Mia murmured.

"Ha! There is a lot y'all don't know," Micki said, thinking back to what Jonas had told her about Enid and their neighbor.

"What secrets were you told?" Margo demanded to know.

"Nothing!" Micki said a bit too loudly.

"Spill," Mia said.

"Can we go find me a dress already?" Micki strode off to the escalator to escape the conversation. Her sisters soon joined her, but Micki breathed a sigh of relief when they didn't question her anymore.

"Should I go with a cute cocktail dress?" Micki asked when they located the store's gown boutique. "I don't want anything sparkly that draws attention."

"Micki, anywhere you go, you draw attention. You could even be wearing a potato sack," Mia said with dry amusement. "How about this soft pink sheath dress. I like the built-in silk scarf running down the back."

"That's gorgeous!" Margo exclaimed. "Micki, you would kill in this dress, with some silver suede pumps and the silver jewelry set Mom got you from Morocco."

"Okay, that's the maybe," Micki said, doubting the dress. "We should check a few more places before we decide."

A few more places ended up being seven and then two shoe stores before they went back to the initial dress. Eventually, they landed in the food court.

"We could've been out of here two hours ago." Mia sighed. "Micki, why are you not trusting your instincts about this?"

"He's different than any other guys I've dated, for one," she answered. "Then, we're going to be with a bunch of intellectuals and rich donors. I don't want to embarrass him or make him look foolish—he's the new dean."

"Explain to me how you'd do that?" Margo asked.

"Well, hopping from majors and careers for one. When other students were working their way through the program, I was a handyman, remember?" Micki felt nervous and her stomach tumbled. "Maybe I shouldn't go."

"Realistically, Micki, if you're going to be with Jonas, there will be more of these times, so you can't escape them forever," Mia pointed out matter-of-factly. "The reason why you bounced around was that you were bored. You have this amazing super brain in your head and can adapt so easily to anything you do, from engineering to architecture. I think your IQ scared you so you decided to underperform to fit in, even in high school."

Margo smiled and shrugged. "Micki, you can rival anyone that's going to be at that party. Stop doubting yourself."

"And if being with Jonas makes you doubt yourself, maybe I don't want you seeing him," Mia said seriously and met Micki's gaze. "You've always known your self-worth and I don't like seeing you insecure."

Margo squeezed Micki's hand and Micki squeezed back.

"I still say, if you go and they try to make you feel terrible, you just tell them all off and come on home," Mia said with determination. "If you need us, just text the code word and we'll be on our way."

"Is the code word still 'fruity marshmallow Halloween crispy treat'?" Micki asked, amused. "Because I would still like it recognized that I believe it's the longest code word ever. Who has the time to text all that?"

"I have it saved as a custom message on my phone." Margo sipped from her straw.

Micki rolled her eyes. "Are we ready to go to the Dilworth Spa or not? I need to soak in warm clay and be wrapped in their vitamin E muslin wrap."

"Let's go," Mia stood. "Do I have to do the mud bath? It feels weird."

"If you want skin like satin you do," Micki retorted.

They managed to maneuver their way through the throngs of people to make it to Mia's Land Rover. She and Ryan now drove matching vehicles and it was so cute that it could make Micki's teeth ache. Traffic was a beast but finally they got onto the highway, relieved.

"We definitely need the relaxation of the spa now," Margo muttered. "The traffic gets worse and worse each year."

"Do you think it might snow this winter?" Micki wished it would. "It's been years since our grass has been white for the holidays."

"Bite your tongue," Mia scolded. "You know how drivers get when they even hear the mere mention of snow or ice in the weather report."

"I'd like to get a gallon of milk and some bread for Claire and Gideon without a fight in the supermarket," Margo pointed out. "People panic hard when it's nasty outside."

"I agree with you there," Micki admitted, laughing. "I remember that one year where Mr. Marley had a cart full of ribs and Enid made him put all but two back."

"Enid was in the supermarket, yelling, 'It's a little ice, calm down!'" Mia added and they all joined in laughing at the memory.

A concierge they recognized was waiting at the spa entrance for them. This was their treat to themselves that happened every three months or so—a sisters' shopping and spa day. They would hit the shops, then soak, get facials and massages, before their nails and toes were flawlessly cared for by their favorite manicurists.

"I think I'll go with coral pink nails and toes," Micki said as they soaked in the mud. "Elle said she'd have my eyebrows done in no time after the mani-pedi."

"You're having the full treatment today, huh?" Mia grinned. "You go, kiddo."

"I'm careening toward thirty ladies. The big three-zero." Micki could feel the mask on her face tightening as it dried, and the cool cucumber slices would decrease any puffiness around her eyes.

Margo laughed. "Honey, we are rounding the

curve and waving at forty soon. Hush up and be grateful for your youth."

"Guys—" Micki hesitated. "Do you think I'm a screwup? Do Mom and Dad? Mia, when Ryan first got to Charlotte you said that I never finished anything I started. Do you expect the same from me when it comes to law school?"

Micki felt a lump of mud hit her chest and took one of the cucumber slices from her eye to look at a scowling Mia. Another handful of mud hit her from the opposite side, and she took away the other slice to look at a mad-faced Margo.

"I'm sorry I said that, Micki," Mia's tone was soft and apologetic. "You don't know how much, but don't you ever think any of us aren't proud of you. You aren't a screwup that we placate. We will always think you're amazing, because you are!"

"What she said." Margo sounded hurt. "I am so sorry if we ever made you feel that way."

"You didn't—kinda." Micki played with the slice of vegetable in her hand. "I just saw how everyone seemed to be like—oh, that's so Micki and her usual way."

"Sis, we know you have layers," Mia assured her. "Promise us that you will never doubt our love for you, and that we always have your back."

"I promise," she replied, feeling much better. "I'm sorry I put a damper on our relaxation."

"You didn't. You made it better..." Margo smiled and settled back into her mud bath. "Because we know your feelings now and we can be better sisters to you."

"No sisters in the world are better than you two," Micki said with emotion clogging her throat.

The trio reached out and linked hands across the water, and she knew no matter what came, she would have Margo and Mia, and her parents to support her. "Those Ballad girls" would always be their moniker because even when they were old, their bond would never fade.

THANKSGIVING IN ANY family was always busy and a little chaotic. At Ballad Inn, one needed to triple or quadruple that. Micki loved every minute of it. The whole house smelled of the different dishes being prepared. Guests sat on the porch, enjoying the day around the portable heaters, or were hanging out in the family room where the television blared loudly with the live parade happening in New York City. The babies either slept or played. Claire was underfoot, and Omar, who seemed to have shot up like a bean sprout, was the official taste tester or so he told everyone as he snacked on anything he was offered. Mom and Dad doted on the kids and one or two of the guests helped decorate the Christmas trees that would be turned on after dinner. Mr. Bolton was there, and Micki noted the secret loving looks he and Enid gave each other. Micki also noticed that her brothers-in-law and Jonas avoided being in each other's company for very long.

"They are so suspect," she said to herself with a laugh. If they were to be interrogated, they'd all be talking fast under the scrutiny.

It was a festive time. Everyone was dressed up, having fun, and a general sense of togetherness could be felt. This year the holiday was even more special for Micki because Jonas was there with them. Today, she had her person, and each time their eyes met, he smiled or he'd find a way to hold her or hug her tight. Somehow they'd managed to dress in the same colors even though it was never discussed. It made Micki wonder if they were truly linked in a special way. She believed in soul mates; she'd watched her sisters find theirs. Was it her turn to find happiness and did she dare hope it was real?

"I thought you were the one who wanted to escape the juju of falling in love," her mother teased after seeing one of those quick kisses.

Micki bussed her mother's cheek. "I might've been wrong."

"That's my baby girl." Rosie hugged her tight. "If he's the one, Micki, make sure he makes you happy."

"I will," she promised.

"Michelle, could you come over for a moment, please?" Jonas asked politely. "My sister would like to say hello."

"Of course." Micki made sure her powder blue sweater dress was pulled down neatly in the front.

That and her khaki suede boots matched the sweater and slacks he wore. They stepped outside for a quieter spot so Emily could hear them easily. Emily was a redhead with interesting tattoos on her arms and neck. She looked so cool. While Micki was adventurous, she'd never been brave enough to get a tattoo. You could see in the background that Emily was at her hospital.

"Hello, Michelle! Aren't you smashingly gorgeous." Emily's smile was wide and friendly. "Mum is going to absolutely love her, JonJon!"

"JonJon?" Micki looked at him with a wicked smile.

"Ah, I see he's kept his pet name away from you," Emily said. "When we finally meet up, I'll tell you how he got it."

"I look forward to that," Micki replied, also smiling. "It's lovely to see you. Are you at work?"

Emily nodded. "Babies come whenever they

want. We have to be ready for them twenty-four-seven."

"My sister Margo says the same. She's not a midwife, but she did her rotation as a pediatric nurse."

"I hear you're celebrating Thanksgiving. Make sure he takes tons of pics so I can show Mum and Dad." Emily chuckled. "They were in love with the ones where he was dressed like a cowboy. He's loosening up finally."

"Emily," Jonas warned.

She waved his words away. "Fine, fine, I'll be good, but my name is being called, so I must dash."

"Nice talking with you." Micki smiled and waved.

"Bye, Em," Jonas said.

Emily gave him a wink. "By JonJon."

Emily quit the call before he could respond. Jonas gave a groan of dismay. "Please let's not discuss or repeat the name, shall we?"

"Oh, I don't know how I'll keep that secret, it's so good." She tapped her chin with her finger, considering her advantage.

"Another milkshake?" he hinted.

"Plus, a kiss," Micki added.

Jonas pulled her into his arms gently. "Deal."

He pressed his lips against hers and Micki wrapped her arms around his waist as they shared the memorable moment. She lay her head against his chest, enjoying the feel of being in his arms when the kiss ended.

"What are we doing, Jonas?" She liked how he swayed her gently as if music was playing. "Should we feel like this so quickly?"

"I don't know, I've never felt like this before." He lifted her chin with his finger so he could look into her eyes. "What I do know with everything in me is that I don't want to give it up."

"Me either," she whispered, and she leaned up to kiss him once more.

Mia poked her head out of the door. "What are y'all whispering about? Dinner is on the table."

"Nothing at all," Micki blurted. "Come on, Jonas, it's time to get stuffed."

Per tradition, the family divided themselves between two tables when guests were there on Thanksgiving. Gideon and Margo and their kids were at one table with Micki, Jonas and Mr. Webber, while the rest of her family was with the other guests at the second table. The dining room was large, and the windows faced the side yard. Christmas decorations could be seen glittering merrily.

Her father stood and tapped a spoon lightly on his glass. "Let's bow our head and give silent thanks for all we have before us, and the blessings we share by being together. Let's not forget those who are in need, and I ask if you see someone who needs help, be kind. Even the smallest gesture can mean a great deal."

The silence lasted for thirty seconds before his voice boomed out. "Let's eat!"

Ryan carved one turkey with the precision of a surgeon while Gideon carved his like a carpenter who wanted to get the job done as soon as possible. Stuffing, potatoes, rice, cranberry sauce, Enid's famous baked macaroni and cheese and Margo's green beans and bacon casserole were shared at each table. On the sideboard was an assortment of bread, rolls, her mother's spicy jerk chicken and all the desserts from pie to bread pudding. The conversation was loud, filled with jokes, stories and lots of teasing. Everyone seemed to share in a wonderful sense of togetherness, love and community. Micki and Jonas held hands secretly a few times beneath the table, and she couldn't help but feed him a bite of the stuffing from her plate.

"So, Jonas," her father called out. People stopped speaking so they could hear what was coming next. "What are your intentions toward my daughter?"

"Dad!" Micki said, aghast. "You didn't ask Gideon or Ryan that question—at all."

"Kinda did," Ryan said. "If you recall when Mia kicked me out that night."

"You kicked yourself out, but that's neither here nor there," Mia said casually before taking a mouthful of her food.

"Did the same with me the day of the wedding," Gideon spoke up. "What are our intentions, Jonas?"

"I know your secret," Micki whispered to him and watched his eyes widen.

"This is great," one of the male guests said cheerily. "Being an only kid with no family, it's like I'm part of this one. It's a lot of fun. Didn't really know what I was missing. Thanks."

"Um—" Jonas cleared his throat and looked decidedly uncomfortable, while her dad pinned him with a fatherly stare. Margo and Mia looked way too entertained. Micki thought fast. She had to do what she had to do and throw some people under the bus to save her man.

"Ryan and Gideon are keeping a secret and Jonas knows, too, but only by happenstance because he was in their company," Micki said loudly and heard more throat clearing. Gideon reached for his water glass. "Something even Mom and Dad don't know."

"You're trying to blackmail us all because you know!" Ryan replied. The guests' attention moved back and forth with interest while they ate.

"This is better than reality TV," one female guest whispered to her husband.

Ryan gulped and looked at Gideon. "Help me out here, man."

"Can't you see, I'm trying to not end up sleeping on the sofa?" Gideon smiled sweetly at Margo. "But my loving wife, I'm sure, is truly understanding of the rock and hard place I find myself between."

"But am I?" Margo asked skeptically.

"The gaze of my father is off you," Micki murmured to Jonas. "You're welcome."

"You sacrificed the lads for me," Jonas said in a low voice filled with awe. "You get all the milkshakes."

"We're waiting." Her father was staring at both Ryan and Gideon, who in turn stared at Mr. Bolton.

"Don't you dare," Mr. Bolton said.

Enid looked alarmed. "You didn't."

"Plot twist. The second mom and the neighbor are in on it," another guest whispered. "There should be only ten-star reviews for this place."

"Enid and Bolton are hitched!" Ryan announced and then slumped in his chair. "Thankfully, that's over, I feel so relieved."

There was silence before family chaos erupted.

"You're married?" her mom asked. "Why didn't you tell us!"

Enid glared at her husband. "We were going to after the holiday when we move into my house."

"Marley's daughter and her family are buying my home to be closer to him," Mr. Bolton explained. "And I kinda let it slip, Enid. I'm sorry."

"When did you get married and where?" Mia demanded. "I'm hurt we weren't invited or involved."

"We did not want a fuss," Enid said. "I'm too old for that. I just wanted to be married and then move in with my husband on New Year's Day. The day we got married was just for us, our time to say what we felt and to promise to cherish each other."

"Oh, they're in love-love." Margo fanned her face as if to stop from crying while Gideon patted her back.

"If you start crying, we'll all start crying," Micki struggled to say past everything she was feeling.

"That includes all of us," another female guest said.

"Well—that day was yours, Enid." Her father was beaming. "But this has just become a Thanksgiving dinner *and* wedding reception. Let's raise our glass to the newlyweds who were married on…?"

"September twenty-third," Enid supplied as Mr. Bolton took her hand and kissed it.

"You've been married for *two months*," her mom said, shaking her head. "Okay, we're going to talk about this later. Right now, it's congratulations!"

Cheers erupted and her family moved to embrace Enid and her new husband. It was another change, one that Micki was happy to see. Enid had spent her whole life taking care of them; she'd never married or had children of her own. She deserved to be happy with a good man who had been courting her for more than ten years. For Micki, it was bittersweet because soon she would have to tell her family she was also leaving Ballad Inn. Maybe it was best to hold off on her news for now and just celebrate Enid and Mr. Bolton.

"You take care of our Enid," Micki told Mr. Bolton sternly. "I know where you live at the moment. You treat her like a queen."

"You got it," Mr. Bolton said with a smile. "Since you'll be just a short walk away from us, you can keep an eye on me."

Micki hugged Enid next. "I'm sorry for outing you like that."

"I'm not. It was exhausting keeping that secret. Now we can just enjoy each other's company." Enid cupped Micki's cheeks and looked into her eyes while everyone else talked and laughed and went back to their dinner. "You'll tell them yours soon enough."

"How did you know?" Micki asked, swallowing her emotions.

Enid kissed her cheek before whispering in her ear. "Every momma bird knows when her baby is going to fly. And you're ready to soar, but I know one day you'll return to the nest."

"Thank you." Micki buried her face in Enid's shoulder and felt her tears fall.

She pulled away with a watery laugh. "So, where's the honeymoon going to be?"

Enid held out her hand and Mr. Bolton took it before they both spoke. "St. Augustine."

The rest of the evening went on brilliantly, with even more to celebrate than before. The babies woke up as dessert was finished and the crowd shifted to the main room to continue the celebration, making the moment complete. Micki looked around. So many changes, so much love. Jonas moved closer and took her hand. How could she not believe that he was meant to be hers to start a new journey with away from Ballad Inn?

CHAPTER EIGHT

THE DRESS SHE wore was perfect, like her sisters had said, but Micki itched to get out of it and into her regular, comfy clothes. Jonas seemed so confident and impeccably handsome in his tailored suit that Enid broke out her camera to take several photos, blinding them both with the flash.

"Where do you find film for that thing?" Micki demanded to know. "It's a relic. At least let me get you a digital camera."

"I will use this until it falls apart in my hands," Enid told her while her sisters took a few pictures the normal way, with the cameras in their phones. "What would I do with a digital camera anyway?"

"Download the images," Micki answered. "To the laptop you got for Christmas last year that's still in the box."

Enid looked heavenward. "I don't know how to use that thing."

"Okay. So where do you get the film?" Micki asked again.

"I order it from an online shop that still sells actual rolls of film," Margo said, joining them in the inn's foyer.

"So, it's you who keeps helping to facilitate this historical relic?" Micki accused.

"How about you leave before she goes and gets another roll of film," Mia suggested, smiling wryly. "You guys look so power couple-ish together."

Jonas kissed her temple where her hair was pulled back from her face. "That we do."

"I got that on camera," Enid said excitedly and pressed the button again.

"Ack!" Micki raised her hand to block the flash. "Jonas, lead me out. That's enough of this."

"I'm on it," he said, laughing.

"You look beautiful," he said with a smile as he opened the car door for her.

"Thank you." Micki was pleased at his compliment.

All too soon, they were at the big event. Micki tapped the heel of her pumps nervously against the carpeted floor outside the grand room where Jonas signed them in with the guest coordinator. She looked beyond him to see the growing crowd and a number of art pieces, some in glass cases, positioned throughout the room. The floor was polished to a shine that reflected the recessed lighting in the ceiling and made many of the bronze sculptures glow. The Edington Foundation was housed in an impressive building that was nestled between office towers and pricey condominiums in the high-end business district uptown.

Glancing around, she felt out of place being among all these sophisticated scholars and wealthy people. The couple behind them were definitely talking with an air of superiority.

"Don't be nervous," Jonas whispered as they walked into the grand room.

He snagged them two glasses of champagne from a waiter passing by, with a quick thank-you, and handed her one of the flutes.

Micki took a sip. "Easy for you to say. You're the dean, they already like you. And there is Professor Willoughby front and center. Can we avoid him the entire night?"

"We can certainly try." Jonas turned. "Look, there's Jennifer and that must be her husband. We can talk to them all night."

He escorted her over to the couple who looked at them with delight. "Aren't you two like models on a fashion magazine cover?"

Micki laughed. "Right. Then maybe I can pay for law school from my lucrative modeling contract."

"Cain, this is one of our best students, Micki Ballad, and this is Dr. Jonas Brand, the new law school dean," Jennifer said to her husband. He looked just as uncomfortable as Micki felt, except he kept pulling at his tie.

"Nice to meet you both. If you don't see me later, this tie has strangled me." Cain grimaced. A bit of salt-and-pepper at his temples was a nice feature, although the rest of his hair and beard was a rich dark brown.

"I'm sorry, he's being melodramatic," Jennifer said, obviously amused.

"Let me guess, you're a contactor or run a plumbing and HVAC small business," Micki assessed. "You remind me of our landscaper, Hunter."

"HVAC," Cain said, pleased.

"I used to be a handyman at our bed-and-breakfast." Micki smiled at him. "Trust me, I would prefer my jeans right now as well."

"Heads up, Professor Willoughby is on his way over, with someone that looks as pretentious as he is," Jennifer said softly and took a sip of her drink.

"Brand, there's someone you should meet," Professor Willoughby said briskly. "A good friend of mine for over twenty years and a huge donor to our law school."

"I would love to meet your friend, but it's Dr. Brand or Dean Brand, not just my last name."

Jonas's tone was calm but clipped. "Just like the respect I show you any time we meet."

Professor Willoughby flushed red but kept up his bravado. "This is Mary Stockton of the Raleigh Stocktons. They own that huge group of department stores."

Micki wanted to crack a joke but listened silently.

"It's lovely to meet you." Jonas smiled and shook the woman's hand. "Unfortunately, I've not been in North Carolina long enough to know your family business, but I'm sure I soon will."

"That's a certainty." Mary Stockton was tall and thin in her fashionable blue satin dress highlighted by diamonds around her neck and on her ears and wrists. "Tell me, Dr. Brand, you have many gifted academics at this venerable institution, including Professor Willoughby, so why has Aaron not received tenure yet? He's told me that he's been overlooked again."

"While I appreciate your donations to the college, that decision is based on a variety of factors and made not only by me but the board, and takes into consideration his record, the dean of students' recommendations and the views of the students themselves," Jonas replied without missing a beat. "Many of the board are here tonight. I'd suggest asking them, since it's not my place to discuss this with the public."

"I'm not the public, I'm Mary Stockton," she said in a haughty manner.

Jonas nodded. "But that doesn't change the matter at hand. This is not something I can discuss."

"Ms. Ballad, what are you doing here?" Professor Willoughby snapped.

Micki was about to tell him but someone else beat her to the punch.

"Aaron, there are several undergrad and grad students here," Jennifer said briskly. "Please use a better tone. They don't deserve that attitude."

"She's here with me," Jonas said without hesitation. "I agree with Jennifer."

"She is a problematic student. I thought better of you, Dean Brand."

"I think that's up for discussion. And I don't see how you can have any opinion of me at this point," Jonas said. "Although I have heard about yours a few times."

"I questioned one claim in your lecture on evidentiary proceedings and since then you've chosen to come after me in every possible way," Micki retorted. "My grades speak for themselves."

"I can attest to that," Jennifer said. "I've had to change a few of your grades, Aaron. You were being blatantly overcritical of many students."

"Your standards are not as high as mine," he huffed before taking a long drink from his glass.

"Now, listen here, you—" Cain was ready to defend his wife.

Jennifer placed her hand on Cain's arm. "It's fine. There's no need, not for him."

Jonas stepped closer. His tone was soft but somber. "You'll not disrespect any of your peers in my presence. Every other professor is just as or more qualified than you are, with impeccable records. While I understand you're upset about tenure, there is an opportunity here to learn and evolve yourself to make a better claim in future. But you can't do it like this. This old way of pompous disparaging of others will no longer work."

"I don't think you can say that to me," Professor Willoughby muttered through stiff lips.

"Then how about you, Miss Stockton? What do you say on the subject now?" Jonas asked firmly.

Mary's smile was genuine. "I don't think there's a need for further discussion, Dean Brand. I understand you completely."

"Thank you." Jonas smiled in return. "It's good when logic and fairness rules."

Again, she smiled, while Professor Willoughby looked furious and led her away.

Micki saw how Jonas had turned the situation to his favor. Still, the woman had been awful and Professor Willoughby the same. She wanted to slip away and not deal with any of it any longer.

"Nicely done," Jennifer said, clearly approving.

"I'm glad you said what you did, frank and to the point," Cain murmured. "What an absolutely horrible man."

"Well, you catch more flies with honey than you do with vinegar." Jonas grinned. "My mother taught me that. Diplomacy sometimes takes a gentler hand."

"Very true." Jennifer chuckled. "Now I must go mingle. If I don't keep Cain distracted, he'll make a run for it."

"No doubt," Cain agreed with a smile. "Nice meeting you both."

After a goodbye from herself and Jonas, Micki's hand was given a quick squeeze by Professor Linton before she walked away.

"Are you all right?" Jonas asked. Concern was etched on his face.

"I told you this was a bad idea," she said. Her hurt and irritation were evident in her voice. "He's never going to let me live it down. Not just what I did during his lecture but that I'm a nontraditional student."

"He's like that because he fears change, he's

insecure. He's seen not just Micah but others pass him by and knows he isn't measuring up."

"You don't have to be diplomatic with me," Micki said, frowning. "You should go mingle."

"Come with me," he prodded gently. "Michelle, you belong here with everyone else."

"I'll find you in a bit. I just want to go to the bathroom and clear my head."

"Okay. Find me after." He kissed her cheek.

That show of affection made her feel better in a way, but with a nod, she hustled to the closest bathroom to escape. The ladies' room had a small sofa and a pair of wingback chairs in the outer room. She slumped into a seat and put her head in her hands. When did she become so insecure herself? Was this what happened when you truly wanted something so badly in your life? It was so important to her to be a lawyer, to be able to help people who couldn't afford a high-priced attorney. She recalled what her mother had said—that anything worth having never did come easy. A silent but mirthless laugh escaped her. "You got that right, Mom," she said under her breath.

She was about to stand and go when she heard voices coming from the stalls. Micki shrank into her chair.

"Did you see her come in with the dean?" a voice she recognized said. "No jean jacket and sneakers, but dressed to the nines. I wonder if he bought her that dress?"

"Well, she found a way to make sure she gets admitted to the law school," another female murmured.

"But she comes off as so down-to-earth and yet she was calculating enough to start dating the new dean?" the third voice said. "I mean, I thought she could cut it, but I guess it's a facade. She is older than we are—maybe slacking off for years made her realize she can't keep up."

Micki listened in horror as the three younger students discussed her when she thought they were her friends. Silent tears fell down her cheek and she swiped them away furiously, jumping to her feet. Three faces looked at her in shock and then shame, when they stepped around the corner and discovered she was there. She lifted her head in defiance.

"I can cut it, Sarah. Remember, if it wasn't for me, you wouldn't have passed your political science class." Micki switched her attention to the second woman. "Denise, you think I was slacking off, but I had already gained enough credits to go straight into my second year of being an undergrad. So, this is no facade. This is someone who has enough experience and intelligence to put toward her work and pass with all A's. I was doing that before Dean Brand showed up, and I will be doing it after. And Leslie, I'll get into law school on my own. I won't need anyone's help or favoritism."

"Micki—" Sarah began.

"No need to apologize or explain." She shook her head. "I guess I truly don't know who my friends are. My sisters always said I see the best in everyone. Thanks for letting me know your true feelings. I'll go back to slacking off and keeping to myself. Don't expect me at study group."

She turned and left the bathroom, more than ready to ditch the whole event. Between Professor Willoughby and now this trio, the night had taken its toll. She wanted her home and the security of what she knew. Micki's eyes found Jonas in the crowd easily. She moved up behind him and tapped him on the shoulder gently.

"Micki, I was just telling two of our board members about your intriguing theory of cross-refencing precedents. It really raises the bar," Jonas said warmly.

"Thank you for that." She gave a thin smile. "I'm going to head home. I have a migraine brewing."

"If you would excuse me," Jonas apologized and guided her to a private corner. He spoke bluntly. "You don't have migraines, Margo does."

"I developed one from listening to one of my

professors, then three fellow students I thought I was on good terms with but think I can't cut it," Micki replied stiffly. "Apparently I'm dating you to eventually get into law school."

"That's ridiculous. Michelle. You can't let gossip or foolish talk define you," Jonas said, grimacing.

Micki gave him a hurt look. "Says the man who no one is saying anything about. They're practically throwing laurels on your head." She paused, trying to get her spiraling emotions under control. Placing her hand on his chest lightly, she said, "Please stay, and continue your evening with your peers. As I said before, I'm not comfortable here and I should've followed my instincts. Some places people just don't or want to fit into."

"I came with you, I'll leave with you, too," he said firmly.

"I can take a rideshare, it's fine."

"Let me say my goodbyes. Ask the hostess for your coat and we'll be on our way." One of the guests called his name and he turned toward the voice.

She turned on her heel and headed toward the foyer without looking back. The hostess accepted the small, numbered ticket from her and, with a smile, handed it to the coat check clerk behind the desk, along with Micki's twenty-dollar tip. Micki knew how it was when tips made up a portion of your paycheck.

Sarah, Leslie and Denise seemed to be leaving at the same time.

"Micki, please," Leslie said in a soft pleading voice. "We didn't mean to hurt your feelings."

"Don't apologize. It's how you really feel." Micki shrugged.

Jonas arrived, and together they walked outside, where he gave the valet the ticket for his car. The ride home began with silence and tension filled the air.

"You didn't have to leave," Micki said.

"You were my guest. It wouldn't be right, you going home alone."

Micki gave a humorless laugh. "Guest, huh? Nothing else?"

He made a frustrated sound in his throat. "Don't try to read anything into one word because your insecurities made you uncomfortable."

"People made me uncomfortable," Micki shot back.

"Because you went in with doubts about being there. Please believe me, Michelle, your worth isn't defined by others."

"It's like you never had a day of insecurity in your life," she said disbelievingly. "I'm twenty-eight, soon to be twenty-nine, and me speaking my mind—standing up for my beliefs—put me in Professor Willoughby's crosshairs. People I thought were my friends, it turns out, certainly aren't, and now I have you telling me my feelings aren't valid."

"I didn't say that. I would never say that." Jonas glanced at her with a deep frown. "I said diplomacy is best."

"Flies with honey, I get it," Micki grumbled. "Not every problem can be solved with a charming voice and a compliment."

"Michelle..." He hesitated and blew out a long breath. "I just got here. I'm new to this job, still trying to find my footing. It's important to me and to do that I'm still navigating these waters. Maybe now's not the time to make waves."

Micki's laugh was caustic. "Well, by all means do not let me be the source of the waves you make. Forget about it, this me and you thing. Let's make sure that our perfect world has no waves."

"Michelle—"

She refused to answer.

"Michelle," he repeated and she still said nothing. What else was there to say, she thought.

When they got back to the bed-and-breakfast, she was out of the car as soon as he parked. Micki stepped inside the inn, Jonas right behind her.

Margo was passing by, taking some ironed linens to the hall closet "Hey, sis, how was tonight?" she said brightly.

"Ask Mr. I Don't Want To Make Waves, since he likes to catch flies with honey and not vinegar," Micki said as she climbed the stairs. All she wanted was that bedroom.

"Huh, wait—are you vinegar?" Margo asked.

"Who knows? Ask him!" Micki yelled back as she reached the second-floor landing.

"Hello, Margo, how was your evening?"

"Don't you hello me, mister, with that winning accent. What did you do to my sister?" Margo's voice was stern.

"It wasn't my fault exactly," Jonas began, and Micki smirked as he stammered.

She went upstairs to go have a good cry because it felt like she'd just broken up with a guy who was truly starting to take hold in her heart. And it had happened in a matter of weeks, which was a new world record for her. Micki took off the shoes and dress, hanging the garment carefully before pulling on a sleep shirt and throwing herself into her bed. She screamed into her pillow to muffle the sound, and then thought, *Great, I still have my makeup on.*

She rolled onto her back and got under her thick covers that always felt like a comforting hug, before reaching for her wireless earphones and putting them on. She turned the music up loud on her cell phone. The tunes would drown out the rest of her thoughts and keep her from crying more. Micki would deal with tomorrow and the next day as they came.

SHE'D BEEN ABLE to avoid him for a good forty-eight hours, not getting up until he was gone for the day. Now they were back on campus for semester finals. She spent most of her time in the library studying alone, or at least she tried to. Like she'd promised her friends, Micki was no longer a part of the study group, which alarmed the rest of her campus buddies.

"Why!" Erica practically yelled. She was another student who'd gotten a late start on her formal education. "You tell me right now who hurt your feelings."

Micki told her hesitantly, knowing that Erica would interrogate everyone until she'd found the truth. She wanted to be a prosecutor and Micki knew by the way she rooted out the truth, any district attorney's office would be lucky to have her.

"Oh no, ma'am, that will not fly," Erica said angrily. "How dare they? Well, they lost me, too. Us nontraditional students stick together."

"Don't tell anyone and make a fuss," Micki begged. "I just want to get through the rest of this semester with my dignity and a slew of A grades, then celebrate the winter holidays at home with eggnog and warm socks."

Erica gave her a curious look. "That's awfully specific."

"Just how my mind works." She shrugged.

First it was Erica, then John and soon six of the twelve that were in their study group happened to migrate to her corner in the library. Erica swore she hadn't told anyone, but hugs of solidarity and words of support proved the gossip got around somehow. Even in class it seemed that she was flanked by friends left, right and center. She sat away from Sarah, Leslie and Denise now and that morning before class, while she was talking to Erica, the trio approached them.

"What could y'all possibly want?" Erica asked bluntly.

Micki winced. "Come on, Erica, don't be like that, not for me."

"We wanted to apologize. It was pure cattiness what you heard in the bathroom," Sarah said.

Leslie continued. "We acted terribly and those words shouldn't have come from our mouths. You've never been anything but amazing to us."

"We hope you can forgive us," Denise finished.

"I was never raised to hold grudges or be unkind, so I can say I forgive you and mean it," Micki said. "But I was also raised to be honest, and even though I can't say we'll be close friends again, I want you guys to continue to be amazing and have fantastic lives."

Sarah nodded and the three women went to sit on the other side of the classroom. Spots filled up quickly and ten minutes later, Professor Willoughby finally came in. He wore his usual brown checkered coat and look of disdain as he slammed his bag down on the desk.

"This class ends on December tenth, and your final will be today," he said in lieu of a good morning or hello.

A groan came from the entire class, even though most of them expected this twist. He was well known for this kind of surprise. He liked to try to catch students unawares, but after the second time this happened, most knew to start studying in October, right up until he sprung his final test.

He handed out the papers and stood at the front of the class. "Everything off your desks, cell phones in bag. All you need is a pencil—ninety minutes. Begin."

They were silent as they worked. Micki looked at each question and clearly defined the answer in her head before writing it down. She was done in an hour and laid her pencil on the paper. He met her gaze, but Micki refused to look away. Thirty minutes more passed and the timer went off. Papers were passed to the professor and he plucked out a few, glanced at each one and tucked them at the bottom of the stack.

"I can see by your answers—it will be a lot of C's going out." He looked up at them. "Didn't you listen in class?"

"This is ridiculous," Erica said under her breath.

"Who spoke?" the professor demanded to know.

Erica stepped forward. "I spoke, and I said it's ridiculous because we've excelled even though you refuse to acknowledge our achievements or offer any constructive discussion. We are here to learn, we want to learn, but you have made this a toxic environment where none of us want to be."

Other students nodded in agreement and he looked furious. "Do you know who I am, how lucky you are that I'm guest-lecturing in this class?"

Erica's shoulders sagged. "I'm tired of your terrible disposition, especially considering how hard we have been working. Since you say we will all get a C, *you* tell us what are we here for? We're not excelling, we're not learning! I can only speak for myself, but I will dispute my grade directly to the chancellor if I have to."

To heck with not making waves, Micki figured. "Same here."

"Has Dean Brand encouraged you to do this, since you seem so—close." Professor Willoughby smirked.

"Uncalled for!" a male student exclaimed in a shocked voice. "Enough is enough. I say we boycott this class, walk out and we don't come back until we're heard on all matters regarding how he treats students."

"You can't do that!" the professor said, clearly alarmed, understanding that he just might have gone too far.

"We have a clearly defined and protected right to gather and protest unjust actions," Micki said calmly. "The college rules also guarantee our rights as students to protest and I think that's what we're doing."

"We're going to ask students from your other classes to join our boycott, until the administration takes action to address your behavior," Erica added and picked up her bag. "Let our silence be the loudest action that this college has ever seen."

"Anyone who walks out that door fails this class," he threatened.

Erica strode out. Micki followed, and no one said a word as the rest of the group left. Instead, they lined the hallway waiting for his next class to arrive. Most took seats on the floor and joined the silent sit-in. He stalked out of the class, his steps echoing loudly in the quiet hallway. They all filed out behind him, exiting the building while an administrator at the information counter had a grim look on her face and the phone up to her ear. Micki thought about how Jonas didn't want to make waves, but this was one of the biggest this campus had ever seen. *Uh-oh...*

An hour later, there was a group sitting as best as it could in Jonas's office, with five students and Professor Linton, who had been officially notified when everyone chose to leave Professor Willoughby's classes. The not-so-good professor was also there, sitting by Jonas's desk, shooting them all nasty looks. Some students refused to take his final, knowing they were in line for a bad grade. Micki could barely look at Jonas, whose glasses only made him seem even more handsome as he stared at them with genuine concern in his eyes.

Her heart raced. She hoped she'd see some extra kind of emotion in his eyes to show he was missing her just like she was missing him. He pinned her with a stare, and Micki saw a flash of something that was soon hidden under the professionalism that made him who he was.

"He told all of you that you'd be getting C's," Jonas repeated what they'd told him.

Jennifer nodded. "I asked to see the test papers for myself, and he refuses to give them to me, nor will he give them back to the students."

"That's very suspect, Professor Willoughby," Jonas turned his attention to the professor.

"It's my exam," he said loudly.

"No, it's not, it's the university's, and the criminal justice studies department's test. You're a facilitator in this case." Jonas held out his hand. "Pass the tests here."

He gave the stack to Jonas, who called Professor Linton over and gave her half. "Let's see if these deserve such a low assessment, shall we?"

They all sat silently while Jonas and Professor Linton went through each paper, quickly and efficiently. Soon, their faces took on a look of disappointment and disbelief. Jonas sat back and shot Professor Willoughby an icy glare.

"You do a disservice to this whole university by using your classroom as a place to bully and discourage students, especially students with an eye on being lawyers one day. New generations of those with a love and keen interest in how the law is interpreted and practiced is essential for our society to succeed," Jonas said. "I see maybe two C's in the stack. Jennifer?"

"That's what I was thinking, and even those

I would probably change to low B's because it's not that the work was wrong, but the students interpreted the questions in a different way," Jennifer said. "But they all clearly know the material to the letter."

"We're not going back until he has had some kind of reprimand or the board addresses how he treats the students," Erica said firmly. "Even the staff stay out of his way because he is so unpleasant or demeaning to everyone."

"It is not my duty or my job to make people comfortable or to like me," Professor Willoughby stated. "I'm not here to coddle children but to teach the fundamentals."

"We're not asking you to like us, but to treat us fairly and respect us," Micki added. "And age or reasons for being in this class shouldn't matter, only that we have open minds, learn what we need to and do the work. Then use all that knowledge wisely."

"Very well said." Professor Linton nodded. "Aaron, the world is changing, and so is the law, and all the college courses related to it. You can't continue with this behavior of yours with students. I don't understand it. When we first met, you were a completely different person. What's happened?"

"What's the end game here, Dean Brand?"

Professor Willoughby completely ignored his colleague.

Micki shook her head. There were some people who just chose not to change, and Professor Willoughby seemed like one of them. What had happened to him, she wondered. Though she was glad his actions had come to light, Micki was also sad for him. No one should be stuck in that kind of unhappiness.

Jonas straightened. "You'll give your final exams, and you will grade the students fairly. It will all be proctored by Professor Linton, if she agrees, to ensure the process and marks are fair," Jonas said.

"You have no right to do this, my dean or not!" Professor Willoughby declared.

"I do," Jonas said calmly. "The board has given me permission to suspend you, until a review can be made of your effectiveness as a teacher in the undergrad department and the law school, commencing after the holidays."

Professor Willoughby's eyes widened and then with a stiff, angry nod, he stood and left the room.

"Is this acceptable? Enough to stop the walk-out?" Jonas asked the students.

Erica looked at Micki and the others. Everyone nodded. "Yes, we're happy with the solution."

"Good. I'm very grateful," Jonas said and then

smiled wide. "I'd prefer to see students in class-rooms rather than eating junk food in the hall-ways."

"We'll save you a candy bar," Erica teased as the group got up to go.

"Micki, could you hang back a moment so we could speak?" Jonas asked.

"Sorry, Teach, but I need to study for the up-coming exams," Micki said as casually as possible even though her heart raced. She didn't want any gossip that stemmed from her being in his office alone with him, given the earlier talk had been put to rest.

"Another time, then," he said, and his eyes went back to the paperwork in front of him.

Micki opened her mouth to speak, but instead closed it. She missed his laughter, how he found joy in the little things and him calling her by her full name, if she was being honest. But how would they work as a couple with so many pairs of eyes scrutinizing them at every turn? Being in love seemed to be truly messy. That made her stop in shock. *Shoot, I'm in love!*

CHAPTER NINE

ENOUGH IS ENOUGH, Jonas thought as he drove home later that night. He couldn't take the tension between himself and Micki any longer because while he'd been more than a bit frank, he hadn't been wrong. You don't run from the hard parts, you stand with your head held high. *You're one to talk.* The words filtered through his mind and his subconscious wouldn't let them go. But he hadn't run, he'd faced the music, and made sure that he and his family's name had been cleared before he moved to the United States. The stigma of what had happened would've surely followed him everywhere in the UK.

Charlotte, the law school—this was a fresh start and he wasn't ready to give up on the chance to be with her or how she made him feel and vice versa, he hoped.

Now, in front of Ballad Inn, the lights for the upcoming holiday glittered and blinked merrily. The Christmas train went around the track set up between the displays. In the bay windows, he could spot the trees decorated with every keepsake ornament the Ballads owned. It made him miss his family; this would be his first Christmas away. However, he was where he was meant to be.

Walking up to the front door, he didn't have to put in the code because it stood wide open, the interim glass door the barrier that kept the cold outside.

Jonas stepped inside to see Margo and Gideon sitting in the TV room by the fire with their children. Claire's little lips puckered in concentration as she put together a wooden puzzle with her dad. Margo patted the baby's back gently, a book on the floor beside her. Micki, dressed in a teal sweat suit, was at the table, stacks of her books spread out around her as she studied. Margo asked her a question from the book and either Micki answered easily or looked it up before scribbling words in a spiral notebook. They all looked his way when he took a step closer.

"Hi there, Jonas," said Gideon, greeting him in a friendly manner.

"Good evening, there's dinner warming for you in the kitchen, if you're hungry," Margo told him.

"Thank you, I'll have it shortly."

Jonas dropped his satchel by the doorway and approached Micki, who tilted her head upward when he came to stand beside her. Silently he took her hand and urged her to stand. Then Jonas cupped her cheeks and kissed her soundly. She deepened the kiss.

Finally, he pulled away and tenderly moved a lock of her hair from in front of her face and spoke huskily, "We can go forward, yes? I'm sorry that I hurt your feelings."

"But you were right." Micki wrapped her arms around his neck. "I'm sorry I chose to walk away instead of stand with you at the party. Next time we'll be a power couple."

Jonas grinned. "I would like that. I've never been a power couple before."

"Ahem, but did you forget you're studying," Margo asked her sister although merriment was dancing in her eyes.

"I think our part in this is over, honey," Gideon rose and Margo gave him Baby Andy, who burped immediately.

"After all the patting I did, somehow you give him the burp." Margo sighed. "Boys, right?"

"Boys, right," Claire mimicked and then giggled uncontrollably.

Margo stood and handed Jonas the textbook she'd been reading from to Micki. "Tag, you're it."

"Gladly," he said and put the book on the

table. He slipped off his coat. "I'll find my dinner and come back to help. I'm starving after today's events. Your sister here and her friends boycotted Professor Willoughby with a class walkout."

"Wait, what?" Margo asked, her eyes wide with amazement.

"We'll find out about it soon enough," Gideon interrupted. "Grab the girl, you know she's a runner when she gets outside."

"Claire Bear secured," Margo said, smiling. "G'night. Enjoy studying, you crazy kids."

"Night," Micki called to her sister. "And thank you."

Jonas dropped a kiss on Micki's nose. "Be right back."

The night went on; guests arrived to enjoy the lit fire and play board games or read. Other guests turned up from having been outside enjoying the lights and heaters, and said goodnight as they passed by to go upstairs. Micki paused long enough to lock up and set the alarm, leaving the bed-and-breakfast dim with the only light left in the family room. Jonas watched her as her mind worked. The way she could find answers so intelligently and fast, how a tiny furrow in her brow appeared when she seemed to be challenged, or how she folded the corner of her very cute lips. Micki was going to be a fine lawyer one day, and he wasn't being biased. She had a knack and a love for the law. It was plain to see. Few people found their niche, but he saw it in her. She'd be a force to be reckoned with for the clients at that nonprofit.

"What are you looking at," Micki asked softly, bringing his attention back to the present.

"Pardon me?" He felt a blush creep up his cheeks.

Micki smiled. "You were staring at me."

"Because you're beautiful," he replied simply. "So I'm allowed to stare."

"I don't think that's how it works," she pointed out gently.

"Well, it should." Jonas stretched his arms with a yawn. "I forgot how stiff you get from being hunched over, studying for exams."

Micki slapped her hand on the table. "Then it's time for a dance-it-out."

"A what?" Jonas said dubiously. "I will let you know I can't dance."

"You line dance just fine," Micki reminded him. She pulled a little speaker from her bag. It was a dog. "Meet Dot."

"Nice to meet you," he said. "It's shaped like a dachshund."

"Hence the name." She connected to the Bluetooth speaker. "Come on, up you get. Shake it out."

"That sounds dangerous," he teased.

"Unless you plan to breakdance, babe, you're okay." She laughed.

"Babe?" He lifted an eyebrow.

"I think it fits." She smiled and began to move to the hip-hop beat. "Stop evading, just dance."

Jonas, knowing it would not be pretty, tried his best to find the beat.

"Oh my goodness, what's happening to you?" Micki asked, her expression dumbfounded.

"I'm dancing," he said and continued to move hips, arms and legs.

"Oh, uh, let's try something else—" She changed the song to a slower one. "We're going to slow dance, so put your hands on my hips or around my waist."

"Now, this I know how to do," he said softly.

"Yes, you do, because whatever that was, it wasn't dancing." He felt laughter bubble up inside her and she leaned her head on his shoulder, chucking.

"Are you laughing at me?" Jonas asked, teasing again.

"Yes." She lifted her head and there were tears of mirth in her eyes. "Your body was going everywhere all at once."

"You'll regret laughing at me." Jonas kissed her once, then twice. "There. Now you've been sufficiently chastised."

Her lips twitched. "Yes, I've learned my lesson."

"Micki, I wanted to tell you, I understand the insecurity, trying to fit in where some may not want you to." Jonas hesitated. "I left London because a friend used me. I gave him money to help and instead he used it for something else. It caused problems and I just couldn't stand the scrutiny anymore."

"Jonas, I'm so sorry that happened," Micki said with what sounded like genuine concern. "But you're here now and you'll leave the past right where it needs to be. In the rearview mirror, getting farther and farther away."

"I hope so." He pressed his forehead lightly against hers as they continued to dance. "You make me feel like the world just stops and it's only you and me."

"What are we doing here, Jonas?" Micki whispered. "Why do I feel like this when I'm with you?"

He lifted her chin so he could look into her eyes. "I think it's called falling in love."

"Oh."

"Just oh?"

"I'm happy about it, if you are," she said and rose up to kiss him.

Jonas could tell he was falling deeper and deeper into his feelings for her. As if he were in a romantic comedy and just as he was about to kiss the love interest, a song would begin to play, and you knew they were going to find their happily-ever-after. Instead of hearing music, he felt a spray of cold water and then wicked feminine laughter filled the air. The barrage of droplets didn't stop. Jonas lifted a hand to keep the water off his face while Micki made sputtering noises.

"Gah! Quit it!" she finally yelled.

Mia stood there, grinning, watching them. Ryan quickly stepped forward to hand them paper towel to dry themselves.

"Really, Mia? Really?" Micki asked, obviously exasperated.

"I told you one day I would pay you back." Mia rocked on her heels in satisfaction. "Imagine when Margo tells me that you're here, studying with your beau."

"My beau."

"Your sweet British beau," Mia continued. "I knew there'd be a kiss or two and an opportunity for a little payback after you drowned me and Ryan in that tree."

"She drowned you in a tree?" Jonas directed his question to Ryan.

"We were kissing, sitting on a branch, and she took a garden hose to us," he answered. "I managed to convince Mia that a garden hose wouldn't be great on the hardwood floors, so a spritz bottle it was."

"You encouraged this, Ryan?" Micki demanded to know. "I thought we had an understanding."

Ryan shrugged. "All's fair in love and water revenge. Besides, my wife supersedes all."

"That I do." Mia smiled triumphantly before backing away. "Remember this moment in future."

"Diabolical," Micki called after her and there was laughter in response.

"This is one interesting family." Jonas balled up the paper towel in his hand and put it in the trash. "But I like it. Reminds me of when Em and I go at each other."

"With that, I think we're done studying for the night," Micki said. "Thanks for helping me."

"I'd do anything for my girlfriend." Jonas grinned. "I feel like I can say that now."

"You can," Micki smiled, too. "Don't forget about camping—we leave Friday."

"Am I still invited?" Jonas asked, pleased and grateful at how the evening had led to a wonderful result.

Micki closed her books and tidied them neatly on the table. "Of course, you are. I want to see if you camp as well as you dance."

"Oh, that was uncalled for," he said as he followed her up the stairs.

Micki chuckled. "It was an easy setup I couldn't resist."

They parted on the second-floor landing, and with a smile on his face, he watched her go upstairs to bed. Micki blew him a kiss before moving out of sight. He'd tell his family that he'd finally found a love that made him think of forever. Immediately he knew his mum would ask about grandchildren. The idea made him laugh as he got ready for bed.

JONAS WAS WILLING to admit he wasn't much of an outdoorsman. The most outdoorsy he'd been as an adult was a hike up a dusty hill on vacation when he'd been an undergrad. It was outdoors, yes, but they didn't even climb for more than an hour. Now, as he looked up at Kings Mountain, where they would spend the next two days, the sky was cloudy, and the mist hung over the peaks. It was supposed to rain that night; the radio said scattered showers but that hadn't deterred Micki and her friends.

"It makes the adventure all the cozier," Micki said enthused back at the inn, and the others nodded with grins on their faces.

He was unsure but smiled as well. Then they loaded up the gear in their car and followed

Nina and Peter as they all headed out from Sardis Woods in the early morning hours.

"So, you said it's Moss Lake," Jonas confirmed as Micki drove.

"Named because of the huge outcroppings of mossy rocks near the waterfall," Micki said. "You won't be sleeping on moss, though."

"At least moss is mostly soft. It grows wild in all areas of England," he quipped. "They have fairy-tale princesses lying on a bed of the stuff when they're hiding in the forest for a good reason."

She laughed loud and long, which made him smile. "Very true, but don't worry, baby, I'll take care of you. I won't let a bigfoot get you."

"What's a bigfoot, some type of fish?" he asked worriedly.

Micki went on to tell him of the myth of Bigfoot and how he'd been seen in not only Kings Mountain but Uwharrie National Forest as well. Jonas listened with the skepticism of someone who dealt in logic, so he had questions, naturally.

"Okay, so there's one large, hairy animal-type or possibly a group of them roaming all over America, almost seven feet tall, because people have found their footprints?"

Micki nodded. "That's what they say."

"Since they've found footprints, why hasn't

anyone gotten actual proof other than a few hazy pictures? Almost everyone has a phone with pretty decent camera technology right now." Jonas kept on the lore. "Why haven't they found samples of hair for DNA analysis, or a den, or a cave? If these things are real, there should be more evidence. Or this Bigfoot group of animals are the best hide-and-seek players in history."

Micki's laughter echoed again in the car. "I can't believe you said that! It's hilarious."

"But no less true," Jonas said, amused. "Let's just hope we don't see one, for safety reasons alone. Once, in Scotland, I swore I saw Nessie."

Micki glanced at him and raised a brow. "So, you believe in the Loch Ness monster but not in a cryptid?"

Jonas answered easily. "It's quite possible that Nessie is from a line of prehistoric animals that live in the water. The Loch is vast and deep with plenty of caves and areas that make it a completely viable option. It's extremely cold and it has a low visibility because of the soil content. Divers can barely see past the tips of their noses. Your Bigfeet…"

"Foot," Micki corrected.

"What's the plural?" Jonas countered.

Micki shrugged. "Who knows—but continue."

"Well, your cryptids are seen in the daylight,

all the time. They have pictures, so it should be easy to find their dens," he pointed out.

"Okay. Valid point," Micki said, changing lanes on the busy road. "By the way, this is the best conversation on a camping trip drive that I've ever had."

Jonas grinned. "I enjoyed it."

It was another two hours before they pulled into the campgrounds by Moss River. Jonas appreciated the weather in North Carolina. While it was chilly, it wasn't overwhelming. Even when the temperature dropped at night, it would still be comfortable. They weren't the only ones who'd thought of taking a camping trip. Along the river, there were already five other sites set up. He and Micki got out of her SUV, which was evidently better for some of the rockier paths they would have to take. Beside them, Peter and Nina exited their truck, and everyone stretched.

"We should set up camp first, before anything else, in case those scattered showers start," Peter said, dressed in a plaid shirt, faded jeans and a winter jacket. "They said by five or six this evening we'll have some rain."

"Plenty of time to assemble the tents and get hot dogs on sticks over a fire," Micki said.

"Sticks?" Jonas looked around. "As in we gather actual sticks?"

"We used to, but for you, we'll use the metal

skewers we brought." Micki kissed him quickly. "Help me get our tent out."

In a matter of minutes, they were working together, getting their shelter up, which was surprisingly easy. The floor was made of a vinyl mat and for comfort they blew up two air mattresses and positioned them on opposite sides of the tent. Each had a sleeping bag and an extra blanket on top, and in the center was a little portable heater that could be charged in the SUV. The LED lamp illuminated most of the space, and Micki produced a thermos and a metal tin that she said held midnight snacks, just in case. She'd also brought at least two thick textbooks and her notes to study.

"Even out here, you plan to hit the books?" Jonas asked, impressed. "Shouldn't you relax a bit?"

"I will, but when it's all quiet I can read a little if I can't sleep," she replied.

"Is it hard for you to sleep outdoors?" Jonas himself didn't know how much rest he would get out in the wild.

"Oh, I can be out like a light, sometimes." She smiled. "We're all set up, people. Time to find firewood to cook our dinner."

They trekked into the woods, where leaves and small branches crackled under their boots. Fortunately, there seemed to be plenty of supplies dry enough to burn. Each of the four of them came back to camp with a bundle of wood and then went out for extra, which he and Peter tied up under a tarp to keep it safe from the rain. As soon as that was done, the group took a walk along Moss River and he got several pictures on the rocks. Jonas sent them to his mum and sister, knowing they would be shocked he was tramping around in a forest. Back at their campground, they started the fire and by the time the sun was setting, they were grilling hot dogs over flames.

"Why are your hot dogs so good!" Jonas spoke around his first bite and closed his eyes in happiness.

"You've never had a chili cheese dog?" Nina asked, smiling as if amused.

He shook his head and wiped his mouth before speaking. "No, but I plan to have several."

Peter pulled a bottle from his backpack and shook the contents at them. "Luckily, I brought the antacid chews."

"He may need them, especially after hot dogs *and* s'mores." Micki chuckled.

Jonas looked at them curiously, his stomach and his interest piqued. "I'm willing to try any and all camping foods. I have heard of s'mores, naturally, but never had one."

"We could always go old school and forage

for our food, let nature be our grocery store," Nina suggested.

"Anything but that," Jonas amended his statement. "I don't have the skill to catch what we'll need to eat. We'll starve, or I will, at least." They all laughed at that.

Jonas had his first s'more, graham cracker with half a chocolate bar, then a huge marshmallow, roasted over the fire until it melted into a sweet sandwich. After three of them, and a Moon Pie, it was evident to Jonas that he would need to use the gym at the college on a regular basis.

The night took hold, and he played checkers with Peter while Micki and Nina talked and listened to music playing from a small speaker. He glanced at Micki more than once and smiled; she winked back and even managed to make him happier than he'd been in a very long time. The first drops of rain began to fall.

"Time to wrap it up, kids. The rain has come forth," Peter said.

Jonas helped him bank the fire. Micki and Nina packed up their food remnants and put them in the cooler, before it was stored in one of the vehicles. He jogged their trash to one of the campground's designated bins, and by the time they were done, the rain was falling steadily.

"G'night," Micki called out as they ran for their tents.

"See you guys in the morning," Nina replied.

Micki got into the tent first and waited until Jonas got in before she zipped the door closed and switched on the mini heater.

"Here." She offered him a small towel to dry his face. "If we hang the sweatshirts, they'll be dry by morning."

"Sounds like a plan."

Jonas pulled the sweatshirt over his head, leaving his long-sleeved jersey on to still keep him warm. He helped Micki hang both garments on the tent frame. Next, it was their boots, which they put at the bottom end of the air mattresses, before climbing into the sleeping bags and arranging blankets on top. The air warmed up quickly and, helped by the gentle patter of rain against the fabric of the tent and the smell of woodsmoke on his jersey, Jonas felt himself relax.

"Light on or off?" Micki asked, breaking the comfortable silence.

"Off. If that's okay with you," he answered. In seconds it was pitch-black and he lay back with his eyes closed. "Thank you for bringing me. I didn't think I would enjoy this so much."

"Stick with me and in spring we'll go white water rafting."

He could hear the contentment in her voice. "To do what?" he asked.

"Take a guess."

"Ah." Jonas smothered a laugh. "Michelle, I think I'm falling in love with you."

He held his breath waiting for her to answer.

"That's good to know because I'm definitely in love with you."

Micki sounded so sure, how could he not believe her?

"What do we do now?" she asked.

"Hold hands in the dark until we fall asleep, because we love each other?" he suggested.

"Okay."

They found each other's hand in the dark, linking fingers and letting that connection lull them to sleep. Jonas noted that some time during the night, they'd figured out how to hold hands and stay connected despite changing sleeping positions. Her textbook lay at her side. He smiled sleepily and went back to his dreams, knowing that tomorrow he would wake up and it would be a new day in more ways than one.

He was a man in love.

CHAPTER TEN

MONDAY. BEING BACK at school had come with something neither of them had expected. An accusation that could destroy her world and her dreams of being a lawyer, and cost Jonas his job. Professor Willoughby had lodged a complaint stating that she had cheated on her final exam by using Jonas's help.

The exam had happened two days before their trip, and then they'd been gone all weekend. Cell service was not something that was found easily where they'd camped. Sunday night, they went home but crashed immediately, sleeping soundly until the next day. Micki woke up, got ready and went downstairs to find that Jonas was already gone, which wasn't unusual. But as she left for class, to sit for her last final, she turned on her phone and found text after text from concerned friends.

"What?" she whispered in horror, glancing at a message.

She couldn't look at the phone and drive, so

she dropped it onto the passenger seat until she could park on campus. Walking into the arts and sciences building, she found people staring at her, disappointment, anger and curiosity on their faces. Erica was by the classroom door and stopped her in her tracks.

"He's trying to get back at you," Erica blurted and hugged her tight.

"How could I cheat, though? I was right there with the rest of you taking the exam," Micki said. "Do people believe this and how did they know?"

"He lodged the complaint on Friday afternoon. You both had left early," Erica replied. "He was loud about it in the reception area, probably trying to sway public opinion. Classic defense attorney move. He wants you to be judged instead in the court of public opinion."

Micki was practically in tears. "I didn't do this. I wouldn't!"

"I know that and you know that. In fact…" Erica hugged her again. "Lots of us know and I'm going grass roots with this. I'm going to build an army to support you."

"It got worse when she wasn't allowed to take her last final with the rest of her Law in Society class." Micah, Professor West, looked at her sadly. "I'm sorry, Micki, but with an accusation like this, you'll have to take the exam alone, proctored by me and another teacher, tomorrow. Meet me back in this classroom tomorrow at nine a.m."

Micki nodded stiffly and took her bag, trying so hard not to cry, but dashing away the tears that happened to fall.

She texted Margo quickly.

911 be home soon.

As she began to walk, her text notification dinged almost immediately.

Micks what's going on!

Can't talk now, will be home soon and can speak then.

Okay, come to Mia's house. We don't want the guests to see the family in a war council.

It was supposed to make her smile, but she couldn't, only texting back one word.

Okay.

Knowing Mia and Margo, Micki realized they would spread the word to the rest of the adult family and they would all be there. Professor

Linton saw Micki and immediately put her arms around her shoulders.

"I was just coming to find you," she said with concern. "I'm sorry he did this. I never thought he would be that horrible. The chancellor is in Jonas's office, and we need you there, too."

"My life, my goals are so important to me, I'd never cheat." Micki felt more beat up than if she'd been in a prize fight.

Professor Linton looked Micki in the eye. "You never have to tell me that. I know he's acting out of spite and desperation. We will get to the bottom of it."

When they entered Jonas's office, his face was a stiff mask of anger. His gaze didn't soften when he glanced at her and Micki felt even worse.

"Michelle Ballad, I presume," said the woman who sat across from Jonas, wearing a kind smile. "I'm Chancellor Brenda Dyer."

"Nice to meet you, ma'am." Micki shook the woman's hand. "I would never do this. I'm not a dishonest person. My record speaks for itself, my grades too. And Jonas is the most fair and honest person I've ever met."

"Please sit down. While the accusation is serious, Professor Willoughby has offered no direct proof, just allegations," Chancellor Dyer explained. "My office has been flooded with calls and emails on your behalf and in support of Dean Brand. I weighed Professor Willoughby's accusation against what happened last week and the complaints that are in his file. I find his statements lacking in merit."

"Exactly how am I supposed to have stolen his final?" Jonas's voice was clipped.

"He claims that the day before the exam was given, you got into his office, logged into his account and printed off the test," Chancellor Dyer answered. "There is a record of a log-in of his campus account at the time he said there was. He's stated that he was off campus. Regardless, his claims can't be proven, but just lodging a formal complaint will cause enough of a problem that the board and I will have to look into it."

"This will be proven false and his actions, along with all his other infractions, should be enough to remove him from his position and give someone else to a chance to teach the theories and principles that he doesn't seem to mind ignoring because of spite," Professor Linton said angrily.

"I agree. Terminating his contract will be my recommendation to the board." Chancellor Dyer straightened in her chair. "Miss Ballad, you'll have to come before the board next Monday. This gives you enough time to find a professor who will stand with you as a representative—"

"That will be me," Professor Linton offered immediately. "We will be ready."

"I know you will be. Professor Willoughby will also be there." Chancellor Dyer turned to Jonas. "We will see you Monday, Jonas."

Jonas nodded.

"I know that he is trying to use your personal relationship against you," Chancellor Dyer said. "But do not let him be the catalyst that breaks apart something good. We found no conflict of interest and on that the board agrees. Still, he accused you, Ms. Ballad, of cheating, and we must go about this using the proper procedure so he has no room to claim that he was not heard."

"I understand," Micki said as the chancellor stood and shook her hand. "Thank you for this."

"Not a problem at all. Keep your head up, both of you," Chancellor Dyer said.

"I'll see you out." Professor Linton followed the chancellor to the door and closed it softly behind them.

Micki knew Professor Linton was giving her and Jonas a chance to speak privately but silence reigned in the room.

"Why would he do this, really?" Micki finally asked in a broken voice.

"Because hateful, angry people react in kind." Jonas ran his hand through his hair. "This is exactly what I didn't want to happen and yet here we are."

"I didn't want it to happen either, but now we have to fight him and his allegations."

Jonas looked at her. "The point was for me to not have to fight anything at all to keep my—"

"And not make waves," Micki filled in for him. "You sound like you think this is my fault."

"I don't," Jonas said quickly. "But is it wrong for me to not want to be in the middle of a scandal before the first year of my job is even complete?"

"No, that's fair." Micki stood resolutely. "It's how you react to it that shows the true measure of what strength is. I'm going to fight for my reputation and my ability to graduate this program with honors. You can keep your head down and answer this false complaint however you want to."

"Michelle—"

She stopped to stare at him and silence reigned once more. It was evident to her that Jonas didn't know what to say. She left his office, passing many people who offered their support. Micki drove home, numb and on autopilot until she parked her car. She walked the path to Mia's house and opened the door, knowing it would be unlocked. When she stepped inside, everyone was there, even Mr. Bolton and Enid. Her beloved second mom was wringing her hands in worry.

Mia handed Gigi to Ryan and dragged her into the center of the group. "Micki, honey, what's going on?"

It was then the tears fell, fat and heavy. She was wracked with sobs so badly that she couldn't catch a breath. Micki rushed into Mia's arms. From the time Micki knew who she was, Mia was the one who dried her tears, spoke a lot of common sense and made sure she was okay. Mia held her as she crumpled to the floor, seeing everything she worked for about to swirl down the drain, including her relationship with Jonas. She wished her big sister could fix this now because Micki didn't know what to do.

"Micki, hey..." Mia held her tight, and her own voice was filled with tears. "Tell me what's wrong, so I can help."

"No one can help," Micki managed to say through her tears. "I just don't know what to do next."

Her mother knelt beside Mia and took Micki into her arms. "We're here for you, baby girl. There is no wave in the world that we'll ever let swallow you up. You know you can count on us."

Micki told them the story from beginning to end, all about the last semester of dealing with

Professor Willoughby up until today and looking into Jonas's blank eyes. Her tears dried, but it didn't stop her heart from breaking.

"First, me and Jonas are going to have a long talk about loyalty," Micki's father said in a serious tone.

"It's not his fault. It's barely been a few weeks since he got here and already he's dealing with something like this," Micki replied.

"But it's not you, it's that amoral professor who shouldn't be teaching." Margo squeezed her hand.

Ryan, who'd been pacing this whole time, finally stopped. "If they believe him over you, the lawsuit will be massive. He has no proof."

"Needless to say, we'll be at that hearing on Monday," Gideon said resolutely. "Sweetie, pull out my dress blues, we're going in for battle."

"That's my husband." Margo beamed with pride.

"Don't even think about telling us no," Rosie said and kissed Micki's temple. "We'd be there anyway."

Micki gave a mirthless laugh. "I know."

"You stay here tonight," Mia said.

"No. I'm going to my own bed." Micki sighed and then stood. "My blankets await."

"Then we'll be up bright and early tomorrow,"

Margo said. "We're driving you to your exam and then back home."

"Okay." Micki was too tired to debate. "I'm drained, I'm going to bed."

"I'll make you something to eat and bring you up a tray," Enid said kindly. "Your favorite. Grilled cheese sandwiches and soup."

"I'm not hungry," Micki said. "I'm going to hide away from the world for now. If I need something, I can forage… I promise."

"All right, but we're here, call us if you need us." Mia hugged her again. "It's going to be okay, I promise."

Micki nodded, trying to show a brave face, and wanting to believe her family. But even with the chancellor's and Professor Linton's words of support, would any of it really stand up in front of the board? Would that save her? Would they just expel her to get rid of the issue or even if they did believe she was truthful, the mar of being accused of cheating could carry its own consequences for years to come. Should she even try to fight? It would be easy to go back to being the old Micki, doing handyman jobs and working for the nonprofit as a researcher, nothing more. Even as she thought it, Micki realized that she couldn't go backward; this was a dream she was so close to finally making a reality, it was a fight she had to win.

Micki spent most of the day in her room just hiding away, sleeping, looking at the TV or watching funny cat videos on her phone, trying to shore up the wall that made her who she was. A soft knock came, and it was her mother who entered and slipped into bed beside her. Micki turned instinctively into her mother's arms and the comfort it brought.

"I love you." Her mother kissed her on the head.

Micki sighed. "I know, Mama, I love you, too. I remember you holding me like this once when I was sick."

"I should've been here to hold you more," her mother said softly. "Maybe if I was here instead of traveling so much, you'd have been able to traverse life better."

Micki looked up. "Mama, you did what you had to and for good reason. We've put the traveling thing to rest, let it stay buried."

"But I'm still guilty," Rosie Ballad said. "I want to just go give that Jonas a good talking-to. He should be here comforting you."

"He tried to call and text, but I'm not ready to answer," Micki admitted. "I need time to get over the fact that someone could hate me so much they'd want to destroy all I worked for."

"That's not hate, its maliciousness. People like that professor are wrapped up in their own unhappiness too much to care about empathy," Rosie said. "I've met some folks like him through the years. It never goes the way they plan, and neither will this."

"Hope you're right..." Micki murmured.

"Oh, I am. We have justice on our side," her mother assured her. "To let him win would be to undermine all that is good and what we believe in. We Ballads are good people, and we don't run away from a fight. We're going to walk in there Monday with our heads held high."

"I have the best family in the world." Micki hugged her mother tight.

"Now go back to resting. Tomorrow will come soon enough," Her mother kissed each cheek. "I'm so proud of you, darling girl. Always remember that."

"I love you, too, all of you," Micki replied and snuggled under her blanket.

Tomorrow, she wanted to bound down the stairs with her usual enthusiasm and spunk, pretend that everything was all right even as she hid her tears. She went to sleep with that in mind, imagining that tomorrow would be better, and she could face all her fears. But when it rained, it poured, and it seemed so for Micki, despite leading what some could call a charmed life.

Hours later, the knock on the door was soft and Mia poked her head inside.

"Hey, Micki," Mia said quietly.

She sat up and wiped the hair from her face. Looking at her sister through gritty eyes, she asked, "What time is it?"

"Just before seven thirty and you may need to throw on some clothes and come downstairs," Mia told her. "A can of chaos has opened on our front lawn."

"Chaos?" Micki slipped from her bed and looked out the windows to news vans and throngs of reporters out front.

"If you step on any of my decorations, I will send a bill to every station out there," Margo hollered. "Gideon, get the hose!"

Micki stared at Mia. "All because of a cheating allegation?"

Mia shook her head. "All because of Jonas. He hasn't been telling us everything."

Micki threw on her sweat suit and pushed her feet into her bedroom slippers before rushing downstairs and out onto the porch with Mia on her heels.

"Rio Rondell, *Highlight News*," the man said with a malicious grin. "Thought you'd never see me again, didn't you, Jonas Donovan?"

"One could hope," Jonas answered.

Micki was standing there in shock, her eyes on Jonas. "Who are you?"

"Michelle—"

But that was all she heard. His words that followed were drowned out by the yelling of reporters and the sound of more of the media arriving. Her defenses crumbled all the way down to their foundation as she and Jonas stared at each other amid the chaos that reigned at Ballad Inn.

NOTHING HAD PREPARED him for the sounds of so many vans coming up the inn's driveway. When he got to the window, Gideon was already yelling angrily to the reporters to not even dare park on the grass. The gates of his past had opened up and when he pulled on his sweater and jeans and strode outside, the bane of his existence was there front and center. Rio Rondell of *Highlight News*, the most disreputable "reporter" there ever was, with his hair greased back until it looked as slick as his personality. He was the one that had broken the news about Ben and ended up dragging Jonas and his family through the mud. The worst part was that the man seemed to enjoy it. Rio was again going to destroy another aspect of his life because that was what he and others like him did—burned lives and used the ashes to fertilize their careers.

"It took a bit for me to find you, Jonas," Rio drawled. "Using your mum's maiden name, very smooth."

"It sounds like you have a vendetta, Rio, not an actual story," Jonas said, trying hard to stay calm. Rio was trying to rile him up—it was all for show and the cameras. It was best to not let him succeed.

"I hear you're embroiled in another scandal. This time it's with your girlfriend and college," Rio continued. "I thought you'd have learned from your wayward ways after Ben, but here you are once more flouting the rules and cheating."

"Are you in fact, Jonas Donovan, son of Sir Hershel Donovan," one reporter shouted out. "Did you lend money to your friend to bribe a faculty member of Oxford?"

"That was two years ago, and I was cleared of any improprieties," Jonas said calmly. "I'm sure Rio Rondell has told you differently. The evidence is there and for all to see."

"Except daddy was the one who got you cleared, didn't he, Jonas? Being a man of great influence, it was easy for him to do so," Rio goaded him.

"My father is a man of great honor and respect. I think the last time you tried to soil his name, you had to pay one hundred and fifty thousand pounds in a defamation lawsuit," Jonas shot back. He couldn't help himself; besides, that was on record as well if anyone wanted to look it up. "It may happen again if you continue on like this."

"You heard it, he threatened me!" Rio pointed at Jonas. "You heard it here first, on *Highlight News*."

Ryan stepped forward. "I think we all heard a man tell you that you're going to lose another court case if you persist."

"Oh, Jonas, have you snookered this family, too, or is this a way to funnel your ill-gotten gains?" Rio asked.

"Now, that's where you're wrong, Mr. Rondo," Mia advanced down the steps.

"Rondell," he corrected her.

Mia flicked a cold glance at him. "Listen to me. If you choose to involve my business, home and family in your fishing expedition, it won't be just one defamation lawsuit you're facing."

"Which one of the Ballads has Jonas Donovan cheated for?" Rio asked. "Professor Willoughby said—"

"Ah, so that's where you found your information," Jonas said with a nod. "He went searching and then gave you a trail of breadcrumbs."

"A professor who is embroiled in his own controversies," Micki spoke up. "I can assure you that Dean Brand did nothing that could be considered cheating on my behalf. The college will stand for him and more than one professor will do the same."

At that point, Micki, Margo, Gideon and everyone else moved forward onto the lawn and Rio Rondell visibly gulped and shifted back. "This is private property," Micki told the crowd. "None of you are welcome here. I suggest you leave, or my next call will be to the authorities. Also, if any of you damage our lawns or decorations, we'll be billing your employers for it as well, like my sister said earlier."

"Give me the story, Jonas, the full exclusive. I won't stop coming until you do," Rio said, heading for his car.

Jonas gave him a cold stare. "No."

"There's no story here, guys," one of the local news reporters said in disgust. "Just a news bite about something that happened two years ago. Big deal."

"Get over it, Rondell, we don't rehash gossip," another muttered. "Keep that for your crappy rag across the pond. We don't do this here."

"Sorry for the intrusion," another person said from the leaving crowd.

Jonas and the Ballad family watched as each van or car drove away. Then they all turned to face him, Margo was shooting daggers at him with her eyes.

"So much for keeping your head down, huh?" Micki gave an incredulous laugh. "You meant to save yourself."

"No, the chancellor knows what went on when I was in London," Jonas replied. "Full disclosure, I didn't hide it."

"Only from me," Micki said. "I can't believe this. You left because of a scandal."

"And fell right into another, yes. But Micki, I was going to tell you," Jonas implored.

"Rio Rondell got here first." Micki shook her head. "I have a test to take. Mia, can I borrow your car? Stands to reason he probably knows what I drive."

"Sure, I can switch the car seat to your RAV4," Mia said. "What time will you be coming back?"

"I'm not, not for a few days at least. I plan to stay with Nina. I have a few things to wrap my head around." Micki folded her arms. "I appreciate your support, everyone, but I'll do the test today on my own. If anything, I'll meet you at my hearing on Monday. I'll keep in touch."

"Micki, let's talk about this," Jonas pleaded.

"I think I'm all talked out."

She looked at him with sad, defeated eyes that broke his heart. *I did this*, he thought miserably. With his words and actions he'd caused

234 A HOME FOR THANKSGIVING

a person he loved harm. It seemed to be a trait in him, to do damage. *I have to make this right.*

"This is a lot," Mia said gently. "And you need a moment to gather your thoughts. That Rio Rondell doesn't look like the best character."

"I thought he was out of my life for good," Jonas muttered brokenly and watched Micki go. "He's on a mission to take everything from me."

"Why?" Mia asked with concern.

"Why not?" Jonas gave a hollow laugh. "I'm the son of a well-known Member of Parliament, and Rondell's the type to sink his teeth into false rumors and twist stories to ruin people's lives because it makes him famous and puts money in his bank account."

"What does your family think about all of this?" Margo asked, worry showing clear in her eyes. "I'm still mad at you, but you're a friend. Plus, you and Micki care for each other. Anyone can see that."

Horror struck him then. "I have to call my family—my dad. This will just make the wedge between us even wider."

"Go do that, and then move forward from there," Mia said. "Give Micki time. It's an avalanche of things that came down on her in two days."

"We came back from a great camping trip and now this…" Jonas gave a frustrated sigh. "Life."

"Is what you make of it, and this is going to work out," Margo said firmly. "It seems our war council might be getting bigger."

"Thanks for that. I'm sorry I brought this to your door," Jonas apologized. "Really."

"It's never boring here, that's for sure," Ryan murmured. "Go do your thing but tell us later how we can help."

"Thanks." Jonas ran upstairs and got his computer out of his bag and used the video feature to call his parents. It was almost noon there, so he didn't have to worry about waking anyone up. This time it was his father who answered the call, and just seeing his face made Jonas remember how close they were. He wanted that again, but with Rio causing trouble it seemed farther away than ever before.

"Jonas." His father looked happy to see him. *For now*, he thought.

"Hi, Dad. Wait. Why are you home and not in the flat in London?" Jonas asked.

His father shrugged. "I wanted to be here with your mother, enjoy the place a bit more. I don't want to spend every day traveling so much or stuck in my stuffy office in Parliament. It's lovely here with the fire going and we've decorated the tree."

"Who are you and what did you do to my father?" Jonas asked.

Hershel Donovan laughed. "I'm learning to relax in my old age. I miss seeing you around the place, son, more than you know."

"You might not think that when you hear my news," Jonas replied. "Rio Rondell found me here and he's trying to stir things up again."

"Let him. We've dealt with all that, it's in the past. No one cares." His father's tone went from casual to excited in seconds. "Guess what? I bought a cappuccino maker and I'm going to learn to make the perfect cup, even with the little designs in the milk."

Jonas frowned. "Dad, I'm telling you that Rondell is going to start his gossip show again, mentioning the family and what happened with Ben."

His father smiled. "And I'm telling you that means nothing to me. It's the past, it's been settled, and Rondell is just a nasty man looking for any reason to stay relevant. Unless it will affect you negatively, in which case I'd fly over to help you handle it."

"I think I can manage," Jonas said, confused. "I expected you to be more upset."

"I wasn't last time," his father replied. "My anger was because you were trying to help a friend and he betrayed you. No one does that to my son."

"But Parliament—"

"Would still be Parliament with or without

me," he finished. "I'm planning to retire, son. Would've resigned two years ago, in fact. You are what matters. My wife and family, my children. So, he can shout it from the rooftops."

"Dad, I've been avoiding you this whole time because I thought you were disappointed in me," Jonas admitted, feeling regretful.

"I know and I also knew that you wouldn't believe me that it was all right until you were ready to," his father told him. "My love for you and Emily surpasses all things."

"Dad, thank you."

"Now, how is Charlotte? What's it like?" Hershel Donovan asked.

"I met someone great, and I think Rio might have ruined it already." Jonas had to be honest with himself. "I also contributed, of course. Her name is Michelle, but she goes by Micki and she's like a sunflower, Dad. Beautiful person, inside and out, with her face lifted up to the sun. She makes me feel like I can conquer the world."

"Being in love has made you into a poet," his father said. "Is she the one that you were at the country dance with?"

"You saw those pictures?" Jonas asked, surprised.

"Your mum showed them to me. You looked very authentic cowboy." His father grinned.

"She's having them printed up and framed for the house."

"Oh no," Jonas groaned.

Hershel laughed. "I hope to meet Micki sometime soon. She sounds as if she's very special. Maybe me and your mum will come for a visit."

"Come in the springtime, I can introduce you to disc golf." Jonas let out a laugh. "I haven't played it yet, but I hear it's fun."

"Looking forward to it. Now, don't give up on Micki. Love is a wonderful thing—just look at me and Mum."

"I won't." Jonas felt uplifted after speaking with his father. "Love you, Dad."

"Love you, too, son, I'll let your mum and sister know you're in love, they will be thrilled." His father stuck a hand in his tousled hair. "Hmm, where did she put the biscuit tin?"

"Cupboard to the left of the kettle," Jonas offered up the solution. "Bye, Dad. Talk soon."

"There it is! Thanks, Jonas. Bye, take care."

Jonas disconnected the call just as his father was eagerly opening the tin. Speaking to his father gave him hope again. He wasn't working off panic any longer—there had to be a way to beat Rio at his own game. He would make sure Micki knew that he loved her, and they could work past this hurdle and any others together in the future. He wasn't going to give up; this time he wasn't about to keep his head down and run away. Jonas Brand was ready to fight for what he valued most. His love for Micki Ballad.

CHAPTER ELEVEN

"OKAY. MICKI, you've been gone for two days. Time to come home," Mia said.

She frowned at both her sisters as they stood in the hallway of Peter and Nina's newly built town house. Micki considered getting her own place in the same subdivision, but it was still too close to home. She'd told her friends about what had happened with Jonas, and while they said they could understand her sense of betrayal, they encouraged her to go back to the inn and sort it out. How exactly was she to do that? She looked up Rio Rondell on the internet and he was a shark that could smell blood in the water. No matter what she or Jonas did, he would find a way to make it salacious.

"You've got to come back, we're having a war council at my house to help you and Jonas," Mia said firmly.

"I thought the WC was for family," Micki retorted in a sullen voice.

Margo gave her a sympathetic look. "He's family, too, hon. Anyone can see y'all are in love. This is part of it. Trouble comes, and you lick your wounds then you face the problem head-on."

"Um, you didn't face it head-on," Micki pointed out. "You ran all the way to South Carolina."

"And you all sent Gideon to find me," Margo shot back.

"I was going to meet Ryan, but he got to me first," Mia added. "The fact is, us Ballad sisters have a knack for running away, but it's how we come back that shows who we are."

"Micki Ballad, you have a stubbornness in you that's admirable. You'll go to the mat to prove a point," Margo replied. "But this is a time when you need to learn the give-and-take of love and relationships. Do you love Jonas?"

"With everything inside me," Micki replied and sighed.

"Then you should hear him out," Mia said, her eyes hopeful.

"I guess I wanted perfection, for everything to go smoothly, be easy. Life isn't perfect." Micki led them to the living room where Nina was.

"I'll get coffee for us," Nina said and all but leaped off the sofa.

"Life is definitely not perfect, but when things

fall into place, this life—being in love—is a blessing," Mia confirmed.

"Aw!" Nina put down the tray she'd carried in and set it down on a table. Together, the women had a four-way hug. "You guys are the best."

"I think that means Nina is an honorary sister," Micki said with a laugh. "We just need to change that *N* to an *M*, and you'll be Mina."

"As long as I'm not Nina Rabbit Cage." She pulled away and grinned. "I've heard the joke about Peter."

They all looked at each other and laughed some more. Peter came through the door and they froze. They all stared at him.

"What?" he asked, looking confused.

That sent them off on another round of laughter but he just shrugged and took his grocery bags through to the kitchen. Ten minutes later, Micki was on the road with her sisters, heading back to Ballad Inn and to her destiny.

Would she and Jonas be able to make it? She would give it the good old college try, to borrow the phrase.

Micki was going up the front steps of the inn with her sisters when Jonas opened the door. She glanced back and her sisters seemed to disappear into the ether.

"Wow, they're like ninjas when they want to be," Micki muttered. She blew out a breath and took the last few steps until she and Jonas were standing face-to-face. One soft word left her lips. "Hey."

"Michelle," he began. "I'm sorry I didn't tell you—"

"I shouldn't have run away—"

They both smiled a little and looked sheepish. He took her hand in his.

"Rio made it seem sordid, as if I was some type of criminal, but that is far from the truth," he said earnestly. "You have to believe me, please."

Micki cupped his cheek. "I know. It's because you didn't tell me the truth, when knowing about it would have made me feel less alone, more like a team. We've both been treated unfairly, but now we have to stand together."

"We will." His words reassured her and when he leaned in for a kiss, she gladly leaned in, too. And after, murmuring against her lips, he said, "I love you, Michelle."

"I love you, too," Micki promised.

Jonas held her tight. "I found a place that I think would be perfect for me to put an offer on. It's a new condo close to the North Davidson District."

"NoDa," she said, reminding him once more of the local name for the area.

"I'd like you to think about moving in with me one day." Jonas's gaze was solid and true.

Micki hesitated. "I will definitely consider it, okay?"

He looked taken a back. "Okay..."

"It's not that I don't want to, but I'm a simple soul beneath all of this awesomeness and this is a lot," Micki admitted honestly. "Let's get past this challenge before we try to tackle another one."

He kissed her again. "I can understand that. Will you come with me to look at it? I have an appointment to see the place again at two."

"Sure, let's turn and burn." Micki linked her arm through his. "We'll have what we call a war council with the family later."

"We'll come up with a solution to both our problems. I might have one for Rio."

"Then let's look at this condo that you might call home." Micki tried to sound upbeat, while all the while she prayed they would be able to overcome whatever was tossed in their way, like everyone had said.

Driving through NoDa made her feel happy. It was the area of Charlotte that was considered a haven for artists of all kinds. Because of it being a community of creatives, their style choices were always bold, imaginative and striking. There was an acrylic painting of Santa dressed to surf, the waves instead of piles of snow behind him. One artist had moved his equipment outdoors and was creating glass-blown snow globes. Some held water and inside it looked like real roses with snow and glitter on the petals. It was so intricately done, all with fabric. And while they sat at the light, a potential buyer shook one and the petals moved.

"That's beautiful," Micki murmured.

"Hey! That's Orne. He made your resin origami animals." Jonas put the window down and yelled, "Hello, Orne, how are you?"

"Fantastic!" Orne called back. "Did you get the girl?"

Micki laughed and yelled, "He got the girl!"

"Outstanding!"

They parked outside of one of the newly completed town house condominiums that she was always curious about. The large floor-to-ceiling windows and the brick exterior gave it an urban feel within the charming historic district. The combination of the two vibes made for a unique neighborhood, one she could live in. She wasn't ready to say yes to Jonas yet. *Old-fashioned? Yes, I am, I know, but it makes me who I am.*

They stepped into the management office that was on-site and soon Jonas was looking around at what could be potentially his new home.

"The master bedroom has a great view of Main Street," Micki called out and waved him over.

"The lovely thing about your windows is that

they are privacy-coated," the Realtor said enthusiastically. "You could put a small sitting table right over there and relax with a glass of brandy and just people-watch."

"Nice idea," Jonas said, peering outside. "What do you think?"

Micki looked at him. "Me?"

"Yeah. Hopefully, you'll be here just as much as me," he said with a smile. "I'd like you to be around as much as possible, if that's what you want?"

Micki nodded. In fact, she wanted to jump and shout out that she'd move in tomorrow but knew that wasn't her way. She needed to take things one step at a time. Suddenly, the idea of having brandy by the window or movie nights on his couch leaped to mind and she smiled to herself.

"Three bedrooms upstairs, a main living room and an office off to the side. The kitchen is gourmet-style, with double ovens, recessed lighting and plenty of counter space," the Realtor told him. "What do you think?"

Jonas looked around. "I like it a lot. It's completely roomy compared to what my flat was in London. The purchase price is reasonable as well. Can I think about it a few days before I give you an answer?"

"Please do but know that two other buyers are looking at this town house later today. If you like it you might want to consider putting a small deposit down on this unit and if you choose not to buy, it will be returned to you, minus five percent. And if you do decide to buy, it goes toward your principal."

Jonas nodded. "I can live with that."

They spent another hour in the office with Jonas filling out his paperwork before he wrote a check. Back in the car, they headed for the inn. It wasn't until three hours later that they were all seated in Mia's living room. Micki sat next to Jonas, and he took her hand. Micki didn't pull away, she couldn't; this was one of the most important times in her life. Jonas looked at her then and she knew they would make it.

"I think this discussion should start with your story, Jonas." Ryan's voice was casual.

Micki squeezed Jonas's hand as he looked at the assembled group. "My close friend Ben was with me at Oxford. He wasn't much for studying and everything was a party, but he always managed somehow to finish with almost perfect marks. I shrugged it off and said his method is his method. But he was there on a scholarship—his family wasn't well off then, so I gave him money sometimes. Looking back, it happened more than I realized, maybe more than it should. But as I said, he was my close friend. Knew him since primary school."

"Primary is like elementary school here, right?" Gideon asked.

Jonas nodded. "He and I wore uniforms and caps. Starts around three."

"Aw, Andy could wear a uniform and a cap." Margo looked happy at the thought.

Gideon shook his head. "That's called the military, sweetheart. He won't be making that decision for a very long time. Continue with your story, Jonas."

"His family calls him JonJon," Micki offered up.

"Do they, now?" A slow grin spread across Gideon's face.

"Different story for a different time, lads," Jonas said. "When Ben came and asked for a lump sum to help his dad, it was an automatic yes. His father being ill, it had always been just the two of them and he did more than any man should to ensure Ben had what he needed. Ben took things for granted and more than once I told him off for speaking to his father in a rude manner. I thought I was helping a friend and his father, I didn't know that Ben had been cheating at Oxford the entire time, by paying someone to do his work."

"Oh, unfortunately, I can see where this is going," Brian Ballad said.

"A faculty member found out and was going

to oust him, but Ben in his infinite wisdom decided to try to bribe him with my money. When it all came out, he had no problem throwing me under the bus and that in turn put my father in the limelight." Jonas took a beat and continued. "He is Sir Hershel Donovan, and he is a long-serving member of the British Parliament. Rio had no problem attempting to falsely implicate him in this scandal for his own personal gain. We were audited, and my father almost had to resign. Such was the public outcry at first. The less-than-honorable members of the media hounded my mother and my sister. It wasn't about Ben anymore but a family that Rio was intent on bringing down. But we were up-front and truthful, proven innocent and Ben was drummed out of Oxford. Public scrutiny ratcheted up when Ben did a tell-all interview with Rio, claiming I knew about his cheating, and that I'd given him sums of money over the years."

"Oh, he's the worst," Micki seethed.

"I didn't know that when we were friends," Jonas replied. "But when he made those claims, me and my father sued them for defamation of character, stalking and harassment. We won and Rio had to pay and face the consequences. Ben tried to beg off, asking me to forgive him, but the judge ordered stiffer penalties. We have had no contact since then, though Rio being called out in public caused him to start this vendetta against me and my family. I guess Professor Willoughby used that to have his revenge as well."

"The fact thar Willoughby must have gone out of his way to find Rio, who in turn flew all the way here, is despicable and whatever they have cooked up will not come to fruition," Rosie Ballad said fiercely. "We're already going to be there for Micki when she's in front of the board. What can we do for you?"

Jonas sat forward and Micki could feel the excitement rolling off him. He had a plan and, from the look on his face, he thought it would work.

"There might be a way to deal with both Professor Willoughby and Rio," he said. "Tell me what you think."

Jonas explained his plan in his usual fashion—concise and practical. With each word, she could feel hope rise within her. It wasn't just a good plan, it was a great one, and they all sat grinning happily at each other.

"That will do it," Ryan said finally.

"Brilliant," her father put in. "This will work, and no one can find fault in it. It's on your terms, both of you," he said, referring to herself and Jonas.

Jonas lifted her hand to his lips and kissed

it. "I'm not going to let Rio or Professor Willoughby ruin her chance at her dreams. I don't need to be dean of any law school. I'll take a teaching job if I have to."

Micki gasped. "I'm not ever going to let you do that. We're in this together or not at all."

Rosie smiled. "This is the type of teamwork that makes the dream work."

"We're doing this," Micki said, enjoying being on the offense for a change. "I'll call my friend Erica and she will do her grassroots thing."

"Does that mean another boycott?" Jonas asked.

Micki smiled. "Something better."

"This will be an interesting few days," Mia murmured.

Micki felt real joy for the first time since this whole entire mess started. She'd gone from heading to school to take a final and ending up embroiled in an international scandal. But there was a way out of their predicament, and no matter what, she and Jonas would stand by each other.

HE NEEDED A break and a moment to breathe after the last few days, so it was an easy yes to Gideon and Ryan's invitation to play pool. Friday would be here soon enough and then a mad dash on through the weekend and Micki's meeting with the board on Monday. Right now, taking this time to catch up and commiserate with two men he called friends was a helpful getaway from his thoughts. *Maybe my plan won't work*, he thought. *No, it will.* He had to stay positive, not just for himself and Micki, but for all the Ballad family. They'd been so kind and loving to him.

The three of them were back at *Dreamboat* and had taken over the pool table in the corner. Jonas had to admit he was a fan of "just apps" as Ryan called it. Chicken wings and mozzarella sticks, onion rings and something called hush puppies, while having a pint of Guinness. Slowly, Jonas could feel the tension leaving his neck and shoulders.

"I didn't think I would like a dark stout, but it's not bad," Gideon said approvingly. "I've always just passed these over on a menu."

"Welcome to the other side." Jonas lifted his glass. "Cheers."

"So, Micki's home and it looks like both of you are back on track," Ryan said as he lined up his shot on the pool table. He propelled his stick forward and the balls cracked as they hit each other and scattered across the green fabric.

"Maybe. She seemed hesitant about something yesterday and I don't know if it's me or if she's slowing us way down because of all we've got going on," Jonas answered. Ryan made another shot and missed, so it was his turn.

"May want to tell us about it and get our staunch advice," Gideon commented with a grin. "I'm playing whoever wins this game and demolishing them."

"Just because you played in some league when you were in the Marines doesn't mean you'll be able to win each and every time," Ryan replied.

Gideon reclined against the wall. "Doesn't it, though?"

"It doesn't," Jonas said, joining in the banter. "I played in competition for five years, I'll give you a run for your money."

"And—here—we go," Ryan said triumphantly. "I will watch this with glee."

"Just tell us why you think Micki is stepping back?" Gideon raised his brows.

"I asked her to think about moving in with me, and then we looked at a town house I might buy," he explained. "She seemed taken aback by it all and became distant."

"This is a two-part problem," Ryan said after a minute of thinking. "First, Ballad Inn is the only home she's ever known, and she might have a problem with moving."

Jonas accepted that but knew that wasn't the problem. Micki had been wanting to move away from the house for a little while now. He couldn't tell them that, partly because it wasn't for him to tell, and based on previous events, it was obvious none of the guys, himself included, was good with keeping Ballad family secrets.

"Micki has contemporary views about most things but when it comes to guys, well…she's not going to live with anyone without being married first," Gideon replied bluntly. "I've overheard conversations between the sisters. Micki might have dated, but she's only about having a serious relationship. Most of her boyfriends turned into friends by the end. Except you."

"That's high praise. I mean she dated Peter and then ended up at his wedding as a good friend," Ryan added. "I think she instinctively knows when something is not going to work out and you asking her to move in without a commitment put her off."

"Isn't moving in together a commitment that leads to marriage?" Jonas gulped. "I'm not sure if I'm ready for 'I do.'"

"You don't have to be. It's all very new, this relationship. But don't expect her to change her beliefs either," Gideon said around a mozzarella stick. "You guys can date and live apart."

"Right. Of course, we can," he said, still thinking nervously about white gowns and champagne popping.

"That was a good shot!" Ryan pointed at Gideon with his pool cue. "Take that, bro."

Gideon laughed. "One good shot and you've gone all cocky on me."

"Guys, focus," Jonas snapped. "What do I do here?"

"Oh, I thought you got the answer." Gideon smiled. "Date for as long as you need to before you want to or you pop the big question."

"But don't lead her on to think it's going to happen for you guys, if it isn't." Ryan moved around the table, looking for his next shot. "If you want someone or something different, say so, and give her the chance to move on." He took his shot and missed. "But remember, you don't know what you have until it's gone, and that goes for love, too. You may be living in Charlotte, doing your law school dean thing, and she could be traveling the world and falling in love in Italy."

"Why Italy?" Jonas's heart lurched at the thought.

"She was talking about traveling there for a few months after she graduates, before she settles into that job she really wants," Ryan explained. "Isn't that the dream? Young women going abroad and coming home with a suave gentleman who can charm all in a smooth accent."

"Bro, that's literally Jonas," Gideon pointed out.

Jonas straightened with pride. "Exactly."

"But you're not ready." Ryan looked at him sympathetically. "Such a pity."

"Just beat him already for that remark. Stop playing with him, Jonas," Gideon coaxed him.

Ryan looked appalled. "I'm your brother-in-law."

Gideon shrugged. "And I like winning, so there's that. Jonas, why use Brand?"

"It's my mother's maiden name," Jonas replied. "Does it mean something to you?"

"There's this movie about a woman who dances her way through college and eventually, she meets this guy, falls in love with and teaches him to dance in a meadow," Gideon explained. Ryan looked shocked. "It's once of *Margo's* favorite rom-coms and yes, I have watched it with her. Not everyone watches alien blobs eating people."

"First, don't judge other's viewing choices, and second, all the sisters love that movie," Ryan retorted.

Jonas sank his teeth into a tasty chicken wing. "These are brilliant."

"Hey, put the food down. You still need to kill off this game, man," Ryan called out to him, slugging Gideon on the shoulder.

In the end, Jonas won three games, Gideon

two and Ryan was shoutout, which Gideon did not let him live down on the ride home. The guys left him in front of Ballad Inn. Jonas took his time walking up to the main house, inhaling the cool evening air after the warm, stuffy lounge of *Dreamboat*. He didn't expect to see Micki walking along the pathway that led through the property. Was she enjoying the night air just as he was?

"You're back," she said with a smile as their paths intersected. "How was pool?"

"Your brothers-in-law can get very competitive, then seem to lead to various types of harmless threats involving things that smell bad," Jonas remarked. "I imagine if I had brothers, it would be like that."

"It happens with sisters, too." Micki laughed. "How was growing up with Emily?"

"You're right, siblings are painful, regardless." Jonas shuddered. "Mom has stories."

"Those I would have to hear." Micki took his hand, and they began walking together. "Did you decide on the town house?"

"Yes, I'm going to take it. It's exactly what I'm looking for." In his usual fashion, he lifted her hand to his lips and kissed her smooth skin. "I just want to say that I understand about you not being ready to consider us living together."

"It's not that I don't want to, but I have to be

honest, Jonas," Micki said softly. "I won't live with someone that I'm not married to. I know it happens all the time and lots of couples do it, but I'm not built that way. I guess I'm a vintage throwback. And I only want you to commit to what you're ready for, nothing more. I'll do the same. Besides, dating is nice."

"Isn't vintage all the rage now?" Jonas teased.

"Not for a lot of people. But it's who I am, and I can't—no, won't change that."

"What are your dreams?" Jonas asked suddenly. "After you murder law school and ace the bar, I mean."

"Travel for a little bit, I think," Micki said. "Though I was talking to Mom and Dad about going to Rome this summer. Why wait until after school? I could see it now and come home relaxed, ready to start law school, wherever that is."

"I want you to know, I dream of you every night now."

"You're in my dreams, too," she smiled brightly. "I'm looking forward to the future, whatever it will bring."

"I don't care so long as you're in it with me," Jonas said with an assuredness that he felt to his soul. "I love you, Michelle. That won't ever change."

"And I you." Micki kissed him gently. "We'll take it one day at a time, yes?"

Jonas nodded. "I agree."

They shared another kiss under the bright stars, in the midst of trees with no leaves and a crisp December wind. An owl hooted and the cheery tune from Margo's automated decorations drifted in the background. Everything seemed to be happening so fast. From the moment he'd stepped inside Ballad Inn he'd felt like he was in a race. Jonas wanted to be sure about all the changes in his life, every step he took, but maybe instead of a careful stroll down the path, he should lean in and run toward his destiny.

CHAPTER TWELVE

THURSDAY. IT WAS twenty-four hours before he was to meet with the chancellor and the board. He thought he would be more nervous, but a calm settled over him, maybe that came from dealing with almost the same issue two years before. Except this time there was a man who had chosen to use Jonas's past to hurt not only him but the woman he loved. That could account for his steely determination. There was no way he was going to let Professor Willoughby or Rio ruin the positive way his life had turned.

Until it took another turn. Maybe one he wouldn't want.

He was still the dean of the law school, so he met with Debbie, and started conducting business as usual, meeting with teachers and students, finding the best faculty and new ideas for courses and programs.

Jonas recognized how good a job Deborah was doing and praised her. "Professor Fey was pleased you talked to her about her paper that was published in the law journal. You are in-dispensable."

Deborah smiled. "Thank you for allowing me this chance to be an assistant. It's beyond what I imagined it could be. I thought I'd be on that front desk until I retired."

They left the meeting room and walked down the hallway toward his office.

"Your door is ajar—it shouldn't be," Deborah said with suspicion. "Did you lock it?"

"I did," Jonas affirmed. As they drew closer, they could hear someone inside. "I bet I know who it is. I'm going to record this on my phone. Will you stay right here as well, listening in, just in case I need a witness?"

"You got it, boss." Deborah gave a quick nod.

He grinned at her before his smile faded and he opened the door to reveal Professor Willoughby sitting casually in one of his chairs, tapping his foot on the floor in a soundless rhythm.

"Who's breaking into an office now, Willoughby?" Jonas asked, moving behind his desk.

"I found the door unlocked."

"I'm sure," Jonas said dryly. "What do you want, and I might add this is an odd way of going about it." Jonas chose to ignore the man's lack of common sense.

"To offer you an accord," he told Jonas. "I see now that things have gone a bit too far."

"When did this occur to you?" Jonas asked curiously. "When you made the false cheating allegation or when you called and divulged my personal information to a gossip columnist who chose to come to where I live and harass all the people there?"

"It can be solved simply. If you recommend me for tenure, I will drop the cheating allegations and Rondell will disappear," Professor Willoughby offered.

Jonas sat back and pinned Jonas with a stare. "In essence, you want me to submit to blackmail and save your job and professional reputation, which are both rapidly vanishing, mind you. Reward you for awful behavior and trying to ruin my life so that you'll get rid of a man who has done nothing but spread false stories for the past two years and had to pay me money for defamation of character? Make that make sense, Willoughby."

"H-he had a judgment against him?" Professor Willoughby seemed to go pale.

"Ah. He didn't tell you that, or the fact that the man he used to try to destroy my family is also still making amends back home." Jonas shook his head, deeply disappointed in the man before him. "I guess you're unaware that by doing this he has broken the terms of the judgment and that now the judge can raise the amount of the settlement."

"This wasn't—" Stopping abruptly, Professor Willoughby didn't seem to know what to say.

"I will not be recommending you for tenure, Professor, but I will fight your fraudulent allegations and when they are proven to be lies, I will then recommend your termination for not following the ethics policy and code of conduct for this college." Jonas stood and pointed to his door. "Leave now. You started this, but I intend to finish it."

"Now, look here, Brand, I'm a man of—"

Jonas didn't let him finish. "Leave."

With a sour glare, Professor Willoughby turned and departed, striding past Deborah in the corridor. She entered the office once the professor was gone.

"Did you hear all that?" Jonas asked.

"The audacity of that man," she said, aghast. "I can't wait to see the back of him for good."

"I have the feeling that this entire law school and all of the students on campus would agree," Jonas replied. "So, what's next on the agenda?"

"If that one's leaving, you might want to look at a few résumés we've received recently from a bunch of really qualified academics."

Jonas smiled. "Sounds good. Have I told you yet how indispensable you are?"

She grinned. "I can never hear it too much, and can you also call my husband plus the three teens at my house and let them know."

"Anytime," he said. "Before we get into this, can I ask you for a bit of personal help? Michelle has taken me to tons of things to do in Charlotte and I want to take her somewhere special in return. Any ideas?"

Deborah looked delighted. "Tonight? There is this wonderful event where they turn the baseball stadium into a winter wonderland. It opened the day after Thanksgiving and it's usually booked solid, but I think I can get you in. My cousin works there, and he owes me a favor."

"If you can make it happen, that favor transfers to me," Jonas promised.

"Consider it done," she said. "Let me make a call."

Jonas sat in front of his computer and went back to work. The rest of the day went by quickly. When Deborah gave him the yes for the winter wonderland, he texted Micki.

Dress warm tonight, we're going out.

Where?

Wait and see, I'll be there after work.

Color me excited!

He smiled at her words: he couldn't wait for the evening to come. There was one more task he had to complete before he left for the day. Jonas picked up his phone to make a call to a number that was seared into his memory, but not in a good way.

"Rondell," he said when Rio answered in a brisk voice.

"If you want a story, then you'll meet me in my chancellor's office tomorrow at nine," Jonas said, his tone just as clipped.

"Jonas, is that you?" Rio sounded excited. "Are you finally going to sit down and tell my readers the truth?"

"You'll get a scoop," Jonas promised.

Rio needed to get a little bit of comeuppance and Jonas was about to serve it to him. He quit the call, turned out the office lights and made his way to his car. Driving away from the campus, Jonas let his mind wander. He thought of Ballad Inn, the distance to the town house, Micki, his parents, and ultimately what they all had in common. *Marriage*. While he didn't want to voice it to anyone, the thought of it was becoming more and more appealing. His parents and Micki's had found a way to make their forever love last, why not he and Micki? She was waiting in the family room at the inn with some of the guests when he arrived.

"Give me a second to change, back in two shakes," he promised.

"I'll be here, then you can explain to me what two shakes are," she called out with a laugh.

He shook his head, amused, her light and fiery personality giving him a second wind after a long day. Jonas changed into long johns and jeans, then added a sweater and coat, then boots. He bounded down the stairs to spot Micki and pulled her into his arms for a kiss and a dip.

"You're getting quite proficient at that," Micki said, her soft brown eyes sparkling, and it was just for him. "Going to tell me where we're headed?"

"You shall see." He led her out the door. "Your family gone for the night?"

Micki nodded. "Yes, the new night-shift clerk started today and so far, he's doing well."

"He?" Jonas looked behind him at the reception desk. A tall man stepped out of the office and smiled before giving a quick wave. "He's staying here at night?"

"He's at the desk in case a guest needs anything at night," Micki replied, grinning. "The dynamic is changing at the inn. Come the summer, none of the family will be living at the inn but in the other houses on the property. But we'll still keep family dinners as they are now, although things are changing to suit the growth of the business and my sisters' expanding families."

"What about you? How do you feel about it since the last time we spoke about it?" he asked while he waited for her to get into the car.

Micki shrugged. "Life changes, I get that. I hope they understand that when I tell them I'm moving away for a while, closer to campus."

"That's still on the table?" he asked, climbing behind the wheel.

"Of course." She nudged him with her shoulder. "At least we won't be driving so far to see each other."

Jonas tried to think positive. She was fine with his choices, and he would have to be okay with hers, including her decision to not move in together right away. To be the person she loved and married one day was an amazing gift, and the thought made him cherish her all the more. Jonas took the entrance marked for the stadium. Winter Wonderland was spelled out in big bold letters made of Christmas lights.

Micki cheered and clapped her hands. "How did you get tickets? They're sold out every day until Christmas. I was trying to get us tickets for weeks."

"I had a special in." Jonas smiled. "I feel quite proud, actually, that I was able to find an event in Charlotte you didn't have to get us into."

"Look at you!" Micki opened the car door to get out.

"I was going to do that." Jonas rushed around the car to her side to take her hand. "Let me be chivalrous."

"As you wish." She took his hand and left the car in a flourish. "This is an awesome surprise. Thank you."

He took her hand and they began to walk. "My work here is done. I only ever want to see you happy and know that big beautiful smile is because of me."

"It is!" She smiled at him. "Now, let's go have fun."

Her brand of fun consisted of ice skating and a ski hill that looked quite dangerous while they stood at the top with snowboards strapped to their feet.

"I'm rethinking this idea," Jonas said, anxious to not hurt himself.

"It's not a big hill. Look! There are kids doing it," Micki pointed out to him.

Jonas squinted at the children. "Like the girl down there, holding her knees, bawling her eyes out?"

"Poor kid, but she'll be okay. It happens to everyone starting out," Micki said, holding out her hand. "We're in this together and I won't let you go."

Jonas chose to see deeper implications in those simple words, so he put his hand in Micki's and squeezed. "I'm counting on it."

They stood on the precipice of the ski hill together and with a slow push they went down, Micki whooping loudly and him yelling for his life. The cold wind rushed by, and it seemed that all too soon they fell into the soft snow and one of the attendants helped them remove the snowboards strapped to their feet.

Micki leaped into his arms and smacked a kiss on his lips. "Wasn't that a blast?"

He held her around the waist and twirled her in his arms. "It was—marry me?"

"What?" Micki gasped as Jonas set her on her feet.

"Marry me?" he said again and placed a soft kiss on her lips.

"Jonas, that's a quick turnaround," Micki said skeptically. "I'm okay with how things are, taking it slow and just being together when we can."

"But we could be more. Isn't that what you wanted?" Jonas cupped her cheeks. "It occurred to me how much I love you, while we were flying down that hill of doom…"

"Doom?" she repeated the word, grinning again.

"Okay. Not so much doom, but more like a hill of bad decisions." Jonas grinned back. "But in that moment, I thought, what is life without being with the woman I love? Her in one area and I in another, meeting up a few times a week and after a sweet kiss, we part and go to separate places. What about wanting to spend each minute with a wonderful woman who wears green neon sneakers just because they make her happy?"

"Plus, they are extremely cute," Micki pointed out with a smile.

"Very. I might get a pair of my own." Jonas nodded.

Micki wrapped her arms around his neck. "I know exactly where to take you."

"Thanks, but…" Jonas kissed the tip of her nose. "Now let me continue with my proposal."

Micki inclined her head. "You may do so, since I am quite intrigued."

"You're so smart that you could work in a top-notch law firm and end up in a corner office, but instead you would choose a nonprofit and help those who can't afford legal services." Jonas paused, hoping he was making his case. "I told my father I was in love, and he said he hoped that I would have a love like he and my mother. I can't do that without you by my side each and every day of my life. So, marry me, my darling Michelle, and make my life complete."

Micki nodded. "Yes, I could say it a thousand

times and shout it from the rooftop. I love you, Jonas Brand, and I will marry you."

"Let's seal it with a kiss," he said, and they did.

When Jonas stepped away, he could feel the smile pulling at his cheeks. Like the flip of a coin, it was moments ago that he was telling Gideon, Ryan and also Micki in his own way that he wasn't ready to be a husband. Now after Micki had told him yes, Jonas knew it was yet another right step toward the future he'd always hoped for. After all the hurt and chaos that had followed him, this new beginning had to be built to last. Micki was the cornerstone of that foundation, and their love would keep it whole.

DAY ONE OF not running from the past, Jonas thought as he stood outside the chancellor's office. He calmly fixed his tie and knocked on the door, ready for whatever would come his way.

"Come in," the chancellor's voice rang clear.

He opened the door and stepped inside. "Good morning, Chancellor Dyer."

"Good morning, Jonas Donovan," Rio said brightly from a chair in front of her desk.

"Rondell." Jonas inclined his head. He wasn't surprised to see the man there early.

"I was filling in the chancellor here about all your activities." Rio's face was pure malicious glee.

"Ah, anything new, Chancellor?" Jonas asked as he sat down.

She shook her head. "No, it's everything you revealed to me and the board at your initial job interview. It just sounds more sordid coming from his lips."

Clearing her throat, the chancellor continued, "I think it's best that you give your side of things to the public. That way the facts will be out there and people can see that neither you nor the university are hiding anything."

"I understand that, and I'm ready to speak my truth," Jonas said.

"Great." Rio slapped his hands together. "We can get a camera set up and shoot this piece today."

"Fine," Chancellor Dyer said. "Susan Cooley will be here shortly."

"What?" Rio looked confused.

"Susan Cooley. She writes for *Global News* out of New York," Chancellor Dyer explained.

"I'm doing the interview, Rio, but not with you," Jonas said, facing him. "I won't have the story tainted to suit your narrative. Two years after the Donovan family survived a manipulated scandal, their proud son speaks about the corrupted gossip columnist who invaded his world once more."

"You can't do that," Rio seethed. "This was meant to be my interview, my comeback."

"I'd like you to leave the campus now, Mr. Rondell," Chancellor Dyer said coolly. "We don't wish to have you spread chaos at this good institution any longer."

"You forget Professor Willoughby." Rio sat back with a smug look. "I can get a story from him, or when my tell-all book comes out."

"He might. But I'm not sure it will benefit his reputation, which he knows is under scrutiny at this moment," Chancellor Dyer said.

"Write your book, Rondell, my family and I don't care but our lawyers will, and the judge as well," Jonas said in a neutral voice. "When you're back in London, you'll likely get a call to come back into court. This will be the last time we speak, Rondell, goodbye."

Rio looked livid as he stormed from the chancellor's office. Jonas turned to his boss. "That went well."

A small smile appeared as she gave a firm nod. "Susan will be arriving shortly so you can tell your story. Right now, we go talk to the board and tell them exactly what went on and why Willoughby made those accusations."

"I have proof and a witness who will back me up. And then this will be over, not just for me and Michelle, but the students," he said, getting to his feet.

"What should we expect when it's her turn on Monday?" Chancellor Dyer looked worried. "Even when we prove that your past isn't damaging the college's reputation, the accusation of cheating, with you as an accomplice, is something she has to face."

"And she will, with her head held high," Jonas confirmed. "The truth will come out."

"I look forward to it so we can get this resolved, go on vacation and come back for the spring semester ready to work."

"I feel the same," Jonas replied.

His meeting with the board took almost two hours. During that time, Professor Linton came to speak and brought Micki's student record and the complaints against Professor Willoughby. Students also came as witnesses to give accounts of his poor conduct in and out of the classroom. Deborah came and recalled hearing the conversation where Professor Willoughby tried to coerce Jonas into approving his tenure in exchange for making the cheating allegations and bad publicity go away. Members of the board showed empathy for the situation and appeared openly suspicious of Willoughby's actions and motives. But like the chancellor predicted, Micki would still need to face the board on Monday. To Jonas it was just another formality because the dominoes were falling in their favor and soon it would be time to focus on their future. When he got back to his office, Micki was waiting for him, looking worried and wringing her hands.

"Well?" she asked as he sat behind his desk.

"The board agreed that I will continue as the dean of the law school." He'd tried to keep his emotions in check but at this point he couldn't help feeling relieved. "One hurdle down, one more to go."

"What time is the interview with Susan Cooley? Do you want me to go with you?" Micki asked, claiming a seat.

"I would love that, knowing you're close by."

Micki pointed at him. "Consider me there."

The interview wasn't something he'd enjoyed, but when it was over it felt like a weight had fallen from his shoulders. To celebrate turning a corner, he and Micki had lunch at a downtown restaurant and after, strolled the streets, doing a little window shopping. Outside a small jewelry store, they stopped and admired a display of engagement rings.

"Nothing too fancy, please," Micki pleaded. "I'd be terrified wearing anything big and expensive. I'd probably be clumsy and lose it down a drain or something."

"Do you tend to lose engagement rings down sinks?" Jonas teased.

Micki laughed. "This would be my first. We should tell my family about our plans, including moving out of the inn sooner rather than later."

"I thought you wanted to wait until after Christmas." He was curious as to her change of mind now.

Micki glanced at him as they resumed strolling. "It's not a sad thing, but I was looking at it that way, that I should tell my family after Christmas so as to not ruin the season. But I'm getting married, and only moving across town, not to some faraway country. Dad and Mom are back from their latest trip. I think we should start living and loving the way we want."

"What about a honeymoon in Greece, say around May?" Jonas squeezed her hand.

"Could happen, if we have a wedding on May eighteenth?" Micki suggested.

"We've got a date, so now let's get a ring," he said, realizing it all felt so right. "We have to go back."

Micki reversed course with a happy smile on her face.

The place was called Claddagh Jewelry, which Jonas saw as a sign of good fortune. He blamed his mother for that. Being a native of Scotland, she loved to believe in their myths and lore, so this was the perfect shop for him to find a ring for his forever love. Ring after gorgeous ring was shown to them, but none felt right until they spotted an engagement ring whose setting was shaped like two hands making a heart. It was encrusted with diamonds. The matching wedding band, made of rose gold, had a solitaire diamond. The two rings interlocked perfectly. He and Micki looked at the set and then at each other.

"This is the one," they said in unison.

The older man behind the counter beamed. "Let's try them on."

Jonas took the engagement ring and slipped it on her finger, and it was as if it was made for her. The wedding band for Jonas fit as well and he considered it a sign, so bought them right then and there.

"I can't wait for you to have that ring on your finger when we tell your family we're engaged." Jonas kissed her finger where the ring would be placed.

"After we finish with the board on Monday, we'll get your family on video chat and tell them our news," Micki said happily. "Then we'll tell my family about our moving out. We'll have a lot to celebrate for the holidays even if this news is bittersweet."

"I think it will be just fine, love," Jonas assured her. "Let's get back to school. I have work and you still have exams to study for, my lady barrister."

"I do like the sound of that." Micki sighed. "Think they'd let me practice here under that moniker?"

"I doubt it very much, tea thrown into the harbor and all that." Jonas laughed.

His mother would cry her eyes out, his father would grin from ear to ear and Emily would praise the heavens that the attention was off her for grandchildren for the foreseeable future. But most of all he was happy to be in love and his family would be, as well. Maybe he should thank Rio for shoving him back into the spotlight.... *Nah*. That man was still rotten to the core.

CHAPTER THIRTEEN

Micki caught a last glance in the mirror before leaving her bedroom and heading downstairs. She was dressed for her day in front of the board in a simple black pin-striped business suit with a neat fishbone skirt and a tapered jacket with an elegant satin blue camisole top beneath. Micki took the time to pin her unruly hair up and left a few soft curls framing her face. She didn't carry her book bag this time, but a brown leather satchel that held her papers, all her work and statements from her previous professors. And if they wanted her laptop, it was in there as well and she'd hand it over.

Jonas and the rest of the gang were waiting in the family room. A gasp escaped Mia, and Margo gave a low whistle while everyone else just stared in shock.

"What?" Micki tugged the hem of her blazer down. "I can dress up."

Jonas spoke softly. "You're beautiful and you look like you're stepping into the courtroom."

"I kinda am," Micki answered.

"If there was ever a power suit, that is it," Mia said, with her hand clasped over her mouth. "Micki, this is so you. You are going to be a heck of a lawyer with all your skill and smarts."

"You sure are," Margo enthused.

"Who's watching the kids?" Micki asked, hoping to take the attention from her; it was making her feel uncomfortable.

"Ellen is. They're with Claire in the nursery at her day care," Mia replied. "Are you ready to go?"

Micki blew out a breath. "As I'll ever be. Let's do this."

Jonas took her hand. "We're going to smash it today."

"I hope so," Micki said.

"I know so." Jonas kissed her hand.

They filed out of the historic Queen Anne inn and got into separate cars and formed a caravan heading toward the campus. They parked alongside each other and as Micki got out of the car, she realized her stomach was hurting because she was so nervous. What if this didn't work? Her family formed a group around her as they walked into the building that had the chancellor's office where the board would be convened. Her steps halted at the central door just as Professor Willoughby came up the other steps from around the corner. He looked at her family, from Jonas to the hard stares of her father, mother, sisters and brothers-in-law.

His eyes widened and he visibly gulped. Did he really think she'd come alone? Even if the day didn't go as she wanted, having her family's support and Jonas's was a gift, and she would cherish it. But there was much more than that to make her feel loved.

Professor Willoughby had gone ahead but stopped. Stepping inside, she could see why. Students lined the hallway, all holding signs on her behalf right up to the meeting room that she would enter. They said nothing, just stared at Professor Willoughby as he briskly walked past. Micki saw warm smiles of encouragement.

Even Sarah, Denise and Leslie were there. Sarah came forward. "You got this."

"This is amazing," Mia said in a low voice. "Did you know this would happen?"

Micki shook her head. "My friend Erica had to have put this together, but even so, I never expected—"

"This," Margo said gently from behind her. "If good people do nothing, evil wins and these are all good people."

Erica waved and Micki moved to embrace her. "You did all this, I'm assuming."

"You bet I did, I wasn't going to let that guy

win and continue to treat us like this." Erica smiled. "It's not just you. If the board agrees with him and he wins, none of us are ever going to succeed in this program and I happen to love this campus."

"I'll do you proud," Micki promised.

"Great. Because our study group needs you." Erica's smile grew.

At the door to the meeting room, her family wished her well before she went inside, Jonas beside her. It was set up like a mock courtroom, with Professor Willoughby on one side and she on the other with Jonas. Professor Linton and a few others, including Micah West, were there as well. In the center, behind a long oak table, was the chancellor and the board.

"We should get started," Chancellor Dyer said.

She looked at the board and there were nods of agreement. "Very well, Professor Willoughby, we'll start with you. Why would you accuse the student Micki Ballad of cheating, using Dean Brand's help to do so? You accused him of being in your office and taking your final. What evidence do you have of this?"

"She had a perfect score," Professor Willoughby said. "She and Dean Brand have an ongoing relationship."

"You lodge a complaint solely because of a

personal connection and the student's grade?" one of the board members asked slowly.

"That seems more than enough to me. It's a conflict of interest," Professor Willoughby answered.

"Might I ask a question?" Micki spoke up. "If I am going to be judged I should be able to defend myself."

Chancellor Dyer inclined her head. "Of course, you will have the chance to be heard."

"I have all my grades, and I have had classes with Professor Willoughby in many where I got a B, which coming from him is high praise. Why would I cheat now to get an A? It doesn't make any sense."

"I'm not on trial, here," Professor Willoughby sputtered.

"Okay. So, let's ask this question, why does Professor Linton have dozens of complaints about your grading system and why did she choose to correct those grades?"

"Well, let me say this—"

Micki cut him off. "How many disciplinary write-ups have you had, Professor Willoughby?"

"I don't know," he blustered.

"Seven. And many of us students have heard you say quite clearly in class that you have friends in high places, and would never be fired." Micki turned to the board and chancellor.

Another of the board members chose to speak. "We have all this information here, Miss Ballad, thank you. Including the details about how Professor Willoughby tried to coerce tenure. How can we resolve this matter with you and determine a fair grade?"

"Let me take the final again, on my own. One of the board members or the chancellor can proctor me," Micki said simply. "If I can pass it with a perfect score before, I can do it again."

"You know the questions now. It would be easy to just use the same answers," Professor Willoughby snapped.

"Then create a new test," Micki replied. "With a five-point differential. I can assure you I can make ninety-five or higher."

"That seems fair," Chancellor Dyer said.

"That's ridiculous," Professor Willoughby said, outraged.

"Why would it be?" Jonas asked. "I'm sorry for speaking out of turn but every professor in here has their own exam questions that could be used, if they agree. He can propagate a new test quickly under supervision, of course, print it, and since the student is willing to retake the test, he either gets proven right or Ms. Ballad wrong."

Chancellor Dyer and the board conferred for a moment before she spoke. "I will go with you to my office, Professor Willoughby, and you will create a new final. Miss Ballad, you will wait for me in meeting room three and I will bring you the test. I will supervise the exam and then Professors Linton, Thomas and Murray will help you grade the answers."

"I don't think that's fair. Those three don't like me either," he retorted.

"It's not a personality contest, but an exam," a third board member said. "Or are you impugning these professors' credibility as well?"

"No, I'm not." Professor Willoughby glowered.

"Then this is what we'll do," Chancellor Dyer said. "I suspect that none of those silent students in the hallway plan to go anywhere until this is over."

"My family is out there too," Micki added.

"I'm sure you had this show well organized," Professor Willoughby accused.

Micki gave him a direct look. "No, sir, I didn't. I was as surprised as you, but people know me and know I'm an honest person. They support the changes that would see your students treated fairly and not have your personal views used against us."

"I'm sure, nontraditional students are always looking for extra breaks," he muttered.

"No, we aren't. We work hard to prove we deserve to be here," Micki answered. "The thing is, Professor Willoughby, I liked your guest lectures, which is why I kept coming back for them. I could've chosen other ways to spend the time, but you made me think, not just about the theories we were taught but the real-world applications. But eventually no one can enjoy learning if the person who is to nurture your knowledge treats you with disrespect."

"Well said." Jonas looked like he was going to leap out of his chair and cheer. Her heart felt full.

It was an hour before she was sitting with a new final in front of her, seven pages long to be exact. Professor Willoughby did not intend to make it easy for her.

"You have two hours and thirty minutes," Chancellor Dyer said. "Begin."

Micki let out a slow breath and turned the pages to scan the first few questions. In a minute, she was in her own head, seeing the answers form, and began writing quickly as the details flowed. As per usual, the world fell away, and she was engrossed in the knowledge and the moment. All too soon, Micki wrote the final word on the paper and sat back with a sigh.

"I take it you're finished?" the chancellor asked, sounding amused. "I started to wonder if you were going to move past writing on the last page and continue right onto the desk."

"I didn't go over the time limit?" Micki asked, alarmed.

"Not at all, and besides I would have warned you if that was the case. You have forty minutes left if you need to go over it again," Chancellor Dyer offered.

Micki passed the exam to her. "I'm pretty much okay with my answers."

"Fine. Then let's trade places with the professors." Chancellor Dyer stood and inclined her hand to the door. "How was the test?"

Micki shrugged. "Standard for one of Willoughby's, but I enjoyed it. As always, you had to really think about the answers, but I love that. Any topic to do with the law is cool."

"You are a very unusual woman, Micki Ballad, I can see why you're well liked."

"I'm just being me. Now, let's see if my answers hold up under scrutiny."

The handing over of the completed exam happened and she sat nervously tapping her foot while it was graded.

"It's going to be okay, love." Jonas squeezed her hand.

She frowned. "If this is how it feels to be on trial, never put me down for being on the wrong side of things."

"You'll never be. You'll be defending those who need you."

"I guess I need to give up my wicked ways," Micki joked.

"Stay just as you are, darling." He grinned.

The conversation was meant to keep her mind off what was happening in the other room, she knew, but she still noticed the tension in the room. All the professors had returned to the first meeting room, where they were seated, although without the chancellor and the board. But then there was the sound of the doors opening, and Micki turned. She could still see her family and supporters in the hallway. The chancellor and the board took up their spots again while her stomach twisted into more knots. Everyone settled and she held her breath, waiting to see if she would be able to finish her undergrad degree at the university she loved.

"After the review of the final exam given by Professor Willoughby, proctored by me and graded by the three alternate professors, Micki, you got another perfect score," the chancellor said with authority. "It has been determined that Micki Ballad is innocent of any cheating allegations and that Dean Brand was not in any way a part of such a plan."

Professor Willoughby sat sullen-faced.

Jonas stood. "I ask that Professor Willoughby's contract be terminated. We've discussed his record and breaches of the code of conduct. It would not be in the students' best interests for him to continue at this university." He glanced at the professor. "I'm sorry, Willoughby, but those are the facts."

Chancellor Dyer looked at the board members and no one objected. "The board and I agree that is the best action to take. Aaron Willoughby, your contract is terminated, and you will leave the campus immediately. This meeting is adjourned."

"Thank you so much," Micki said, and breathed a sigh of relief. She put her papers in her bag and blinked away the tears in her eyes. "I mean it, thank you so much, you don't know what this means to me."

"I think we do," Professor Linton said. "At least let us get out of this room before breaking the news to everybody in the hallway and we can't pass."

Seconds passed and the room was now silent. Jonas pulled her into his arms and lifted her off her feet. Back on the ground, he kissed her lovingly and she knew she'd never forget this moment.

"You were outstanding, love, just brilliant."

"We were brilliant," she smiled at him. "Let's go break it to the gang."

As they stepped out of the room, everyone looked at her hopefully and Micki didn't keep them in suspense. "Vindication!"

Like Professor Linton had predicted, the crowd erupted in cheers and applause, with her family at the center. They hugged her tight and her mother was openly crying. She and Jonas looked at each other through the celebration and it was love and relief that mirrored back to her. It was finally over, and they could move on together to a future with endless possibilities.

As she and Jonas walked hand in hand, the crowd followed them outside. It might be the beginning of winter, but the cold was far from their thoughts, it seemed. She kissed Jonas in front of everyone, while laughter and whistles rang out. Why not, there was no reason to hide their love.

"OKAY, EVERYONE MEET in the family room!" Micki called out to the people she loved the most.

There was no better place to announce their news than the space where she'd once played with crayons and Tonka trucks over dolls. Where she cut her chin trying to fly and then hiding from Enid when she'd gotten into trouble. Where she had her first kiss and the memory of feeling like a grown-up.

Enid joined her and Jonas. She smiled because Enid always calmed her down when big changes were brewing or when she'd been caught out for a bad decision, like that flying stunt. Instead of a punishment, Micki would get a sit-down with Enid and they'd talk while having ice cream. Sometimes she did have to take a grounding for a few weeks, but that was okay, she deserved it most of the time for being a brat. Micki stared at the familiar walls and the spot on the doorframe where the Ballad sisters' heights had been marked after each growth spurt.

She tried to take it all in. The banisters where she had slid down to the landing, and then fixed decades later as part of her job at the inn. Same for the hardwood floors that got scratched by her roller skates, Mia's skateboard and Margo's cart of pets and strays that she cared for. She would miss the place she called home for the first twenty-eight years of her life, but sometimes you had to step away to appreciate it all the more. This was her time to do that, and with Jonas's laptop on the crocheted doily spread over the coffee table's surface, her growing family arrived.

Husbands, kids and babies, plus her parents were now there, too. With so much love around them both, Micki knew that she and Jonas would always have a solid foundation. The assembled gang looked on curiously as everyone found a seat.

"What are you eating, Omar?" Micki asked the young boy who was growing as fast as the honeysuckle did in the spring.

"Ice cream with crushed Oreos, caramel sauce, chocolate sauce, gummy bears and choco puffs." He grinned and gave Claire a bite from his spoon.

"You're going to give her a sugar rush, dude," Micki pointed out. "It looks good, though."

"Trust me, it is," Omar said awkwardly around a bulging mouthful.

"Don't give her too much or we're dropping her off at your house when she can't sleep and wants to run around in circles, giggling," Gideon warned in a good-natured tone.

"You know you're going to go make the exact same thing, Gideon Holder," Margo shot back and laughed. "You can chase her around."

The whole family joined in the laugh. Seconds later, her mom looked at her soberly. "What's going on, sweetie, another war council?"

"None of those for a very long time or ever again," Micki said. "But we have news. Jonas, hit it."

He pressed the connect button and his family's faces came into view. "Hi, Mum, Dad, Emily. Can you all hear me, okay?"

"Perfectly, JonJon!" his mother said.

"Oh, wow, really?" Mia gasped. "We could have been calling him that all this time and we've missed it." She smirked and Margo slugged her sister's shoulder.

Jonas continued. "Mum, Dad, Emily, you've met Micki. This is her family. Let's start with her parents."

Introductions were made and the usual gushing and talking over each other happened before she or Jonas could wrangle control of the conversation again. Jonas's mother gushed over the babies and looked at Emily and pointed a finger at Jonas accusingly. Micki smiled as Jonas reached for her hand and waited for the antics to die down.

"All righty, so, Jonas and I have to tell you all something important," Micki said loudly, and the discussion fell away. Micki held up her hand and Jonas slipped the engagement ring on her finger. "We're getting married!"

Chaos erupted. Her mother bawled. Jonas's mother cried just as loudly. Both sisters embraced her at once in all the excitement. The men could only shake Jonas's hand because the babies were in their laps. Everyone seemed to be laughing and trying to talk at the same time.

"I knew it, I just knew it when you said you

wanted us all to come over here," Margo said in singsong.

Her father, possibly the only one to hold on to his cool, stood and hugged her silently before speaking with a choked-up voice. Evidently, the emotion of it all had gotten to him, too. "My youngest is getting married! I'm so happy for you."

"I'm happy that you're happy, Dad. It means a lot to me that you and Mom, and all the gang like Jonas 'cause he sure likes all of you." Micki smiled through her tears. "And you're gaining another son."

"I am." Brian held out his hand to Jonas, who shook it. "You take care of my daughter."

"Micki, welcome to our family," Beverly said warmly over the video call. "Oh, I can't wait to meet you all in person. Do you and Jonas have a date in mind?"

"May eighteenth," they said together. "We want to go on our honeymoon for a few weeks in the summer."

"Sounds like a fabulous idea. And so many romantic places to choose from," her mother said.

"Ohhh, I will make a list. Great thinking, Rosie," Beverly said excitedly.

Her mom nodded. "I like the way you think, too. This is going to be some family."

"I'll finally have the sister I've always wanted." Emily gave a little cheer.

"Well, more like three sisters. You have to take the whole set," Micki said, shooting a grin at her sisters.

"Even better. I'll come see you all, and then you'll all come see me! A return girls' trip!" Emily gushed.

"I guess we take a boys' trip with this guy," Gideon chuckled and pointed at Jonas.

"We'll have fun with JonJon." Ryan's smile reached from one ear to the other.

Jonas sighed. "And so it begins."

"Spring wedding!" Mia announced. "The honeysuckle will be beautiful and the gazebo you built, Micki, will be a gorgeous spot to say your 'I dos'."

"I didn't know you built that," Jonas said, his voice full of admiration. "Is there anything you can't do?"

"Eat rhubarb. I'm allergic," Micki teased, and he laughed.

Margo looked worried. "Seriously, she's allergic. Don't give her rhubarb anything."

The conversation went on for another half hour before Jonas was able to say goodbye to his family and end the video call. Then it was time to give her family the second part of their big news. Micki wasn't looking forward to it, but it had to be done. She glanced at her mother, who gave her a slight nod, and she took a deep breath.

"There's more that we have to share." Micki cleared her throat. "We're not going to live on the property. Jonas bought a town house in NoDa, and we plan to make it our home."

Her heart almost broke when her sisters' faces went from happy to sad.

"Why—Micki, there's plenty of space on the property for your house," Margo said.

"Is this what you want or what he wants?" Mia asked bluntly, sending Jonas a cool gaze.

"Mia, that can't be right," Ryan said gently. "No one makes Micki do anything she doesn't want to do."

Micki moved to sit between her sisters on the sofa and took their hands. "This is all me. I was thinking about it long before Jonas got here. I wanted to cut down on the commute and life is changing so much around here. I need to find who I am and not as part of those wild Ballad girls. You have families and lives..."

"Micki, our families are yours. We're sorry if we made you feel excluded." A sob escaped Margo.

"Hey, guys, let's get the kids a popsicle." Ryan rose. "This is for them to work out."

"We'll come, too," her mom and dad said.

"I'm staying," Enid declared, as if defying anyone to argue with her.

The room cleared. Micki wiped her tears away, glad she could be this open with her sisters and their beloved second mom. It was how the idea for this first started—Mia, Margo, Enid and herself, the foundation of Ballad Inn.

"Margo…" Micki said her sister's name huskily.

"I know you have to do this, but it hurts," Margo whispered and gave a little laugh. "I'll come over here and know that you're not up in your room dancing to your music or at the table studying."

"You won't be just down the path when we need a girl session," Mia said. "What if you need me or I need you?"

"I'll be a phone call away and I'll come running," Micki promised. "I know how to find my way home, I always do."

Enid huffed. "I always knew you'd be the one to leave, but it is only NoDa, not across the world like I feared. You have to do what's in your heart, Micki. And you better come home for at least Sunday dinners."

"You guys will see so much of me, you'll wonder if I really moved out," Micki added. "Don't be sad, be happy for me. I'm in love with a good guy and I'm getting married. I'm settling down, just like you wanted."

"But not here with us," Margo said. "I don't know if I can handle this."

"Margo, I'm not going to the moon. I'll be close by," Micki said with a chuckle. "I will show up randomly to kiss my nieces and nephews often."

"Okay, Micki—okay," Mia breathed out. "We love you, and we'll support you, but always remember home is right here waiting."

"I'll be back, you can count on it." Micki gave a watery laugh. "This place will never be empty for long. I just need a chance to spread my wings and fly for a little bit."

"Then you soar high, Micki Ballad, and we'll always be here to cheer you on." Mia put her arm around Micki's shoulders. Margo did the same.

Enid leaned over to wrap her arms around them the best she could. "I'm so proud of the three of you. My heart is bursting with love."

"And it's time you have your happily-ever-after, Enid," Mia said. "You and your new husband have a lot of living to do. Enjoy every minute of it."

"Our lives may go in different directions but we always know Ballad Inn is here for all of us in good times and bad," Margo said. "One day we'll sit on that porch, watching our grandkids and talking about old times."

"Ryan, Gideon and Jonas will be playing checkers or doing who knows what with that tricky trio." Mia laughed.

"And we'll be there, rolling our eyes," Micki added. "Till then, our family can survive a few miles apart, it's survived so much more."

By the time folks left the inn to return to their own homes for the night, Micki was exhausted. Her bed beckoned. She and Jonas held hands as they went upstairs together and stopped on the landing for the second floor.

"Good night, soon-to-be wife," he said with a smile. They held each other for the longest time, until he asked, "Are you okay, Michelle?"

"I am," she answered and smiled at him. "I found my new home in your arms. How couldn't I be? Just a few more months and we'll be married. Thank you for sticking around in my world."

"Thank you for inviting me in." He kissed her then. "Dream of me?"

"Always."

Micki met his gaze once more before he went to his room. She lingered, taking in the quiet of the house, her eyes falling on the twinkling white lights and pretty green garland decorating the banister. This was home base, but she was ready to fly and see what life had in store for her. It was time for this Ballad girl to leave home.

CHAPTER FOURTEEN

THE SCENT OF honeysuckle filled the air and the birds called to each other in the trees. Ballad Inn stood proud in the sunshine, empty of guests except for the ones that were there for the wedding. Jonas's family were in from England and thoroughly enjoying the warmth of a sunny day in May.

"It's still chilly in London," Emily said. Micki didn't think she'd worn anything but shorts and T-shirts since she and her parents arrived ten days ago.

Micki and her soon-to be father-in-law formed an instant friendship and took to playing checkers with Mr. Marley and Mr. Bolton. Mr. Webber joined in and Gideon's former father-in-law, Grant, was there as well. He was invited to the wedding, his wife having passed, as it gave him an opportunity to see his granddaughter Claire, who was just about to turn four.

It was the day before the wedding, and the

men had gone off for a fishing trip to bond and relax. It was okay with Micki. She and the rest of the females had their own agenda. Besides, the guys were underfoot more than the babies scooting around in their walkers. The atmosphere around the inn was charged with a wonderful type of energy and sense of community, mostly because the wedding had turned into a neighborhood affair.

Invited guests combined her friends and classmates, Professor Linton and Professor West, overseas mates of Jonas's as well as family friends and aunts and uncles, cousins—the lot. Rows of chairs would have to be spread out across the entire main lawn, around the gazebo. The rest of the space would be for the buffet and rented chairs and tables set up under large white tents with strings of tiny lights strung overhead. The reality was that she couldn't invite someone in the neighborhood without someone else wondering where their invitation was. It was just the nature of Sardis Woods, and she was glad about that. A closely knit community had seen her grow up and doing everything from helping with an apple cider stand to roller-skating up and down the streets in summer, singing at the top of her lungs. She was Micki Ballad, and she was getting married, although it did make her wonder if half of the guests were coming to see if she would go through with it or be some kind of runaway bride.

"There better not be a betting pool going on with respect to my getting wed," Micki had warned Mr. Webber when they'd been playing checkers.

"There's not," he proclaimed with an innocent expression and a bit of outrage. "Micki, I thought you knew me better than that."

"I do," she'd said sweetly, "which is why I'm asking."

Margo, Enid and Beverly had taken over the kitchen completely. They were preparing food for the reception, making the wedding cakes— plural— and were still managing to come up with a family dinner each night. How they did it and so well, she didn't know, but when she'd tried to help, she was shooed away each and every time. *You're the bride! Go sit and relax,* she was told one too many times. If she sat anymore, she would only start to worry about whether things would go as planned. Her dress was hanging upstairs, the hairdresser would be there bright and early tomorrow and here she was, sitting in the family room alone.

"Okay. Enough of this," Micki grumbled and hopped off the sofa.

She picked up her Bluetooth speaker and found Mia with the others in the kitchen, tick-ing items off a long list. Micki could see it even from where she stood by the door.

"Micki, what are you doing in here?" Enid asked with a frown.

"Trying not to die of boredom," Micki said. "You guys know I'm no good at sitting still for too long."

"So, what are you doing?" Mia asked.

Micki scrolled through her playlist and hit the play button for one of their favorite tunes. "Finding the perfect song for us to dance it out."

"Micki, we don't have time for this," Margo bemoaned.

"Don't we? I see Emily's hips shimmying over there," Micki grinned. "And Beverly's tapping her foot."

"She's right," Emily said and began to dance with Micki. "We need to stretch our backs just a bit. I feel like I've been delivering babies for fourteen hours straight, rolling these spring rolls."

Mia began to dance while walking around with her notepad and a smile on her face. "This song always makes me want to move. A mix of Latin and reggae, it's a groovy song."

Micki laughed. "Groovy? You'll be wearing tie-dye clothes in a minute."

"Those were good times," Beverly said. "I used to be a fan girl for The Cougars. We traveled everywhere."

"Mum," Emily gasped. "Does Dad know this?"

Beverly laughed and took a sip of her cold sweet tea. "How do you think I met your father, sweetheart?"

That garnered laughter from everyone, and Micki stole Enid away from icing the eclairs to dance.

"I've got seven dozen of these to finish in as many hours," Enid said helplessly.

Micki kissed her on her cheek with a loud smack. "I'll help you after the song."

"You're the bride…" Enid began.

Micki hugged her. "This is *my* wedding, I'm helping my family prepare for it. No more leaving me bored and alone. Now dance with me, your favorite Ballad."

"Hey," Margo, Mia and their mother said simultaneously.

"You're very lucky, having a mum and another mum," Emily said. "Wait. Do they both ask you to have grandbabies?"

"I got lucky," Micki said and pointed to Margo and Mia. "They gave both of them exactly what they wanted, thankfully."

"Oh, I just love holding your grandkids," Beverly said as she danced around the island. "They're so chubby and I want to nibble their little toes."

"See!" her mom laughed. "It is not weird that I want to put their little feet in my mouth."

"Ha. I used to do that to JonJon and Emily." Beverly laughed.

"Oh, Mum, no, don't tell the world that," Emily begged.

"I love my family," Micki cried out happily. "Let's finish this song and get back to work."

It was the break they all needed, and Micki, blissfully content, settled into filling the next batch of eclairs with pastry cream, and then took over assembling the spring rolls from Emily because her fingers were cramping.

The landline rang and Margo picked up the receiver. After a cheery hello, she listened, then frowned. "Oh, Gideon, it's a day before the wedding," she said. "If you guys aren't back…you know what? We're coming to get you all. Yes, all of us and just so you know, you're taking us away from the food that will feed the many, many guests at my sweet sister's wedding."

When she got off the phone, Margo put her head against the wall and moaned.

"What?" Micki asked in alarm. "Who's hurt?"

"No one." Margo sighed. "The men in our lives have managed to put the truck into the lake when they were trying to take the boat out."

"Oh no." Mia's jaw had dropped.

"But wait, there's more," Margo said. "In their

infinite wisdom, instead of calling someone, they thought, well the SUV is a four-by-four with good traction..."

"Please don't say it," Micki pleaded.

"Gideon waded out, attached a rope and they tried to pull it out, a boat and a truck," Margo told them.

"And they got pulled in instead," Mia finished the thought. "Honestly, do they not think? And they have so much knowledge between them. Seriously, do they really think?"

"They don't," her mom said. "Us older gals will keep the momentum going here, you girls go get them before they manage to drown themselves."

"Come on, Emily, you can see the lake close up, and get to point and laugh at your brother," Margo encouraged.

"Absolutely," Emily said enthusiastically. "This is the best holiday we ever had."

IT TOOK AN hour and forty-five minutes to get to the lake and then another thirty to find the primo fishing spot as Gideon had called it. Eight men looking boyishly embarrassed stood in a line, their hands stuffed in their pockets. Behind them you could see about half of the SUV sitting out of the water. Micki got out of the car. Emily was already practically skipping up to her brother, while Margo and Mia brought up the rear.

"I called the county's marine services," Mia said. "After the laughing, they said they'll be here in thirty minutes."

"Our insurance company is going to love us." Margo put her hands on her hips. "Why, why did you all think this would be okay?"

Gideon shrugged. "It seemed plausible."

"I mean the math seemed to fit," Jonas added.

"You're a law professor, not a physicist," Micki pointed out to her groom.

"Well, Dad is…"

"Also, a lawyer." Micki was on a roll. "Dad, you're a financial analyst, Gideon—well, you're a contractor and deal with angles and stuff, but still, this is very way off."

Ryan raised his hand. "I would like to say I told them this was more than likely not going to work."

"But you directed the whole thing," her dad said. "Who was the one that was saying, 'Gun it, gun it'?"

"Did anyone account for the fact that this lake has a very strong undercurrent and so it's more than likely pulling the boat and truck further into the water?" Micki asked, incredulously.

They all looked back at the lake and sure enough the SUV was sinking farther into the water and mud. Once water rescue services, the tow truck and the sheriff's deputy arrived, they could see more than the front of the truck finally.

"A caravan under the water. That's not how these vehicles work," the tow truck guys with the big wench said with humor.

"We tried telling them that," Micki said, amused.

Margo stepped up. "Our insurance rep was screaming on the phone. I'm pretty sure I could hear that vein by his temple pulsing."

"Okay. Let's get'er done," the man said jovially. "These vehicles are a wash anyway—get it, wash—water?"

"You're hilarious," her dad muttered.

Jonas's father was busy taking pictures with his phone and seemed quite jovial. "The lads back home won't believe what we did."

"At least your father is having fun," Micki said to Jonas dryly. "And look at you, you're almost sunburned. We need to get you a good SPF and slather it on this summer."

"'At least he wasn't wearing sunglasses and looking like a racoon now." Gideon chuckled. "Imagine the wedding pictures."

Micki glared at him.

He raised his hands and stepped back. "Okay, not funny."

It took another two hours, and an Uber that

cost a pretty penny to get all of them back to the inn where they were chastised a bit before being dismissed. The group split off. Micki wanted her and her sisters—her matrons of honor—to stay here with her tonight. It seemed apt given all the memories and how special the place was to them. In what was once Margo's room, they lay on the four-poster looking at the ceiling where a canopy was formed with stringed lights. The sisters held hands like they used to when sharing a bed, talking about their dreams, desires, doubts and triumphs. Now Micki was in the middle, her bigger sisters flanking her, and while it felt like an end it was also a beginning.

"The lights were a good idea, Margo," Mia said. "It makes it so pretty, so hopeful. The gazebo will look amazing for the ceremony."

"The only one of us who chose a late evening wedding," Margo said with a smile. "Why didn't I think of that?"

Micki gave a dramatic sigh. "I've always been a visionary, ahead of my time, with an eye for the future."

"Oh, shut up and take a compliment," Mia nudged her with her elbow, while Margo squeezed Micki's hand.

"I *am* taking the compliment," Micki said, smiling too. "Were you guys as nervous as I am about tomorrow?"

"You were there for my wedding—it was so impromptu I didn't have time to be nervous," Mia recalled.

"Mine was a different kind of nervousness. Was I making the right choice and was I marrying for the right reason?" Margo said and squeezed Micki's hand again. "But you guys had months and months to plan and to learn and love each other more. Yours is the best kind of nervousness, Micki, the one that comes with the first day of the rest of your new life with your husband."

"Unless you want to bolt, then it's a whole other story," Mia said. "Please don't be a runaway bride, I've got twenty on you staying."

"I knew those two old coots were betting on me to do a runner," Micki said, faking the outrage. "Can I uninvite them to the wedding?"

"Too late now, sweetie." Mia pulled a quilt over them. "And don't forget how you bet on me to fall off my skateboard. Remember when I landed and hit my tailbone?"

"Coc—"

"Don't say it," Mia warned.

"Our lives have really taken off these last couple of years, haven't they, ladies." Margo's voice sounded dreamy. "From each of us tied up in our own world, to finding love and sort of joining all those worlds together. And now Jonas and his world. It's been exciting. All the love around us now. Being grown-ups and married, having our families and finding new paths."

"You guys might feel older, but I'm still only nineteen in my head," Micki said, giggling.

"I can't wait for you to hit thirty-five and wake up one day, roll out of bed and something twinges in your back and you're like. Wait. What was that?" Mia laughed.

"Don't you wish that on me!" Micki said.

Both sisters turned and wrapped an arm around her. Micki felt complete. There was no love like the one between sisters and she had the best two a girl could ask for.

"I love you both so much," Micki whispered.

"We love you, too," they both replied.

Micki closed her eyes and let the feeling of closeness surround her. Tomorrow she would be leaving Ballad Inn, but the love she knew now would never go away.

MICKI CHOSE THE evening for her wedding because it was always her favorite time of the day. You could watch slivers of a burnt orange sunset through the leaves as the warm breeze wafted like a soft whisper of happiness from nature. In the evenings the scent of the honeysuckle was always heavy in the air, and it blended with the sweet magnolia from the white flowers of the trees. Tonight, lights glittered among the yellow blooms that covered the trellis of the gazebo, reminding her of the fireflies she'd caught in mason jars as a child or the fairies she thought once lived among the gardens of Ballad Inn.

She stood on the balcony of her bedroom, looking out at all the guests, grateful they could all be with her to see her take her vows. Below she could hear soft clicks of a camera from one of the photographers, no doubt getting picture after picture per Mia's request.

"Okay, I'm going back inside," Micki said, glancing at her sisters. "Mia, there will be seven thousand pictures to go through if those photographers keep it up."

"I'll enjoy seeing each one, even though I know there are a few with you poking your tongue out," Mia told her. "Yes, they told me about that. I could never understand why you always hated taking pictures."

"But you look breathtaking." Her mom wiped her eyes again. "Your dad is going to be so proud to walk you down the aisle."

Micki looked at herself in the mirror. Her hair was done in rope twists and pulled back from her face. Small stems of baby's breath were placed carefully in her hair, and matched the shade of her dress, a strapless gown with layers of satin and shimmering lace that went down to her yellow satin pumps. In true Micki fashion the outfit needed a spark and what better way than to include the beautiful color that was the signature of Ballad Inn. Mia, Margo, and Emily as her bridesmaids made up her half of the wedding party. They lined up in order, their wispy, dusky pink dresses flattering them all.

"Come on, Micki," her mom said, "it's time." She smiled and led them downstairs where her father stood waiting. When their eyes met, she almost cried noticing how he mopped his eyes.

"You look like an angel," her father whispered, clearly caught up in all the emotion. "For a moment, I flashed back to you running out on the porch to meet us, dressed like a fairy with the wings and all. Now look at you, my beautiful daughter, asking me to escort her down the aisle to see her off into marriage and I don't know if I can."

Micki kissed her dad's cheek. "You're not getting rid of me that easily, you know that, right? You and Mom are just sharing me with the man I love. You're the one that taught me to only expect the best from anyone I chose to love, and that it wasn't half measures that made a relationship work. It has to be all or nothing. And I thank you for that because Jonas loves me and it's because of you I know how to recognize that love."

"How are you so smart?" her father asked.

"Raised from good stock," she replied. "Let's go get me married."

"Fine, but it's under duress. I like the boy but he still doesn't deserve you," her dad teased.

Micki tucked her arm through his. "You're wrong there, we deserve each other."

The music began. Instead of the traditional wedding march, it was a love song that encompassed what she and Jonas meant to each other.

Claire was once again a flower girl, but this time she had Omar in a tux to catch her when she tossed the rose petals and took off like the runner she was. Everyone laughed as she was brought back to her seat with a grin and waving her little basket as if she'd won a prize. Gideon came to walk down the aisle with her mom before taking up his post again at the front. They were followed by Emily, Mia and Margo. Each slow step brought Micki closer to her destiny and the man who wearing a tux with a shirt and suit jacket that matched the hue of her dress. His trousers and bowtie were black. The look suited him and when she caught sight of his yellow high-tops that matched her shoes. A laugh escaped Micki's lips.

His groomsmen all had silly grins on their faces. Ryan and Gideon, her brothers-in-law, of course had love in their eyes for their wives.

Micki knew they were thinking about their own marriages and how everything had come full circle. Meanwhile, Micah, who was Emily's partner for the ceremony, had made a good impression on her, she knew. Could there be another wedding here next May featuring the other Brand sibling? Micki smiled at the lovely thought.

The song was nearing its end, and she was almost at the gazebo to pledge her life, her loyalty to the man she loved. Jonas, looking strong, elegant, fixed his glasses and beamed a mile-wide smile just for her. Finally, Micki stood beside him and her father kissed her cheek.

"Take care of my girl," her father said to Jonas. "Welcome to the family."

"I will, sir, I can promise you that." Jonas looked at her, and she saw him swallow as if he was holding back a lot of emotion. "You are the most beautiful woman I have ever seen. How did I get this lucky?"

"I mean, after all the bachelors, you're the one I picked." Micki shot him her spunky grin.

The reverend they chose was a friend of Micki's who'd promised that if Micki ever got married, she would officiate the ceremony. Dominique Moore was a historian and archivist who'd majored in religious studies and also wore the best angel costume with halo and wings for

Halloween that had spooked Sardis Woods. Her hair was a curly pixie style, ruby red, and she had black round-framed glasses and a rose gold nose ring that glittered with a simple diamond in the hoop.

"Dearly beloved, I am so very honored to marry this couple today. My good friend Micki has found her soul mate." Dominique began the ceremony and they focused on her words until it was their turn to speak. "The bride and groom have written their own vows."

"Michelle Ballad…" Jonas hesitated for a moment as his emotions seemed to take over. "You blew into my world like a whirlwind with neon green high-tops on your feet. I couldn't help but be caught up in your passion for everything you threw yourself into. Your kindness, the love and empathy you have for everyone and the way you've loved me is truly special. Through my stumbles and mistakes, and then watching the shooting stars with me, I am humbled by how you've brought me into your life and have never let me go. That night when we made the wish, mine was for you, to be able to spend each day in your presence, and my wish has come true."

"Wow. How am I supposed to follow that?" Micki said with a watery laugh and the guests joined in, but her tone became serious as she offered her own vows. "I was a baker, worked in an ice cream parlor, was a handyman and I even pressed apple cider for the holidays in the fall. My life has been a series of adventures, from falling off the roof to convincing my sisters we could ride the cows in Crawford Field."

"We always knew when the Ballad sisters were around!" Mr. Webber called and someone else whistled.

"Will you behave," Micki said sweetly. "Anyway, pardon the interruption."

Jonas laughed. "I'd have it no other way."

"In all my adventures, nothing was scarier but also made happier than when I fell in love with you," Micki continued. "Jonas 'JonJon' Brand, you get me, on a level that very few people can. I was always seen as the carefree one who never took anything seriously, but you saw past that to the real me. I love you, Jonas, more than I could possibly imagine. I see my life taking a clear path, one that I gladly walk with you. So, let's get this show on the road, babe, I can't wait for our journey to begin."

"Wonderfully said, both of you. Now, time for the rings." Dominique gestured for Jonas to go first. "Do you, Jonas Brand, take Michelle Ballad to be your wife?"

"I do." Jonas placed the wedding band on her finger, and it locked neatly into place with the engagement ring.

"Michelle Ballad, do you take Jonas Brand to be your husband?"

Micki slipped the matching wedding band on his finger. "I do."

"Then by the power invested in me by the state of North Carolina, and this fantastic couple, I now pronounce you husband and wife," Dominique announced happily. "You may kiss the bride."

"May I?" Jonas asked her. She smiled and nodded.

"Kiss the woman!" Ryan said with a laugh.

Micki closed her eyes as Jonas's lips met hers and the world slipped away for a moment. Wild applause filled the air. Jonas lifted his head, but only briefly. He smiled and then dipped her one more time for a kiss.

"Did you get that?" Micki heard Mia cry out excitedly. "Please tell me you got that photo!"

The kiss ended. "Hello, wife," Jonas said softly.

Micki grinned. "Hello, husband."

They walked down the aisle, hand in hand. Micki stopped at Mr. Bolton and Mr. Marley. "And you two had said there was no betting."

"Blame Mia, she won it all anyway," Mr. Marley grumbled.

Micki beamed. "I love you, too, old—gentlemen."

"Have the most wonderful life imaginable," Mr. Bolton said and kissed her cheek.

"You bet I will," she promised.

"It's time to celebrate the Sardis Woods way," Mia called out and everyone cheered.

"By dunking Gideon in a tank full of water like we did once?" Micki teased.

Gideon grinned. "How about we enjoy your wedding reception, kiddo."

"Yes, let's do that instead." Micki leaned into Jonas and off they went.

As they walked to the tents, where the reception would be held, Micki looked up at the stars and realized she couldn't be happier. The Ballad Inn love juju had struck her after all, and she was truly glad for it.

THE WEDDING RECEPTION was in full swing. The food was sublime. Jonas was still in awe that the combination of their two families had put out such a fantastic group of Asian and American dishes. From the handmade spring rolls to the sesame chicken, American cheeseburger sliders and mini buffalo chicken sandwiches, he tasted it all. He knew the guests would leave happily full and talking about the cuisine for a long time to come. He sat next to Micki at the wedding party and more than once his eyes met hers and they stared deeply into each other's soul. He had a wife, a caring, talented, amazing wife and yet there had been a point when he'd wondered if life would ever be normal again. Well, here he was, and it was a lot better than normal.

Jonas admitted that what he'd thought was lost with his family had instead grown. Jonas couldn't see his life without any of the Ballad clan, not to mention his mom, dad and Em. The universe was aligning for something wonderful, and their past trouble was just that—the past. It seemed Micki was right as usual because between mingling with guests and watching how his father laughed or Emily danced, they were in their element, and it was blissful.

"It's time. Gather the men," Gideon said in his ear.

"I'm a bit nervous, actually," Jonas confessed.

"Hey, you talked us into this, so we're doing it right. This is how you decided to step out of your comfort zone and go a little wild. I just hope no one takes a video of this."

"There will more than likely be tons of recordings, let's face it." Jonas got up and pulled on his jacket.

"Great, just great, it will haunt me forever," Gideon muttered.

Micki looked up at them. "Where are you two off to? No shenanigans at the wedding, I don't need a tow or fire truck, nor ambulance here."

"None of that is going to happen," Jonas assured her.

"It may happen," Gideon said under his breath as he signaled to Ryan and Micah to follow him.

Jonas passed his mother and placed his hand on her shoulder, bending low to whisper. "It's time. Can you get Micki to her seat by the dance floor, please."

"How exciting," his mother said and clapped her hands.

"Where are they off to?" Mia asked loudly over the music.

"Who knows? But trust me, it will be shenanigans." Micki's answer made him chuckle.

He and Ryan, Micah and Gideon stood near the dance floor, getting ready to make their entrance. His two new brothers looked more apprehensive than anyone.

"Come on, lads, perk up. This is going to be fantastic," Jonas said cheerily.

"But will it, though?" Ryan sounded doubtful.

"We watched the video, and we've been practicing the moves for the last six weeks," Micah said firmly.

Ryan snorted. "Says the guy that can glide across a floor. I am not built for the dance."

"The dance? Really?" Jonas was amused.

"Step up, we got this," Micah said again. "Remember, we're calm, cool and collected. We look like four top movie spies, channel that."

"Debonair, got it," Gideon said. "Well, let's get it done."

"When I announce us, you guys come in and throw me my hat and cane." Micah straightened his tie. "Throw it lightly, not like it's a javelin—Jonas."

"Once, it happened once, and I apologized profusely," Jonas reminded him.

"Uh-huh."

Micah went out onto the dance floor. The mic made a screeching sound and then he spoke. "Hey, Mr. DJ, cut the music and stand by with track four."

"Gotcha," was the reply.

Jonas blew out a nervous breath. He couldn't afford to show the guys his heart was racing, too. This was his way to break the box he'd put himself in long ago. When better to do it than for his wife, at their wedding. He cast his eyes upward in a silent prayer. *Do not let us make a complete fool of ourselves.*

"Bro, are you praying?" Ryan asked.

Jonas shrugged and put his top hat on. "Couldn't hurt."

"True." Ryan mimicked his actions.

"Sorry about the music, folks, but you'll want to gather around for this one," Micah said grandly.

"The men of Ballad Inn present a dance through time featuring the groom himself. Micki Ballad, this one's for you."

Micki was grinning but looked worried. Jonas said another quick prayer.

"Hit it, Mr. DJ!" Micah called out.

The music blasted from the speakers and Jonas stepped onto the dance floor and threw the cane to Micah flawlessly. Micki, sitting in the front row, was applauding the loudest.

"You go, babe," she yelled and clapped her hands. "Grab my phone, I need my own video of this!"

The routine began with a classic song that took you back to the age of iconic musicals. Their canes and top hats were props as they moved in unison. When the music changed to rock and roll from the sixties, those items were tossed aside along with their jackers while their dance changed to fit the era.

"I didn't know you guys could dance," Mia hollered.

Margo laughed. "I don't think they could before Micah taught them."

Jonas plucked a hair band from his pocket and slipped it on. He noticed his fellow dancers doing the same. Rocking out to the popular tunes they'd chosen, Jonas was on his knees, air guitaring like his life depended on it. As the applause grew louder, it gave him the extra bit of bravery to think their little show was being enjoyed. The nineties brought hip-hop, and these were the moves that were most difficult for them.

Jonas plucked a rose from a centerpiece, kissed it, touched it to Micki's cheek, then placed it in her hand. The music of the two thousands started with a pair of popular songs until the big finish that was a flourish of steps and flash moves. Jonas ended the dance in a cool crouched position in front of the rest of the guys. The guests erupted in cheers and Micki came forward to help him to his feet while using a napkin to wipe the sweat from his forehead.

"That was fantastic!" Micki beamed and pressed kisses all over his face. "When did you have time to learn all that?"

"Let's just say we weren't playing disc golf the last six weeks," Jonas replied with a shy grin. "It wasn't too much?"

"It was just right," she assured him. "How did you get Gideon and Ryan to sign up for this, especially Gideon? Margo was obviously in complete shock. She started yelling, 'That's my boo.'"

Jonas looked over to where Gideon stood grinning with a red-cheeked, embarrassed face while Margo fawned all over him. "I used begging, bribery and an assortment of guilt tactics until they said yes."

"Good for you," Micki said with a laugh. "This is the best night of my life."

"Because of the dance?" he asked.

Micki caressed his cheek. "No, silly man, because I married you. The dance was just a bonus."

"We have a bone to pick with you, Jonas," his father said, coming up to him with his father-in-law in tow. "How were we not invited into this little routine to get the adoration of our wives?"

"I...um, well, the thing is..." Jonas was at a loss for words.

"What he's trying to say is that you two would've stolen the show, especially in the first two decades," Micki said quickly. "Those were eras when gentlemen like yourselves made ladies swoon."

"That's right," her father agreed proudly. "Just remember, Jonas, next time, we want to be included."

"You will be the first call, sir," Jonas promised, and the two older men both looked satisfied as they strolled toward the bar. He blew out a breath. "Thanks for that."

"It was better than, 'We were afraid you'll hurt yourselves,'" Micki replied. "Dance with me."

"Always and forever." Jonas took her into his arms. "Thank you for giving me your love. I'm looking forward to our future, Michelle."

"The good and the bad, we'll do it together," she promised, and he twirled her across the dance floor.

The party went on around them, but they were in their own little world as they slow danced to song after song, no matter the tempo. He'd found a home at Ballad Inn, new friends, a family and so much more. The sun would rise and set, they would get older and wiser, but the moment he met Micki at the reception desk would be enshrined in his memory. It was the day she changed his life forever.

EPILOGUE

"Michelle, where is your passport?" Jonas called. "We need it for the tour of Rome today."

"Pocket of my fanny pack," she called back from the bathroom over the noise of the hairdryer. "I got my stuff together, stop worrying."

She switched off the hairdryer and went out to the living room.

"Stop worrying, she says," Jonas muttered. "We have a packed schedule."

"And we will unpack it, not to worry." Micki came up behind him and wrapped her arms around his waist. "This is a honeymoon, not a diplomatic tour. We can take our time. We're not going home until the end of the month."

Jonas turned in her arms. "I want to make sure you see everything."

She smiled, loving how this felt so right. "And if I don't, we'll come back. I don't think that Italy is going anywhere."

"I thought our next trip was to the Bahamas," he countered, smiling back at her.

"Then we'll go the next year," she retorted. "And don't say Scotland. I know, we'll just take two trips in one year. We're young, semi-wild and free—there's no limit on when we do what we want."

Jonas snorted. "*Semi-wild* always amuses me."

"I'm glad I could help." Micki smiled and moved away to find her shoes.

Having spent seven days in glorious Greece, this was the second week of their honeymoon slash vacation, and they were having the time of their lives. The rented villa in the small, picturesque village outside of the Italian capital was another gift from both sets of parents. Micki felt the cool tiles beneath her feet. The balcony overlooked rolling, lush-green hills. Each day they walked to the town center to buy bread, cheeses or eat breakfast at a rustic café. Their evenings were spent strolling along the cobblestoned streets, poking their noses into shops, churches and whatever else caught their interest.

She found a seashell trinket box for Margo on one of those excursions and some old books for Mia that she would go gaga for. She had bought a little something for each of her family members that was a true reflection of their personality. She was so immersed in the culture and to be there with Jonas, that she could understand why her parents traveled so much.

"You're deep in thought," Jonas said. "Missing home and the family?"

"A little bit, but I'm enjoying this much more," Micki admitted. "Our honeymoon in a place like this, with you, is more than I could've ever hoped for. And now we're going into the capital and Vatican City, places that are steeped in history. I love Charlotte, but there's a whole big world out there I want to see. I think it will help me appreciate home more as well."

"It does." He followed her out onto the balcony.

The light breeze pulled at her hair and sundress; savory scents were in the air and her stomach rumbled, reminding her that they'd slept through breakfast that morning.

Jonas chuckled. "I think that's our cue to leave, so we can eat before we go. Do you have everything in the overnight bag you need?"

Micki rolled her eyes, teasing, "Yes, I do, husband. I can't wait to see Maurizio's menu today. Come on, food is calling me."

"Let's get gelato tonight," Jonas said. "I could eat that stuff every day."

Micki picked up her tote and her fanny pack, slung them over her shoulder and stepped out the door, which Jonas was holding open for her.

"We can never tell Enid or Margo how much we enjoy the food. Everything is delicious."

"The paella we had last night, that was sublime." Jonas tilted his face up to the sun.

While she and Jonas strolled to the restaurant, Micki gave him the news that she'd gotten that morning via email.

"So, guess what?" she said, lacing her fingers with his.

"When it gets too cold in Florida, the hibernating iguanas fall from their trees, so they have falling iguana advisories," he answered.

Micki looked at him in shock. "What? No—wait, is that true?"

"Fact." Jonas grinned.

"Well, don't tell Margo that tidbit, or Monty will wind up with a bunch of siblings." She laughed. "But that's not the answer."

"Then what is?"

"I got into Drysdale College," Micki replied. "I'm going to law school!"

"Oh babe, congratulations," Jonas said enthusiastically and pulled her into his arms for an embrace. "I knew you'd get in. You were worrying about nothing."

"I was worrying that I might have to commute to Georgia in the fall if I didn't get in. But now, we don't have a thing to worry about, two separate colleges and no conflict of interest. And both are close by to our place, so the rush-hour drive won't bother us in the least."

"I wasn't worried about the drive." Jonas pressed a kiss on her lips. "I just wanted you to be happy with the choice of law school. Are you sure you're happy, I can look for another dean's position—"

"I'm thrilled and you're not going anywhere, they need you over at that campus," Micki said with conviction. "This is good for me, and it feels like the perfect fit, just like we are."

Jonas kissed her knuckles as they started walking again. "I'm so proud of you, love. Now, let's get something to eat before your stomach gets any louder."

"How can you hear my tummy over yours?" she teased.

Maurizio's was a quaint bistro that served the best coffee. Micki paused and thought how she hadn't tasted a bad cup of coffee yet since they'd arrived there. Idina, Maurizio's cousin and business partner, greeted them warmly. She and Jonas were now familiar to almost everyone in the village, and they sat outside under the blue canopy so they could people-watch as they ate.

"I don't know why you look at the menu. You always get the same thing for your first meal of the day." Jonas grinned.

Micki peered at him over the top of the laminated paper she held in her hand. "You don't know, maybe I'll be inspired to try something else today."

"Michelle Ballad-Brand, what are you having for breakfast?" Jonas asked. His smile and the love in his eyes always took her breath away.

"Fine, the usual, Idina, please. Maurizio's special frittata, and a coffee. Make that a large coffee." Micki smiled.

"How is all that caffeine not keeping you awake at night?" Jonas joked. He ordered the same items, except he did it in fluent Italian. She shook her head. Idina thanked them and went inside.

Jonas reached for her hand. "Are you happy, love?"

"So happy I'm afraid I'm going to wake up and it will have been a dream. But then, I believe in dreams now."

"Mine's come true, Michelle, thanks to you," he said and kissed her fingertips.

"This is a dream, the best kind. We are so lucky to be right here, right now." Micki laced her fingers with his. "I adore you, Jonas Brand."

They talked and ate and laughed a lot—a sound that filled her with happiness as it echoed in the small square. He was hers and she was his no matter how far they traveled or what they would see. Micki knew that they'd always find their way home, to the place where the honey-suckle grew wild and untamed, just like their love was meant to be.

* * * * *